Sugar on the EDGE

Felicia,

Thank you for your
Support!

Sawyer Bennett

Sawyer Bennett

SUGAR ON THE EDGE (The Last Call Series, Book #3)
By Sawyer Bennett

ISBN: 978-1-940883-21-2
Interior Design by NovelNinjutsu.com

Find Sawyer on the web!
www.sawyerbennett.com
www.twitter.com/bennettbooks
www.facebook.com/bennettbooks

CONTENTS

ONE

Gavin

"And, as you can see here, all the panels of glass slide so you can open the entire back wall to the beach."

"Not a real handy feature in the winter months," I grumble under my breath as the woman... my realtor... prattles on about the features of this 2.7 million dollar beach house I just purchased—sight unseen—in Duck, North Carolina. Stupid fucking name for a town, but I'd live with it since the house met all of my requirements.

And there weren't many. It had to be oceanfront with no other house near it for at least two hundred yards. I like my privacy, so in order to afford said privacy, I had to shell out a shitload of cash to purchase it.

"Excuse me?" I hear from behind me. I turn to see the woman looking at me with her blonde eyebrows arched high. What was her name again? Casey Markham, I think.

"Excuse me what?" I ask, trying to keep my features bland. I'm normally not passive aggressive. In fact, most would call me just aggressive, but I'm hungover as hell and not as combative as normal.

"You just mumbled something. I didn't hear what you said," she challenges me. I know damn well she heard what I said but, she wasn't about to let the smart-ass comment go unnoticed.

"I said," I drawl out in a strong voice laced with my own special brand of assholery, "not a real handy feature in the winter months. I apologize if you didn't hear me, but what I meant by that is it's a pretty fucking stupid feature to have on a house that has cold winter months. I mean… if this house was in the tropics, sure... I get it. But what wazzock installed that knowing it would only be used maybe half the year?"

I'm a prick, I know it, and this woman, Casey, knows it too. I've been dealing with her from my flat in London over the past several weeks while she's diligently tried to find a piece of property to suit my needs. I really don't give a fuck if I hurt her feelings though; I've gotten beyond caring what anyone thinks of me and besides, she's earned a hefty commission off this sale, so she has no reason to whine.

Rather than stick out her lower lip and pout, she does the opposite instead. She throws her head back and laughs from deep within her chest and suddenly, the woman becomes a bit more interesting to me. She's beautiful, sure. Long, blonde hair, streaked pale in some areas from the hot, Carolina sun. Perfectly sun-kissed skin and runway model features. Her smile exudes happiness and contentment with her life, sparkling with brilliance. She apparently also has a backbone as well, which is intriguing because that means she's breakable, not just bendable, and sometimes, I find joy in breaking things.

Still chuckling, Casey shoots me a wink as she walks past me. "I thought the same thing when I saw that. Our summers are very nice here, but we can get some nippy winters, no doubt. Now, let's go upstairs, and I'll show you the second level."

Shaking my head, I follow her up the stairs, definitely eyeing the way her ass sways under the slender, cream-colored skirt she's wearing. It makes me think about bending her over and fucking her with it hiked up around her waist.

Maybe.

If my head wasn't pounding and my stomach wasn't threatening to expel up the half bottle of Scotch I drank last night.

I follow her around, letting her point out the features of the house... zebrawood flooring throughout, five bedrooms, each with its own bath suite, and a third-floor office that has its own private deck overlooking the Atlantic. It came completely furnished, even stocked with pots and pans, so I don't have to do anything but unpack my suitcase. There's even an entertainment suite on the basement level that houses a private cinema, billiards room, and fully functioning bar.

The bar is my favorite feature in this house by far.

By the time we make it back down into the kitchen, I've pretty much tuned my realtor and her perky, sweet disposition out and start calculating how quickly I can get her out of here. There's another half bottle of Scotch calling out to me, and be damned that it's only one o'clock in the afternoon.

"Here are your keys, and congratulations on your new home, Mr. Cooke."

I look at Miss Casey Markham standing there, holding out the house keys to me, all sunny and bright, and realize it's not worth trying to get in her pants. My brand of fucking is dark and rough, something a sweet girl like her would never understand.

Would never tolerate.

"Thanks," I say as I take the keys and pocket them.

I walk her to the door. Once she steps out onto the front porch, she turns to me with a huge, sparkling smile and says, "Is there anything else I can do for you, Mr. Cooke?"

How about a blow job, sunshine?

Yet, her sunny personality is exactly the reason she doesn't really appeal to me. I don't like my women smiling, happy, or carefree. I like them quiet and passive, taking what I give them, and otherwise leaving me the fuck alone.

"Nope. I'm good. Cheers," I tell her and start to turn away to close the door. My last glance at her shows her smile to still be fixed in place, but there's a hint of a smirk she's showing that tells me she very much knows I'm a supreme asshole, yet she couldn't care less. She just made thousands of dollars in commissions off me, and that will keep her in rainbows and unicorns for many months.

After the door closes, I lean back against it and survey my new kingdom. It's massive… four stories if you include the basement and way more room than any one man could ever hope to possess, or live in for that matter. It's going to be a bitch to keep clean, and that's the last thing I'm looking forward to because all of my attention needs to be focused on trying to stay away from the bottle and working on my manuscript, which is due to my editor in two weeks.

Pushing away from the door in a spur of the moment bout of insight, I pull it open and call down to Casey, who has made it to the bottom of my porch staircase. "Wait a minute."

She turns back around and pastes a pleasant smile on her face. "Yes, Mr. Cooke?"

"It's Gavin," I say, tired of the formality, because Mr. Cooke is my father and it makes me feel fifty rather than twenty-seven.

Casey cocks her head to the side in curiosity.

"Do you know of a cleaning service you can recommend that can come in a few times a week?"

She chews on her lip in thought and takes a step back toward the staircase. Looking up at me, she says, "There are a few here in the Outer Banks, but I actually have a friend… my roommate actually… who might be interested."

Shaking my head, I say, "No, thanks. I'd rather have a professional company."

Casey's brows draw inward, and she steps up on to the bottom of the staircase, poising one hand on the bannister, the other sliding into the pocket of her skirt. "She's really fantastic. She cleans a few other houses on the island. She's very unobtrusive, and she will do a better job for a better price than the professional companies do."

"Is she as talkative as you?" I ask skeptically, but what I really mean is she bubbly, perky, and outgoing. "Because I don't like to be bothered."

"Quite the opposite. She's shy and a little withdrawn. You probably won't even know she's in your house."

Drumming my fingers on my thigh, I think about her offer. My gut says to decline and insist on a professional company, because if they don't work out, there are no awkward feelings if I have to fire them. But then I think… what the fuck do I care if there are awkward feelings? If I don't like her, I won't have a single qualm about booting her arse out.

"Okay," I capitulate. "Give her my contact information and have her give me a ring. I'll discuss the details with her."

Casey pins me with a huge smile and says, "I'll do that. Her name is Savannah Shepherd. I'll have her call tonight."

I nod at Casey and turn away from her, walking back into my house and straight down to the entertainment suite, where I pull out the bottle of Scotch and pour myself a "welcome home" drink.

Just a mere hour later, and I am fully unpacked in my new home. All I had was two suitcases of clothes, and a box of office supplies that I had shipped over from my flat in London. I pour another two fingers of Scotch in my empty tumbler, which is actually a plastic glass with a big, pink flamingo on it that I found in the cupboard, and take a sip as I sit down behind my desk. The office chair creaks and moans, causing me to make a mental note to get a new chair. This one will drive me nuts if it makes this much noise.

Reaching over into the almost-empty box of office supplies, I pull out the last item in there. The only piece of decor that I had shipped over.

The small frame feels light in my hands. As I turn it over to see the picture inside of it, I'm wholly unprepared for the sharp stab of pain in the center of my chest. I haven't seen this picture in over two weeks, and it opens up a fresh wave of longing and bitter feelings. I take another sip of the Scotch, willing the peaty burn to start numbing my mind and my heart as it slides down my throat. I gently set the picture on my desk in front of me.

Reaching out, I rub an index finger lightly over the glass and swallow hard so as to prevent the buildup of tears that will often hit me when I stare at Charlie's picture. It's my favorite one of him... taken just a few weeks after he turned two. He's sitting on the front porch of our house in Turnbridge Wells, a midsize town about sixty kilometers from London. Charlie had his elbows resting on his knees, his hands clutching on to his favorite stuffed animal... a ridiculous-looking, bright blue octopus. He's smiling big, his little baby teeth winking at me, while his blue eyes sparkled in the morning sun. I remember he was smiling so big because I was dancing around and making a fool of myself while Amanda snapped pictures. It took almost no effort on my part to get Charlie to smile and giggle, but I always hammed it up hard around him. It was just my thing as a dad.

I can almost feel his soft, brown hair on my fingertips if I think hard enough. My favorite times were when he'd lay across my lap to watch TV, and I'd stroke his head. He'd never make it very far, often falling asleep within minutes, and then I was free to just watch his tiny chest rise and fall with every breath he took.

I miss him so bad that I ache in my bones, and it's the main reason I turn to my good friend, Macallan, to help numb the pain.

Speaking of which, I lift the plastic glass to my lips and swallow the rest of the smoky liquor down in one huge swallow. My eyes burn in response, but then I become gloriously warm all over. Reaching for the bottle, I pour another two fingers and set the glass down, reaching instead for my laptop. I need to check my email before I get too drunk. My agent, Lindie Booth, will want a status update from me to make sure the house closing went off without a hitch. She's been afraid that I'll change my mind and head back to London to the life of dark debauchery that I've been living for the past several months.

It was actually her idea that I move here. She said my writing wouldn't survive my lifestyle, and that I needed to get away to craft in peace. She suggested the Outer Banks, having vacationed here herself many times.

Maybe she's right. Maybe she's full of shit. Who knows, but here I am.

Lindie is a power hitter in the world of traditional publishing and snapped me up quickly when my last book, *Killing the Tides*, hit number one on the New York Times Best Sellers list. I had self-published it, having spent four years being turned down by every agency and publisher in the United Kingdom and the United States. My brand of dark, paranormal thrillers with a heavy dose of erotica was not something anyone was willing to take a chance on. But apparently, the readers knew something that the big publishers didn't, and my book stayed on all the major best-seller lists for weeks and weeks.

Just four months after its release, I was represented by Lindie. Three months after that, and I had one of the big five offering me a huge, eight-figure deal for another two books. Even though I was drunk and high as hell when Lindie pitched the deal to me, I recognized it as the money train I had always been waiting for in recognition of my work as a writer. I'm pretty sure I was stoned out of my mind when I signed the contract. In fact, I was pretty tanked when Lindie flew to London to confront me, telling me that I needed to get my shit together, get away from the sordid lifestyle I was living, and move away from the UK so I could concentrate on saving my fledgling career. I agreed to all of those life changes without really having any good lucidity whatsoever.

And, so here I am, in a new country, a new home, with a manuscript that is just about forty-thousand words shy of completion and only two weeks left to finish it.

Staring at the bottle of Scotch before me, I know I'm going to have to set it aside starting tomorrow.

I hope I can set it aside.

I don't want to, but I need to.

TWO

Savannah

"About time you got home," Casey says as I step inside the door to the small beach house that we share. It's almost nine o'clock in the evening, and I'm pooped. No... beyond pooped. I'm utterly exhausted, as I've been working since seven this morning.

"I know," I say, my voice laced with fatigue. "The photo shoot went much longer than I anticipated."

"And just exactly how much of that time was spent trying to avoid the douche bag's cheesy come-ons and lame innuendos?"

"A good thirty minutes, at least," I answer her with a wry grin, but then I give a tiny shudder. I do some contract work with a local portrait photographer and he's an absolute slime ball, constantly hitting on me in the most inappropriate ways. Unfortunately, I need the job desperately, having just been laid off at the newspaper where I was the staff photographer. The paper couldn't afford me full time, thus the layoff. At least they promised to contract certain projects to me, but it's microscopic peanuts compared to the regular ones they were paying me.

Heading into the kitchen, I drop my purse on the kitchen table with a thud. Opening the refrigerator, I peruse the contents, but I'm too tired to make anything substantial to eat. So I pull out a bag of carrots and an apple. When I turn back around, Casey is leaning up against the counter with her arms crossed over her chest.

She's so beautiful that I feel dowdy next to her, but Casey is never one to flaunt herself... at least not around other women. Sure, she's the biggest flirt when it comes to men, and her motto has always been "love 'em and leave 'em," but she's one of the nicest, most down-to-earth women I've ever known. I'm so glad we became roommates, because without her added help with the rent, I wouldn't have been able to afford to stay here.

"What did he do this time?" Casey asks, her eyes narrowing at me.

"The same... casual brush ups against me, dirty comments," I tell her wearily. "You'd think he'd come up with something original, right?"

"Well, your luck is about to change, girlie," she tells me with a grin, dropping her hands to rest on the counter at her hips. "I found another house for you to clean... it's huge and the guy that owns it is super rich. With that, you can leave the douche bag forever."

I take a bite of a carrot and, with my mouth full, demand, "Tell me more."

"His name is Gavin Cooke, and he's kind of weird... well, he's kind of an asshole. He's some big-time, British author that moved here to finish writing a book. He needs someone to clean his house a few times a week, and he told me to have you call him."

Munching and then swallowing the carrot, I consider this. Between the contract work at the newspaper, the part-time work with the douche bag photographer, and the two other houses I clean, it will mean even longer hours for me. I'm barely functioning as it is, and this will mean less sleep and sorer muscles.

Unfortunately, I really don't have a choice. Between my student loans, living expenses, and the brand new transmission I had to put in my car last month, I barely make enough money to feed myself much more than carrots and apples. On top of that, cleaning houses and hauling camera equipment provides me with too much of a workout for the very few calories I'm able to consume each day, and I've lost weight I couldn't afford to lose.

Still, the alternative isn't appealing either. If I can't make it here on my own, my only other choice is to move back home to Clearview, Indiana, and become that weird twenty-five-year-old woman that still lives with her parents. And while my parents are the nicest, sweetest, Midwest couple you can find, my life will absolutely stagnate back home. I worked hard to get out of our little town, so I could travel the world and take photographs of all the wonders I would behold. Granted, I haven't made it any further than the Outer Banks of North Carolina, but that is practically a world away from my humble upbringing.

Yes, I don't have a choice. I'll have to slot another job in. Once I get the transmission work paid for—which, thankfully, Smitty down at the local garage is letting me make payments on—I can ditch the douche bag and have more of a manageable life.

"I'll call him after I eat my dinner. Do you think it's too late?"

"Nope. My guess is that as a writer, he stays up late. At least, that's my impression from when I went to pick him up at his hotel room to have him sign the closing documents and then show him the house. It was around noon, and I'm pretty sure he just rolled out of bed."

Setting the carrots aside, I pick up the apple and take a bite. It tastes like chalk going down, my interest in food waning over the past several weeks. I've been so mired in hard work, coupled with a rising sense of panic that I'm not going to be able to survive on my own, that my appetite has been off.

"I have some leftover pasta in the fridge I made tonight," Casey says as she eyes me eating the apple. I don't know what expression is on my face, but I'm guessing she can tell the apple isn't doing much for me.

"No thanks," I tell her with a small smile. I'm too proud to take help from her, and even leftover pasta is still charity to me.

"You're wasting away to nothing, Savannah," she gripes at me. "You can't go on much longer like this."

"I'm fine," I drawl out with false confidence in my voice. "Like you said… this house cleaning job will be enough to put me in the black on my expenses."

"You're not fine," she practically barks at me with narrowed eyes. "You're working yourself to the bone. What are you up to now… like three jobs, plus you volunteer every week at The Haven with Alyssa and Brody. You're hardly eating. Seriously, you're putting your health in jeopardy."

Now… I'm normally a polite, sweet, Midwestern girl. It takes a lot to rile me up, but having these reminders of my failures thrown into my face gets me a little irritated. "Back off, Casey. While I appreciate your concern, I've got this handled."

She blinks at me in surprise, because I think this may be the first fight we've had as roommates. Out of my core group of girlfriends, Casey, Alyssa, and Gabby, I'm the least likely to get irritable with anyone. Some would even call me a pushover.

"Fine," she grumbles. "But it was just a small bowl of pasta I was offering."

Taking a deep breath, I let it out slowly. Gentling my voice, I say, "I'm sorry. I appreciate the offer… I really do. But I'm one of those people that just have to do it on my own. You should know that about me by now."

Casey nods her head grudgingly, because she does know that. In the four months that we've been roommates, she's come to know me well enough to know that I have a streak of stubborn pride about a mile long and just as wide. It's why I haven't told the douche bag photographer to piss off, because yeah… while I need the money, I more importantly need him to know that he can't rattle me. My days of being rattled are over.

My phone chimes from inside my purse and I sit the apple down on the counter, wiping my fingers on my jeans. Pulling it out, I see it's a text from Brody.

My heart instantly lightens.

Brody and his fiancée, Alyssa, run The Haven, a nonprofit, no-kill animal shelter where I volunteer. I love animals—dogs in particular—so much that I spend all of my free time there helping out. With three jobs though, that time has been less and less, and I feel my soul starting to starve. My love of dogs has been long standing, stemming from one, single event that happened when I was just six years old.

I was out playing in the woods that surrounded our house in Clearview. We lived out in the country, so Mom usually pushed me out the door in the morning while on summer break from school and told me not to come home until dark. I was with our family's dog, Petey, who was a Lab. I had gotten lost and couldn't find my way back home, and Petey kept me safe and warm throughout the night. I don't know if it was my child's imagination, but as I sat huddled at the base of a tree, I thought I heard coyotes, bears, and lions coming at me from all directions. Petey would growl periodically, his eyes searching the darkness around us. He would lick me every so often, assuring me that everything would be okay. I snuggled into his warm fur, clutching my arms around him tight, and I knew that I was safe.

The search party found me around dawn the next morning, and Petey was hailed as the town's local hero. He even won a medal.

Since then, I've found myself happiest when I can be around dogs. While I can't afford one on my own, if I can ever get out of this butt load of debt, I'm going to have five at least.

Brody's text is to the point.

Got any time tomorrow to help? Alyssa has to go to Raleigh to pick up a horse.

I shoot a quick text back.

Not sure. I may have new job to start. Text you later.

I stare at my phone for a moment, slightly depressed I can't give him a simple "yes." I'd much rather be up to my elbows in dog slobber than cleaning some rich asshole's house, but that can't be my priority right now.

You could just accept the job we offered you, Brody responds.

Yes, that would be the simple solution, but I can't do that either. There's no way I can let Brody and Alyssa put me on the payroll for The Haven. It's a perfectly permissible thing for a nonprofit to have paid employees, but I also happen to know that adding me to the overhead will cause even harder work for Alyssa and Brody to have to raise money to support said expenditure.

No, my time at The Haven will always be as a volunteer and while their offer meant the world to me, I had to sadly decline. Just as I do once more.

I love you two for it, but my answer is still no, I text.

His response is immediate. *Stubborn.*

I laugh, because Brody has no cause to be lecturing me about stubbornness. After spending five years in prison for a crime he didn't commit, he returned to the Outer Banks a broken shell of a man, that stubbornly refused to let people into his life and refused to believe that he was worth anything. But for the help and love of a good woman—that would be Alyssa—Brody would still be mired in darkness.

I've become especially close to Brody and Alyssa over the last several months, Brody in particular. Ever since he fell in love with Alyssa, and told his family and closest friends his secret about doing time for someone else's wrong, he's become a completely different person. He's warm, humorous, and fiercely protective of those he cares about. I'm just lucky that I happen to be in that circle, and the long hours we spend together caring for the animals has created a closely bonded friendship between the two of us. He once told me that he recognizes inside of me the same pride that he once held before he went to prison, and it was drained out of him. That made me sad and happy at the same time. Sad that Brody suffered, but happy that he compared me to himself, because as every one of his family and friends can attest, there's no one more respected than Brody Markham.

Looking up at Casey, I say, "How about giving me this guy's contact information so I can call him?" Might as well nail down this job and hope it gives me some measure of peace that I'll have some extra income coming in.

"Sure," she says as she pulls out her phone from her pocket and flips through her contacts. When she finds what she's looking for, she holds her phone out for me to see.

I dial the number as I flip my gaze back and forth between her phone and mine.

He answers on the fourth ring, just as I was expecting voice mail to pick up.

"What?" is all he says, but his English accent is clear in just that one word.

"Um… Mr. Cooke?"

"Gavin," he grumbles into the phone and if I'm not mistaken, his voice is a little slurred.

"Uh… yeah, this is Savannah Shepherd. My roommate, Casey Markham, said you wanted me to call."

There's silence on the other line for a moment, and then he says irritably, "Who told you to call me?"

"Casey Markham… your realtor? She said you might want me to clean your house?"

I hear him hiss through his teeth, and he sounds even more irritated. "Fuck… yeah, I forgot about that. Look, I'm in the middle of something and can't talk. Just be here tomorrow at ten, and we can discuss the details."

"Ten in the morning?" I ask, just to clarify, because I have another house I have to clean starting at eight, and I don't know if I can be done in time.

"Of course, ten in the morning," he says, clearly exasperated at my question. "Do you clean houses at ten at night?"

"Sometimes," I answer automatically, and I can tell he doesn't have a comeback. "Look, Mr. Cooke…"

"Gavin," he butts in.

"Gavin," I acknowledge. "I have another job at eight and not sure I can be there by ten. Can we possibly—?"

He cuts me off. "If you want the job, be here at ten. If you don't, don't be here at ten. Choice is yours."

He then hangs up the phone on me, and I'm stuck listening to dead space.

Putting my phone down, I glance up at Casey, who is watching me intently. "He really is an asshole."

"Told you," she says, while nodding her head up and down. "What did he say?"

"Told me to be there at ten if I wanted the job and then hung up on me," I say as I start flipping through my contacts. I pull up the number for Grace Banner, the woman whose house I clean every Thursday at eight. "Guess I better see if I can be at her house a little early tomorrow."

"Great," Casey mutters as she watches me dial

Grace's number. "You're trading in one douche employer for another."

As the phone rings, I cock an eyebrow at her. "I'm not trading just yet. Looks like I'll have two douche employers for a while until I can cut one loose."

Casey nods at me in commiseration.

THREE

Boom, boom, boom.

The pounding in my head causes me to open my eyes slowly, because I know the sunlight filtering through the shades is going to hurt like a motherfucker.

Boom, boom, boom.

Christ, it seems to be getting louder, and I'm regretting polishing off that last half bottle of

Macallan last night. I rub my eyes, which are caked with sleep, and turn my head to look at the alarm clock. Fuck… it's only ten o'clock in the morning, and I was hoping to sleep past the majority of my hangover.

Painkillers… that's what I need right now.

Gingerly sitting up and swinging my feet out of bed, I hesitantly put my fingertips to my temple and try to massage the pounding away.

Boom, boom, boom.

Fucking hell. That's someone banging on my door, which causes the actual pounding in my head to skyrocket. Lurching out of bed, I stumble out of my bedroom, down the flight of stairs, and into the kitchen with my eyes only open to half slits because the sunlight isn't helping the pain either. I manage to crack my hip against the counter, letting out a string of curses as I make my way to the front door.

Boom, boom—

I swing the door open forcefully and glare at the person standing there. "You better have a good excuse for pounding on my fucking door this early," I snarl.

"Mr. Cooke? You told me to be here at ten," the person says… a woman, I can now glean, even though I've yet to fully open my eyes.

Squinting at her hard, my eyes still blurry, I can make out a young woman with dark brown hair and unrecognizable facial features, as I'm sure I still have drunk goggles on. "I did?"

"Um… yes, to talk about cleaning your house," she says quietly. Even in all my hungover glory, I don't fail to notice that she takes a small step backward.

My mind is blank for a moment, and I have no clue what she's talking about. Clean house? Ten o'clock?

Then it sinks in… this is the woman my realtor recommended. It's vaguely coming back to me that she called last night and we arranged a time to meet this morning.

Scratching my stomach, I open my left eye up a little bit more to take a better look, and she starts to come into better focus. Pretty girl… beautiful actually. Not in the sunny, bright way that is Casey Markham, and not in the luscious, centerfold way that is my ex, Amanda. But in a fresh, wholesome kind of way. Long, brown hair with some red glints in it, soft brown eyes, lightly tanned skin, and full lips. As a writer, I'd stereotype her as the girl next door. She'd be the classic character that would immediately get ravaged by one of the monsters in my books, just for the sake of ravaging a fresh innocent.

Taking a step back, I manage to open both eyes and clear my throat. "Sorry, I forgot, but come on in."

She looks at me for a moment, chewing on her bottom lip and clearly indecisive about whether she should accept my invitation. I don't wait around for her decision, instead giving her my back and walking into my kitchen. I hear her step inside and softly close the door.

Busying myself with making a pot of coffee, I watch out of my peripheral vision as she hesitantly steps into the kitchen and stands as still as a statue. I don't turn around to look at her but ask, "What did you say your name was again?"

"Savannah," she says softly. "Savannah Shepherd."

After I put a filter in the machine, I scoop out some coffee, putting in extra to make it strong enough to help chase away this hangover. I take the pot and turn to fill it in the sink, giving her a quick glance. "Well, Savannah Shepherd, Casey told me that you do some house cleaning on the islands. Thought you might be interested in doing my house as well."

She doesn't respond to me though, so I raise my gaze up to her after turning off the water and pulling the pot back. Her wide eyes stare at me in indecision, and I suddenly wonder if she's daft or something. "Cat got your tongue?" I ask.

Shaking her head, she casts her eyes downward. "No... it's just. Maybe you should get dressed first before we talk."

I blink a few times, trying to register what she's saying, and then drop my own gaze to casually peruse myself. Well, what do you know? I'm only wearing a pair of boxers with the fly gaping wide open, and my cock is sticking out half erect.

Oops. Bet she got an eyeful when I answered the door.

Shrugging my shoulders, I adjust myself not so discreetly. I turn my back on her to fill the coffee machine up with water. Setting the pot on the burner, I flip the switch. Turning back around to face her, I lean back against the counter and cross my arms over my chest. She can't help herself... her eyes involuntarily flick down to my crotch and while I'm sure I'm completely covered after my adjustment, I'm betting I'm tenting my underwear nicely. Her face flames pink, and her eyes quickly come back up to mine.

Giving her a tiny smirk, I say, "So... I need you to come probably twice a week to do general housecleaning... probably my laundry since I suck at both."

"You aren't going to get dressed?" she blurts out.

Pinning her with a direct stare, I curve my lips up and say, "No, Savannah, I'm not. Got a problem with it?"

"It's slightly awkward having you standing in front of me half naked for a job interview," she says, and I'll have to give her some credit for having a sass mouth. Oh, the things I'd love to do with a girl that smarts off to me.

"You're lucky I had my boxers on when you woke me up. Half the time I walk around naked," I tell her with a serious look. I don't, but I sort of like the blush she's wearing and I wonder if I can get it to go a shade brighter. "Think of it this way, the less clothing I wear, the less laundry you have to do."

I watch as Savannah clutches her purse a bit tighter to her body, and indecision filters into her gaze. I wait her out, certain that I've scared her off for good, which is no skin off my back.

"I really need this job," she admits, and then her gaze falters to the floor. "But I'd be wasting your time if I stayed to discuss the details. I just can't work here if you're going to walk around naked all day. Thank you, Mr. Cooke, for your time, and I'm really sorry I woke you up."

She never looks back at me but spins on her heel and heads for the front door. I watch her for just a millisecond, and then I push off from the counter to go after her. "Wait a minute," I call out.

She stops and turns to look at me over her shoulder, her eyebrows raised.

"I don't really prance around naked all day," I grudgingly admit. "You woke me out of a sound sleep this morning, and I didn't even realize I only had my underwear on when I answered the door."

Savannah doesn't say anything, just levels those brown eyes... which now that I look at her some more, are really quite lovely.

"Besides... I'll be in my office most of the time, and you will probably never see me," I add on, hoping she reconsiders my offer. I really don't have time to interview other companies, and I'd like to get this taken care of so I can get working on my manuscript.

"What exactly would my duties be? And the pay?" she asks as she turns fully to me.

"Like I said... clean the house, do my laundry. Nothing too hard... twice a week. I'll pay you five hundred dollars."

She blinks at me in surprise, and I realize the money I just offered her was ridiculously generous. I didn't know that until she blinked, but based on the look on her face, it's clear I have no clue what the value of a cleaning service is. Oh, well... too late to take that back now. I'll just have to make sure she earns it... like maybe scrub the floor with a toothbrush or something.

"That's too much," she tells me, and now I'm the one blinking at her in surprise.

"Excuse me?"

"You would be paying me way too much. It will probably take me about no more than three hours a day if I were to come twice a week. That's got to be something like... eighty bucks an hour or close to it. Way too much."

Seriously... this girl... woman, just had a major opportunity to make some serious cash off me, yet here she's telling me that I'm overpaying her? Who the fuck is that honest these days?

"Tell you what... how about you cook dinner for me the days you come to clean?" I offer.

"That's still too much," she says, her eyes determined not to take advantage of me. This is fucking weird? In fact, she'd make a fantastically kooky character in one of my books... a character that was honest to a fault, which means she probably doesn't have much in the brains department. She'd get eaten by one of my monsters in a nanosecond.

But, I'm officially over being amazed by her naivety and tell her, "Take it or leave it. I don't have time to mess around with this further, as I'm already terribly behind on my work."

There she stands again... staring at me in uncertainty, and I can see she's actually contemplating turning down a job that will pay her more money than she's probably ever been paid for a job before. It sort of irritates me this foolishness she's exhibiting, and I start to open my mouth to tell her to get the fuck out, when she says, "I'll take it. When do you want me to start?"

"How about next Tuesday? The house is practically spotless right now... that will give me a chance to mess it up a bit," I tell her with a loose grin. "I'll also make sure to wear clothes every day so you have some laundry to do to earn your paycheck."

She returns a tentative smile. "I can do that. How about I come on Tuesdays and Fridays then?"

"That will work."

"Any particular time?" she asks.

Shrugging my shoulders, I walk back into the kitchen and pull a cup out of the cabinet above the coffee pot. The liquid gold is still brewing, but I'm done waiting for the caffeine. I pull the pot back, noting the hiss and sizzle of coffee that drips to the burner before sticking my cup underneath the stream. "I don't care. I'll give you a key."

My cup doesn't take long to fill, so I pull it back and put the pot back in its place. I take as big of a sip as I can without burning my tongue and turn back to face her. Her eyes are leveled with the fly on my boxers again and they snap up quickly, but not quickly enough to miss her look.

Caught your hand in the cookie jar, little girl, I think to myself and smirk at her while my cock jumps at the attention. I'm surprised by the boldness of her actions, because she's seems to be nothing but a shy slip of a girl. But when I see the worry in her eyes that I just busted her sneaky peek, I realize that her look wasn't bold at all. It was more of an involuntary reaction when I spun around on her, and now she is mortified to have been caught looking at me like that.

Yes, she'd be a lamb left to the slaughter in one of my books. She's the antithesis of everything that I would find attractive in a woman because while I like my conquests to keep their lips sealed for the most part because conversation is usually a turn off to me, I don't like the work involved with someone that seems so unsure of their self. I like a woman who knows what she wants and lets it be clear to me that she's available for the taking. It's easier that way.

Which makes it very odd that my body would even give the slightest reaction to her. It usually takes a lot to get my dick to twitch since my tastes are pretty singular, yet here I've been sporting a semi the entire time I've been talking to Savannah this morning.

Oh, well… no sense in dwelling on it. She's so not my type, so I'll chalk it up to my cock just having general curiosities.

Setting my cup down, I walk over to the set of keys that Casey left me with yesterday that I had tossed onto the back kitchen counter. I see there are three keys that all look the same, so I twist one off the ring and hand it over to her. Savannah steps forward and quickly takes the key, grabbing it with the very tips of her finger so we don't touch.

That amuses me somewhat, and I snicker to myself. Yes, she'd make a wonderful character in one of my books… an anti-heroine of sorts that the reader would feel a bit of kinship to, but would be well satisfied when she met her demise because she'd probably deserve it due to her lack of confidence and complete innocence. Maybe I'll use her as a muse in my current project. I can never have enough bloody and tortured bodies in my work.

Picking my cup back up, I turn toward staircase that leads up two flights to my office. Not looking back at her again, I say, "I probably won't see you on Tuesday because I'll be working, but I trust you can let yourself in and lock up when you leave. I'll pay you in cash on Friday."

She doesn't say a word in response, but that's okay. She's forgotten, and I already have my head wrapped up in the manuscript I'm getting ready to delve back in to.

FOUR

Savannah

It's ten o'clock on Friday night, I'm dressed in the sluttiest-looking outfit I can manage to put on without blushing, and I'm walking into Last Call... the oceanside bar that my friend, Hunter Markham, owns and that has become the hot hangout here on the islands. While the summer season is long gone, there's still a pretty sizable crowd for late January.

I'm taking advantage of it tonight. Meeting my girlfriends, Casey, Alyssa, and Gabby for a night out on the town. It's Gabby's turn to be designated driver, and I intend to get drunk. Well, I really don't do drunk well, but I intend to get buzzed enough on sweet alcohol to try to erase the last half of my day today.

I had another awful portrait session assisting Eric, the douche photographer I work with part time. We shot a local couple for their engagement photos, and my job was simple enough. Handle the lighting equipment, adjust the odd lock of hair that would fall funkily over the woman's shoulder, or smooth out the wrinkles in the horrendous lavender colored drop cloth they chose for their background. It was lame actually, especially when I was used to doing my own work and on far more interesting subjects than happily grinning couples who would probably get divorced in a few years.

After Eric snapped the last picture and sent the duo on their way, he told me he wanted me to start editing the photos tonight. I blinked at him in surprise because he never turned the photos over that quickly, and I knew without a doubt he wanted to keep me there so he could throw some of his cheesy and slightly disgusting moves on me some more.

I easily capitulated though, because Eric pays me by the hour and I need the money.

For the first hour of editing, he pretty much left me alone and I heard him periodically moving equipment around or talking on the phone in his office. But eventually he sought me out, as he often did. I didn't have an office but rather a little cubbyhole off the lobby that had a thin, wooden desk tucked up against the wall.

Eric walked up behind me and leaned over to watch my progress. Putting his chin just inches over my shoulder, I could smell the hot dogs with onions he ate for dinner on his breath and tried hard not to shudder in disgust. He watched me work for a few moments, and then said in a low voice, "Your work is very good, Savannah. It has a very sexy quality to it."

Seriously? I was brushing out acne blemishes from the man's face and he called that sexy? I cringed internally but kept a level voice when I said, "Give me a break, Eric. There's nothing sexy about what I'm doing right now."

He chuckled at me and stood up straight. His fingers came up and rested on my shoulders, digging in slightly in an attempt at a clumsy massage. "It's looking pretty sexy from where I'm standing."

I couldn't help myself, shrugging my shoulders violently back and dislodging his hands. Standing up from the chair, I pushed back at it and it hit Eric in the knees. Spinning on him, I growled, "Enough! I'm sick of your come-ons, corny lines, and touching."

Eric just blinked at me in surprise, acting like he had no clue what I was talking about, but I knew he wasn't that dense. Sadly, he was actually a fairly good-looking guy, but he had no tact, no manners, and absolutely no brains when it came to what women wanted.

"I'm sorry if I did something inappropriate," he said with an apologetic smile.

"Well, you did," I huffed. "And you've been doing it a lot. I need you to stop, or I can't work here anymore."

I held my breath in fear he would fire me, because I really, really needed this job right now. Fortunately, all he did was make another profuse apology, and then his demeanor chilled to near subarctic temps. He told me I could go ahead and leave and that he'd finish the editing. He also told me that he'd call me when he needed me again. So, while technically I wasn't fired, I'm not sure he'll call me for any more work and that has me in a near-panic mode.

Sighing, I walk through the crowded bar, all the way through to the back while letting some peaceful, easy feelings from the Eagles song that is pouring out of the jukebox suffuse through me. As I hit the back bar area where all the pool tables and dartboards are set up, I'm surprised to see Brody behind the bar.

He grins at me as I step up to an empty spot, resting my forearms on the wooden top. "You filling in tonight?"

"Yup," he says as he pours a draft beer. "One of Hunter's bartenders apparently has a case of the crabs so severe that he can't stop scratching at his crotch."

I blink at him dumbly, unsure of what he just said. Just to clarify, I ask, "Are you serious?"

"Nope, completely kidding. I think he has allergies or something, but it was worth it to see that look on your face," he says, laughing.

Who would have thought it? Brody Markham, only out of prison for just over nine months, having been completely broken and withdrawn from life, was now sitting here throwing out jokes at me. I freakin' loved it.

It never fails to bring a smile to my face when I see how easily he's now reintegrating to life. Much of that has to do with him falling in love with Alyssa, but it also has to do with the incredible support system he has. His identical twin, Hunter, and his fiancée, Gabby, and of course, his little sister and my roommate, Casey, as well as his parents and myself. He has a close cocoon of people around him that share his secret… that he took the fall for a drunk driving accident where his ex-girlfriend, Stacy, was actually the one driving. Tragically, a man was killed and Brody became a felon, forever losing his charmed life in one blink of an eye.

But he's back now, and as he told me last week when we were bathing the dogs at The Haven, he has never been happier in his life. Of course, he said that while staring sappily over at Alyssa, who was clipping one of the dog's nails. It made my heart seize up in joy over the love they share. I'm not sure I'm ever destined for something like that, but there is enough of a romantic in me that I have to hope it will happen to me one day.

"The girls are out on the back deck," Brody says as he inclines his head toward the door. "You're the last to arrive."

"Work and duty first," I quip. "Can I get a Screwdriver while you're at it?"

"Sure," he tells me as he passes the draft beer he poured across the bar to the guy sitting to my right. After he takes the guy's money and makes change, he starts making my drink. "Doing work with the photographer tonight?"

"Yup, but I might have lost my job," I tell him sadly.

"Why's that?" he asks as puts some ice in a glass and turns briefly to grab the Ketel One from the back shelf.

"I sort of snapped at Eric after he put his hands on me. He apologized, but I could tell he was a little taken aback that I finally called him on it."

"It's about damn time you did so," Brody growls. "You've been taking too much shit from him."

"Yeah, well… I need that damn job so I was willing to put up with a lot of crap from him to keep said stupid job."

Brody's hand freezes just before he tips the vodka over the glass. His eyes narrow at me, and his voice is dangerous. "What exactly did he do to you that made you finally speak up?"

I give Brody an easy smile of reassurance. "Nothing bad, so don't go all Rambo on me. He just put his hands on my shoulders after making some lame comment about me being sexy. I just sort of lost it and couldn't help myself when I told him to back off."

Brody resumes finishing my drink. "You are totally sexy, Savannah, and one day, you'll find a guy that is deserving of that sexiness."

I snort out loud, and Brody has no trouble hearing it over the music. His eyebrows rise up in surprise. "What? I'm serious… you're totally a babe. Sexy hot," he says with an attempt at a lecherous wink, but it fails miserably because one, I'm so not sexy, and two, Brody is just one of those guys that is so nice, he likes to make everyone feel good about themselves.

Sliding the drink across the bar, Brody says, "This one's on the house. Now go hang with your girls, you sexy thing you."

"No way," I protest as my hand dives into my purse for money, but he's already turned away from me to see to another customer.

Jerk!

Lovable jerk!

Grabbing my drink, I take a quick sip and my eyes water. Damn, Brody made that strong and I know he did it because he just gave me a double shot for free basically, knowing that my budget is limited. He's trying to make sure my girls' night out is fun.

Sweet man!

I head out to the back deck, which Hunter closes off in the winter with drop-down walls and portable heaters. I immediately see Gabby, Casey, and Alyssa sitting at a table with Hunter. He's identical to Brody in almost every way, especially now since Brody cut his long hair and shaved the beard he'd accumulated in prison. He's sitting next to Gabby, his arm around her shoulders and his fingers playing with her long hair. They make quite a beautiful couple with his sunny, surfer good looks and her exotic beauty born of having some Cherokee Indian in her bloodlines. Her slanted, hazel eyes pop against her dark hair, and her high cheekbones make her almost look like royalty of some sort.

As I approach, they all turn to look at me with happy, slightly buzzed smiles. They have about an hour head start on me with the drinking. When I reach the table, I look pointedly down at Hunter. "You're in my seat," I tell him sternly.

"Grab another chair and pull it up," he says with a grin.

"Nope," I tell him. "In case you missed the bulletin, this is a girls' night out, and you Mr. Testes Between The Legs, are most definitely not a girl."

"I can vouch for that," Gabby says with a giggle. "So scram, baby."

Hunter takes it all in good nature, because he knew without a doubt he wasn't allowed to hang with us tonight. Leaning over, he gives Gabby a kiss. It starts out sweet and light, but before you know it, he grips her firmly behind the head and dives in for something that borders on pornographic.

"Ewww," Casey says, wrinkling her nose up in distaste. "That's just gross."

"I think it's kind of hot," Alyssa says while she watches Gabby and Hunter kiss.

"You're just saying that because your man is identical to Hunter and you're wishing you could do the same thing to him right at this very moment," I quip at her.

Alyssa leans her elbow on the table, puts her chin in the palm of her hand, and sighs dreamily as she watches Gabby and Hunter make out. "That's the truth."

Taking another sip of my drink, I smile at Alyssa. Where Casey has golden, beach babe beauty along with a smokin' hot body, and Gabby looks like an exotic princess, Alyssa wears her brownish-gold hair in a really short pixie cut, only a few inches in length all over. Her face is classically beautiful, which means she has no need to wear makeup or jewelry to enhance herself. She's one of those women so comfortable in her own skin that she could be wearing a brown paper bag and still be one of the most beautiful women you'd ever behold.

Yup... I'm surrounded by mind-numbing beauty from my best girls, and while I do feel way out of their league, they've never made me once feel like I didn't belong here with them. I'm clearly the one that sticks out in the group, the one that is just a bit different. For example, my idea of my sluttiest dress and theirs vastly differs. Mine is a simple, black sleeveless dress that has a scooped neck that stops just shy of revealing my cleavage and comes just above my knee.

By contrast, Alyssa has on a short, red mini-skirt and low-cut, black halter top that reveals most of her upper back, Casey has on a tight, white dress that is strapless but cut low so most of her breasts are on public display. That, however, is how Casey likes it, and I can't begrudge her showing off her assets. Finally, Gabby is wearing a silky, flowing top in a blue, tropical print that only has one sleeve, the other revealing a bare shoulder. She has it paired with dark jeans and brown boots. At first glance, it doesn't look like there is much sex appeal to it, but when you look carefully, you see that there is a keyhole cut out of the material in the center of her chest that gives a scandalous glimpse of the inside swells of her breasts. It's just a peek of forbidden skin, but it's probably the sexiest outfit out of all of us tonight.

So yes, my sedate, black dress that could easily be worn to a funeral will never be noticed by men... not in the way that my girlfriends are sure to be noticed tonight, but that's fine by me. I only made a half-assed attempt to dress up tonight because the girls insisted. Otherwise, I probably would have been in a simple pair of jeans and a sweatshirt, along with my comfiest pair of tennis shoes. I wasn't in the market to show off my goods, nor catch the eye of a man with said goods.

Hunter finally pulls his mouth away from Gabby's, leaving her looking slightly dazed and confused. I wonder if I'll ever have someone kiss me that way... someone that would leave me breathless and begging for more.

My thoughts turn unbidden to Gavin Cooke, and my cheeks immediately heat up when I think of him.

When he opened the door to his house yesterday, standing half naked with a massive chest right before my eyes and rippling muscles all around, I about had a heart attack. I probably would have continued my stupid stare at him had he not barked at me, bringing me back to full awareness.

Gah, the guy is such an asshole... all sharp words, snide remarks, and evil smirks. I'm still sort of regretting my decision to clean his house, because he screams danger and stressful times, just like Eric. If I'm lucky... he'll keep himself and his humongous penis that I caught a quick glance of firmly locked in his office whenever I'm there.

But man, what a penis. I've never seen anything like it, and I'd be a complete and utter liar if I didn't admit that I hadn't thought of it a time or two since then. I don't have much experience with men, but I'm not a complete fool either. No doubt, his package is something special.

Giggling at myself, I take a sip of my drink as Hunter stands from the table. "Okay, you ladies stay out of trouble tonight."

He leans down and gives Gabby a sweet kiss on her forehead, and then he's gone. I immediately sit in his vacated chair. No sooner has he stepped two feet away from the table, then Gabby leans over to me and says, "So tell us all about this hot, British author that you're going to be working for. Casey told us a little bit about him."

I take another sip of my drink, feeling the vodka warming me from the inside out. When I set it down, I decide to go full-on girly gossip. "So, he answered the door yesterday in nothing but his boxer shorts, with his Mr. Happy hanging halfway out."

"No way," Alyssa gasps, leaning forward to hear more.

"He's hot, right?" Casey says.

"Totally, and let's just say he's well hung too," I tell them, my cheeks burning a bit over this admission, because I don't normally talk sex with the girls. Gabby and Alyssa are in committed relationships—both engaged to the Markham twins—and although Casey has no qualms with bragging about every one of her conquests, I've never been much of a sharer when it comes to the opposite "sex."

But the alcohol is already working its magic on me, I've had an extremely stressful evening with Eric, and my tongue is feeling a little loose.

"I knew he'd be packing," Casey says with authority. "You can just tell... he has that swagger about him."

"I can confirm that to be true," I say with a laugh, "but he's also sort of a douche too. Really grouchy and has an ego the size of Texas."

"I bet he'd be great in the sack though," Casey says dreamily as she circles her finger around the rim of her wineglass. "I thought about making a play for him the other day, but he has some serious bad vibes coming off him."

"Totally," I agree, and then I amend, "about the 'bad vibes.' Not about making a play for him."

Gabby laughs and reaches over to slap my forearm lightly. "You should totally make a pass at him, Savannah. You deserve to have some bone-melting sex."

"No way," I say firmly. "That guy is way out of my league, plus... he sort of scares me a bit."

"Mmmm," Casey sighs again. "The danger is what makes it hot."

"I disagree with you, girls," Alyssa finally chimes in. "Savannah deserves someone sweet and kind, who will dote on her. This guy doesn't sound anything like that."

Pulling my Screwdriver up to my lips, I take a swallow, the alcohol no longer possessing quite the stinging bite the first few sips did. "I'm with Alyssa. I need someone sweet... like Brody or Hunter. So, let's try to find me someone tonight," I finish off with a huge dose of bravery that I might actually go on the prowl tonight.

Fat chance.

That's just not in my nature, to make the moves on a man. I'm too introverted and unfortunately, I'm one of those women that will just have to wait for my Prince Charming to come after me.

FIVE

Gavin

I tilt the glass back and swallow down the last of the Oban. I've lost track of how many I've drank, but I'm fucking buzzed as hell so I'm thinking it's been quite a few. The bartender, I think he said his name is Brody… looks like he may want to cut me off. Or maybe that jaundiced look he's delivering at me has something to do with the fact that I've shunned any attempt he's made at conversation tonight other than to thank him for every glass of Scotch he's set down in front of me.

The only reason I'm here—in a local bar in a strange town on a Friday night—is because when I finally surfaced from my writing cave after two hard days of work, I realized I didn't have any liquor in the house. I wholeheartedly felt I deserved a drink, seeing as how I banged out a solid five thousand words on my manuscript over the last two days.

Unfortunately, the five thousand words I managed to type didn't get me anywhere closer to finishing this project. Rather, I ended up adding a new character to the book, which twisted my plot line just a bit, and will end up making more work for me in the end, but what the hell… I've been inspired by my new cleaning woman.

Yes, the new character is a soft-spoken, wisp of a woman with dark brown hair and warm, brown eyes. She's shy and innocent, and I intend to serve her up on a platter to the villain in the story, a demonic warlord who peddles in drugs and prostitution and loves to dirty up his prey before he devours them.

"Want another?" Brody asks as he steps in front of me and drags me from my musings.

"Sure," I tell him and pull a twenty from my stack of bills lying before me, pushing it across the wooden surface of the bar. "Make it a double."

He gives me a curt nod and pulls the Oban off the shelf behind him. Tipping it over my glass to pour, he doesn't attempt to make any further small talk with me.

"Do you have a cab service around here?" I ask as he tilts the bottle back straight and pushes the scotch closer to me.

"Absolutely. Need me to call you one?" he asks with a smile.

Shaking my head, I tell him, "Not yet, but soon. I'll let you know."

He nods at me again, another small smile, and I feel like I've made him happy by asking for a cab. I'm guessing he must have been worried I'd drink and drive, but that's a worry he can leave behind. I don't make stupid mistakes like that. Brody picks up the twenty I had pushed toward him and makes change at the register. When he returns, I hold up my hand to stop him. "Keep the change."

"Thanks," he says as he puts it in the tip jar and turns away from me.

Feminine laughter gets louder and I look behind me to see what all the noise is about. A door to the back deck area swings open, and the voice of several women laughing filters through. To my surprise, my new little housekeeper walks in to the bar, her head turned back to the women I can just see sitting around a table littered with empty drink glasses.

"You girls are rotten. I'll see you later," Savannah calls out to the women, then she turns with a huge smile on her face and a chuckle pouring over those generous lips as she walks through the door, letting it close softly behind her.

She doesn't see me, but rather makes a beeline straight to the bathroom facilities to the left of where I'm sitting.

Interesting... looks like sweet Savannah is having a fun night out with friends. She didn't seem to be the type to do that. Rather, I sort of imagined her sitting at home reading a book with an old cat on her lap or something. At least, that's the way I wrote her character in my novel, and I'm usually a pretty good judge of character.

"Want to buy me another drink?"

Turning to my right, I smile at the woman standing next to me. Can't remember her name for shit, but she introduced herself to me a little bit ago and I bought her a shot of tequila. I don't know if it's the scotch working some magic but she's pretty fucking hot. Long, blond hair, a magnificent set of tits, and a slammin' ass that would look fantastic while I fucked her from behind.

"Sure," I tell her with a smile, waving my hand to catch Brody's attention. I point at the woman and call out, "Shot of Patrón Silver."

Can't remember the woman's name, but I can sure remember what she's drinking.

She takes her fingertip and runs it down my forearm as it rests against the bar. "So, leaving any time soon?"

"Probably after another drink or so," I tell her, my eyes straying down to the creamy swells of her breasts, which are plumped out over the top of some type of black, corset-like top she's wearing.

"Want some company?" she asks coyly, but her eyes pin me with direct confidence.

My smile becomes calculated, because it's clear what she's asking. "I'd love some. Want to give me a ride home?"

"I'd like nothing better," she says as she leans her face in toward me, nipping my ear with her teeth. "Come find me when you're ready."

Fuck yeah, game on.

Brody pushes the shot of tequila with a lime wedge on the rim of the glass toward the woman. She takes it, gives me a wink, and walks back over to the group of friends she had been hanging with.

Brody helps himself to another twenty laying before me for the cost of the tequila shot. "Keep the change," I say as an afterthought.

He says, "Thanks."

No biggie. I'm feeling super generous tonight, because looks like I'm about to get laid for the first time since I became a temporary U.S. resident.

"Can you call me a cab, Brody?" I hear from my left, and I don't have to turn in my seat to recognize that voice. But when I do, Savannah is standing at the end of the bar, leaning casually against the swinging service door.

"Sure," he calls back to her, and I watch as he picks up a phone beside the register to dial. When he hangs up, he says, "Be about ten minutes. Want anything?"

"Bottle of water," she replies.

I stare at her, waiting for her to notice me. But she keeps her eyes pinned on Brody while he reaches down into a cooler and pulls out a bottle of water, twisting the cap off and setting it down before her. She tries to hand him a five-dollar bill but he turns away. "It's on me."

"Quit being an ass, Brody, and stop buying me stuff."

"You're cute when you're angry," is all he says as he walks away from her.

Savannah huffs but shoves the money back in her purse, keeping her gaze on Brody with a wistful sort of look in her eyes.

Understanding dawns on me. She has a thing for the bartender. Now isn't that just fucking sweet as can be? And this little exchange I just witnessed has only confirmed my initial impression of Savannah. Sure, she may be out at a bar late on a Friday night to have some fun with friends, but she's still the insecure, withdrawn, and 'too shy to make a move on a dude' woman that I had originally taken her for. A total pushover in my opinion.

Whether she feels the weight of my stare or she knew I was sitting there the entire time, Savannah's gaze slides over to me. The minute we make eye contact, her eyes dart back behind the bar, seeking to look anywhere but at me.

I'll probably later blame it on the liquor swirling in my blood, but I suddenly feel the need to see how Savannah reacts to an unkind world. She is, after all, my muse, and I consider this more research than anything.

"Hello, Savannah," I say, loud enough that I know she hears me.

Turning back to me, she offers a small smile and says, "Hello."

Cutting my eyes briefly over to Brody, who is chatting with a customer at the other end of the bar, a rag thrown casually over his right shoulder, I nod my head toward him. "Boyfriend?"

"No," she says quickly, shaking her head with a blush.

"Lover?"

"God, no," she squeaks out. "Just a friend."

Scooting my barstool over closer to where she's standing, I lean toward her and ask, "Want him to be your lover?"

"What?"

"Lover," I affirm with a low voice. "Someone who will fuck you sweetly every night and whisper sweet nothings in your ear while he pumps away in between your legs."

Savannah rears backward from me, face flaming red and indignation swimming in her eyes that I'd talk so crudely to her. I can't help the grin that comes to my mouth because she reacted exactly as I figured. In fact, I need to memorize that look on her face right now because it's exactly how her character should look when she first gets propositioned for a trick. All affronted and indignant, because it's beyond the scope of the narrow walls within which she lives.

Taking a sip of Oban, I watch and wait to see what she'll do. Running from the bar in tears is my first bet, and I've probably just lost my housecleaner, but I just couldn't fucking help myself.

What I don't expect is the tiny flare of heat that enters her eyes, and quickly transforms into anger. Before I can even set my glass back down on the counter, Savannah takes two steps toward me and leans in close. "Brody is a dear friend of mine. He's engaged and happily in love with another dear friend, and I'm happy for him being in love with Alyssa. You think you know something about me, but you don't know shit, Mr. Cooke. And at the risk of losing my job with you, go fuck yourself."

Now I'm the one that rears backward from the venom in her voice and the absolutely unexpected violence of her convictions. I open my mouth to say something… what, I don't know, but snap it shut when she whirls away from me and stalks from the bar.

"What the fuck did you just say to her, asshole?" Brody asks as he slams his hand down on the bar in anger, right in front of me.

Turning my head slowly, I look at him... eyes flamed in anger, his jaw muscles ticking because his teeth are clenched hard.

Picking up my glass of Oban, I shoot the rest of the liquor back in one swallow. When I set it back down, I pick up the rest of my money on the bar, leaving a last twenty-dollar tip behind.

"Friend of yours, I take it?" I nod toward the door that Savannah just slammed through.

"A very good friend," he snarls as he waits for me to enlighten him on our conversation. He can keep waiting for all I care.

"Well, cheers, mate. I'm off," I tell him with a smirk, so he knows I have no intention of addressing his concerns. He glares at me as he swipes the twenty-dollar tip I left him and stuffs it in the jar. After tucking my money in my wallet, I walk over to the blonde, who watches me with hungry eyes as I approach. She licks her lips, and I'm betting they'll be wrapped around my cock before the end of the night.

I forget all about Savannah Shepherd and her tender sensibilities.

My orgasm is just lukewarm as I watch the blonde head bobbing up and down over my cock. I'm almost dispassionate about the whole event as I unload down her throat, my balls slightly tingling from the effort. I figure maybe because it's the second orgasm I've had with this chick in the last hour, and I am pretty fucking drunk, but if I'm honest about it… the first orgasm wasn't all that great either.

The blonde from the bar with the fabulous tits did indeed give me a ride home. I fucked her the first time standing up against my front door, on my front porch, thankful for the two hundred yards of privacy separating me from the neighbors to either side. Then I invited her in and we cracked open a new bottle of scotch, courtesy of a quick stop at the all-night liquor store. After a few drinks, and ten minutes of me having to listen to her prattle on about how sexy my British accent is, the best way I figured to get her to shut up was to push her face down onto my lap and have her blow me. Yup, with her mouth full of my cock, I enjoyed the blessed silence and the fumbling of her tongue up and down my shaft, resulting in an orgasm that ranked just above not having an orgasm at all, and right below the way it felt to blow my load after a wet dream when I was thirteen.

Still having no clue what her name is, I push the blonde away from my dick and reach for the bottle of scotch, tipping it back so I can suck it straight from the bottle. I hand it to her, but she shakes her head in the negative.

"I got to get going, baby. Told my babysitter I'd be home by two." She stands from the floor of my living room and wipes the corners of her mouth with her fingertips.

I stare at her hard. "You have children?"

"Two," she says with a grimace. "Run me fucking ragged all the time. Half the time, I want to pack them up and send them to live in Virginia with their daddy. They're so draining on me."

Her words make fire swim in my stomach and fury rip through my veins. While still holding the bottle, I lift my index finger and point it at her. My voice is low and menacing. "You should cherish your kids."

She's clearly too drunk to comprehend the warning in my voice, because she snorts over my comment as she bends over to pick her purse up from the floor. "Those brats haven't done a damn thing for me other than give me stretch marks and migraine headaches. If I knew then what I know now, I'd probably have insisted their father raise them."

Setting the liquor bottle on the table to my right, I stand from the couch. She gives me a heated look, probably thinking I'm going to give her a passionate kiss, or maybe drop to my knees and return the oral orgasm. Instead, I grab her roughly by the arm and push her through my living room, right through the kitchen and to the front door, where I open it and push her out onto the porch.

"Time for you to go," I tell her and start to close the door.

"Wait," she exclaims in surprise, and her hands shoot out to stop me from shutting her out. "I mean… what the fuck is all that about?"

My upper lip curls in disdain and while I'm pretty fucking drunk, my words come out clearer than ever. "You don't deserve to be a mother. No one should talk about their kids that way. Now get off my property, you fucking bitch."

Her hand drops from the door in surprise over my words, and I slam the door in her face.

SIX

Savannah

I walk through Gavin's house, surveying the damage that has been done since I was here last Thursday and realize, without a doubt, that this guy is a certifiable slob. The kitchen is a disaster… the sink full of dirty dishes, the garbage can overflowing, and a jar of mayonnaise that was left out on the counter for God knows how long, because it now has a green layer of fuzz across the top when I open it up to inspect it.

His bedroom is no better. He apparently doesn't know how to put his discarded clothes in the hamper as they are scattered all over the floor. The sheets and lightweight comforter on his bed are twisted around one another and kicked almost all the way onto the floor. The man must not sleep very well.

His bathroom isn't so bad with just an open tube of toothpaste and some deodorant lying on the counter, and about five towels laying on the floor.

The rest of the house isn't messy, just in need of general dusting and vacuuming. He appears to limit his time to some select areas... his kitchen and bedroom, and I'm guessing his office on the third floor, since he told me that's where he'd probably be when I came over. I haven't seen him since I got here fifteen minutes ago and familiarized myself with the house.

Luckily, I brought all my cleaning supplies with me, including my vacuum cleaner and mop, because I assumed, rightly so, that he wouldn't have any forethought to provide that stuff. I even brought laundry detergent because I doubted he had that either, and immediately start a load of his laundry after stripping his bed sheets.

After putting in my ear buds and dialing up some Black Eyed Peas on my iPhone, I decide to tackle the kitchen first because it's the nastiest. It takes me a good twenty minutes to wash all the dishes because Gavin didn't even bother to rinse them when he stuck them in there. It appears the man subsists on canned ravioli and ham sandwiches. After scrubbing down the counters, I go ahead and dust the entire house, top to bottom, and then scrub the bathrooms. When I finish that, I creep up to the third floor and see that his office door is closed. I put my ear against it, and I can hear the faint clicking of his fingers on a computer. I hadn't known if he was even here or not until now, but decide against disturbing him. I'm absolutely certain I'd be treated to a whole lot of cranky if I did that, so I carefully creep back down the stairs.

After changing out another load of laundry, I go ahead and start vacuuming the house. All of his floors are hardwood and tile with some scattered rugs, but I find it easier to run the vacuum cleaner rather than use a broom on the hard surfaces. After giving the first floor a once-over, I move onto the second-floor bedrooms.

While I am generally not a fan of house cleaning in general, for some reason I enjoy vacuuming. I think it's the gentle push and pull of the machine that lets my brain seem to lull and my mind to wander, allowing me to escape into a lovely daydream. Sometimes I'll fantasize about an epic romance, where a handsome man with an amazing body sweeps me off my feet and tells me he will adore me for all time. Sometimes, I even let my fantasies stray to the bedroom, where said handsome man with a rockin' body will give me pleasure beyond my wildest imagination.

I'm betting Gavin Cooke knows how to do that for a woman. Sure, he's brash, arrogant, and a jerk, but deep within those eyes, you can tell that part of his ego is what would make him undoubtedly a fantastic lover. I bet he doesn't know how to do a poor job at anything.

Shaking my head with an internal smirk, I try to banish those thoughts. While Gavin may be well equipped in the bedroom, that's about as far as his talents would take him, I'm betting. He absolutely screams "loner," and you can tell he probably has no concept of what a loving relationship would be about. At least in my limited experience. Yup… need to keep his gorgeous face completely segregated over into the sole category of "pornographic fantasies" and keep waiting for my dream man that will hopefully resemble someone of Hunter or Brody's caliber.

Suddenly, something grabs ahold of my upper arm and I scream at the top of my lungs, releasing the handle to the vacuum cleaner and thrusting my elbow upward and back in self-defense. It cracks into something hard, and I leap forward a few feet, spinning to face my attacker.

Gavin is standing there, looking pissed and holding his hand to his jaw while he flexes it back and forth. He says something but I can't hear him, so I hastily pull the ear buds loose and scramble forward to turn the vacuum cleaner off.

"Jesus fucking Christ," he says as he fingers his jaw. "What the fuck did you hit me for?"

"You scared me," I say defensively, my heart still pounding like a jackhammer.

"I called out to you," he throws at me, anger heavy in his voice.

"Well, clearly I didn't hear you or I would have responded."

"Clearly," he sneers. "How could you hear me with all that fucking racket you were making? I'm trying to write for Christ's sake, and you're hoovering the house down."

"Hoovering?" I ask, confused.

"Hoover," he says as he points to the vacuum cleaner.

"It's a Dirt Devil," I say as I look at the bright red model with a devil's tail on it.

"What?" he asks, confused, his eyebrows drawn inward.

"It's a Dirt Devil," I confirm.

"What the fuck ever. We call them hoovers in the UK," he growls, and I have to resist the urge to laugh. But then he brings me back down to earth by saying, "I can't have you making all that noise when I'm trying to work."

"I can't clean properly without vacuuming," I tell him. "Hoovering, I mean."

"Then use a fucking broom so you don't make any noise," he snarls as he turns away from me, "or I'll find someone that can clean my house in a way that caters to my needs, not theirs."

"I'm sorry," I say softly as he starts to climb the staircase, because I truly am. He's my employer and I do need to find a way to work around him and fulfill his needs.

"Whatever," he gripes. "Daft Yank."

I'm not sure why his words set me off. Maybe it's because adrenaline is coursing through my body from having the pants scared off me or maybe it's because I'm tired of being a doormat that certain douche bags walk all over, but I put my job in jeopardy once again when I say, "Why are you always such an asshole?"

The words pop out of my lips so suddenly that I have an insane urge to clap my hand over my mouth. But I don't. I straighten my spine, stand tall, and cringe internally while I wait for him to bring the hammer down on me.

Gavin turns slowly on the staircase until he's facing me directly. His eyes are narrowed and his teeth are clenched. "What did you just call me?"

"An asshole," I confirm. "You're mean. Really mean, actually."

He doesn't say anything, just stares at me a moment. Then my heart really starts pounding when he steps down off the bottom stair and walks toward me. His gait is slow, his eyes holding me in place. He walks right up to me and when I have to crane my neck upward to look at him, I finally take a step backward. It doesn't stop his momentum though, because he takes another step in my direction, even as I back up. We continue this dance until he backs me right up into a dresser. The halt in my progress doesn't stop him though, and he takes one more step into me until there's nothing more than a few inches separating our bodies.

He glares down at me... his eyes probing my gaze deeply. I swallow hard, not knowing if this man is certifiable enough to hurt me, but pretty damn sure he's getting off on the fact that he's scaring the daylights out of me.

He surprises me when he brings a hand up and I struggle not to flinch, unsure if he's going to strangle me or not. Instead, his fingers graze along my jaw before giving it a firm grip to hold me in place. "So, you think I'm an asshole?"

I lick my lips once and swallow again to wet my tongue. "Yes," I whisper.

The frostiness in his gaze dissipates, and he slides his thumb over my chin. The move is soft, sensual, and his breath fans out over my face in a rush of cinnamon scent. "You're an interesting woman," he muses.

"I am?" I ask, my voice still held hostage by fear, but also something else that I can't quite put my finger on. Curiosity? Excitement?

"Indeed," he murmurs. "I thought your backbone was made of jelly. I'm thinking I might have misjudged you a bit."

I don't know how to respond, and I'm slightly offended he would think that. Sure, I'm quiet and a bit withdrawn, and yeah... I've put up with all kinds of shit from Eric, but I'm not without mettle. As evidenced by the fact I just called him an asshole, which admittedly, is a bit of a surprise even to myself that I did it.

"Tell me, sweet Savannah." His voice pours out of his mouth smooth as melted chocolate. "Did I piss you off the other night… at that bar?"

"No," I immediately deny.

"Little liar," he whispers and grazes his thumb across my chin again and, this time, my body shivers in reaction. He sees that and chuckles deep in his chest, clearly delighted to have that power over me. "You're not just interesting. I find you positively fascinating."

Gavin releases his hold on my face and turns away from me, heading back to the staircase. "Use a broom," he orders. "And I'll be ready to eat dinner around seven."

"But… you don't have anything in your refrigerator or cupboards other than ravioli and molded cheese," I lament.

"Then I suggest a trip to the grocer to buy something. I have money in my wallet beside my bed," he says, leaping up the staircase two steps at a time. In just a few seconds, I hear his office door open and slam shut, and I'm left behind with my heart still pounding and my hands shaking.

Giving a last toss to the shrimp stir-fry, I turn the gas off and place a cover over the wok. Reaching into the refrigerator, I grab a bottle of water, taking a small measure of pride in the contents. In addition to buying stuff for his dinner, I took the liberty of buying more lunchmeats along with some vegetables I cut up and put in Ziploc bags for him to munch on. I also made a quick tuna casserole that he can pop in the oven tomorrow night and a Mexican casserole for the following night. At least he wouldn't starve to death before I got back on Friday, and it makes me feel better because he's overpaying me.

His footsteps on the staircase alert me to his impending presence and suddenly, I'm nervous. What seemed like a nice gesture to prepare a few meals for him seems to now be stepping across a line that maybe I should steer clear of. But it's too late now to worry about it.

I hastily turn to the cabinets and pull out a plate, then rummage in a drawer for a knife and fork. Pulling a paper towel off the rack, I have it folded and sitting under the cutlery by the time he walks into the kitchen.

"Something smells delicious," he says, and every bit of anger and animosity, as well as intimate danger he showed me earlier, is gone. He's dressed same as he was, in a pair of faded jeans and an olive green T-shirt that fits his upper body well. His feet are bare and his dark hair is slightly disheveled. I'm not sure if it's the five o'clock shadow he's sporting, or his smoky gray eyes, but he looks dark, dangerous, and utterly freakin' gorgeous. Add on that silky, smooth British accent, and he's what you'd call a classic panty-melter. That is, if he kept his condescending, cranky mouth shut, which would then obviate the sexy accent. Still, his looks alone would make a woman twitchy and damp.

I walk over to my purse on the kitchen counter and grab it, rustling around inside for my keys. Keeping my eyes averted from his, I say, "That's a shrimp stir-fry in the wok and there's some rice in the pot next to it. I um… left you a few other things in the fridge."

Heading for the front door, I hear him open the refrigerator. "What's all this?"

Turning around, I bring my gaze to his and he looks confused. So I elucidate. "I made you a few casseroles. Instructions are taped to the top on how to cook it. That will hold you over until Friday."

I reach for the doorknob, but he stops me. "Why don't you stay… eat dinner with me?"

My jaw sags a little, completely caught off guard. This was the guy that was manhandling and cursing at me a few hours ago, and now he's inviting me to eat with him?

"Um… I really should get home," I hedge, because it just feels totally awkward to share a meal with this man.

Gavin walks over to the stove and lifts the lid off the wok. He takes a sniff and his lips curve upward. Turning to me, he says, "Stay. This is way too much food for just me."

My eyes dart around the room, my brain frantically trying to come up with an excuse to decline his invitation. He doesn't wait for me though, reaching into the cabinet and grabbing another plate. "Come on. I don't bite," he cajoles.

"No, you just threaten and intimidate," I mutter softly.

"I heard that," he says with a grin.

I can't help the smile I give in return and with a sigh, I drop my purse to the floor by the front door. Walking back into the kitchen, I take a seat at the kitchen island and watch as Gavin fills my plate up. He grabs a fork and knife from the drawer, handing it across the counter to me.

"What's with the nice act all of a sudden?" I can't help but ask. I figured if I could call him an asshole earlier and retain my job, he wouldn't be too perturbed over that question.

Shrugging his shoulders, Gavin fills his plate up and walks around the counter to sit beside me. "I guess I had a great day writing, despite the caterwauling noises you were making earlier."

My cheeks heat, but he's opened the door to my own curiosity. I had Googled Gavin a few days ago, and was surprised to find he was a New York Times best-selling author. His first book, *Killing the Tides*, was a huge, international success and sounded so intriguing, I one-clicked that bad boy for my Kindle.

"I bought *Killing the Tides* a few days ago and started reading it in my spare time," I say before popping a shrimp in my mouth.

"Really?" he asks with amusement. "So what do you think of it?"

"It's really great," I say after swallowing my food. I spear a sugar snap pea and open my mouth again.

"No… what do you *really* think about it?" he asks, his gaze probing, his meal neglected.

Setting my fork down, I turn slightly in my chair to face him. "I think it's raw, disturbing, and overwhelming. It reminds me of you."

Picking up his own fork, he stabs a shrimp and gives me a dark smile that sends shivers up my spine. "Good answer."

SEVEN

Gavin

Savannah doesn't know me well at all, but she understands that *Killing the Tides* was borne of a pervasive darkness that's within me. While she'll never know the hell I was mired in while I wrote that manuscript, she understands fully that every word in that book was inked in the blood of my wounds.

But I don't want to talk about that.

"So tell me, sweet Savannah," I drawl. "What did you think of the erotica component?"

I take immense pleasure in the redness that stains her cheeks from my question, and I know without a doubt that she's read enough of the book to get to the first sex scene. While the plot line is simple... a hero with magical powers tries to save modern-day Earth from a demon uprising, I wove some hardcore erotica into the story that was nothing more than my baser desires being revealed. During the time I was writing the book, I experimented in some twitchy kink, visiting various sex clubs throughout London and the surrounding areas. I've pretty much tried it all—BDSM, fetish, swingers clubs, voyeurism, orgies—you name it, I've sampled. I used those experiences to spice up what, I thought, was an otherwise unoriginal story. In fact, but for those erotic elements, *Killing the Tides* would have gone nowhere fast.

In that first sex scene, my hero ends up saving a woman who was on the verge of being devoured by a particularly nasty demon—one that had the spirit of an incubus and who had made the woman so consumed with lust that she was in pain.

I mean... what was the hero to do at that point? Fuck her, right?

And so he did... in a dark alley in the middle of New York City. He pushed her skirt up, ripped her panties off because she was begging with tears in her eyes, and fucked her hard. Her cries of pleasure and relief filtered out onto the streets, and a few miscreants stopped to watch while my hero nailed her over and over again.

Savannah doesn't answer my question, chewing on her bottom lip with her eyes pinned to her plate. I feel the need to make her uncomfortable for some reason, so I push at her.

"Come on, sweet girl," I murmur. "What did you think when Max fucked that woman against the wall?"

I watch as she swallows hard, her hand gripping her fork so tightly that her knuckles are white. I think she's going to ignore me, or maybe even throw her plate at me, but instead, she raises her eyes and her voice is steady. "I think your hero was trying to fuck his own pain away," she says. "After his parents were killed at the beginning of the story, I think he stopped caring about propriety. Yes, he was fueled by an almost unquenchable need to help others, almost as if he was trying to make up for not saving his parents, but he also took stupid risks, allowing himself to lose control."

I blink at her hard, because that wasn't the answer I was expecting. I figured she'd fumble over her words, cheeks flaring hotter, and try to find a way to deny she was turned on. Instead, she saw straight through to the subtle hint of truth in my words and exposed it brightly before me.

"You see a lot," I tell her, turning back to my food.

"It was also pretty damn hot, too," she says as an afterthought, and I can hear the smile in her voice, although I don't look back at her.

We eat in silence for a bit, and that's no chore because fuck... the woman can cook. I can't remember the last time I had a home-cooked meal, and Asian cuisine is my favorite.

"What are you working on now?" Savannah asks and because it's no secret, I tell her.

"New York loved the book so much that they want to turn it into a trilogy."

"So, you're going to leave me with a major cliffhanger at the end of *Killing the Tides*?"

"Actually, no. When I wrote it, I made it a stand-alone. I had no intention of ever writing another book after that... ever again."

"Why?" she exclaims. "You're really gifted... I can't imagine you not continuing on."

I shrug my shoulders again and damn... I would like to claim indifference to her praise. I've had hundreds of people compliment my work, but none of those accolades seemed to cause a warm feeling in the center of my chest like Savannah's simple words do now.

"Well, I'm continuing on now, aren't I? Besides, they waved too much money for me to ignore," I tell her simply.

"I call bullshit on you. I think you would have written another book with or without them offering you a dime," she says before she takes another bite of her dinner.

"Maybe," I hedge, because I'm not so sure. I was so drained after finishing *Killing the Tides*, that I wanted to do nothing but crawl inside of a bottle and drink myself away.

Which is exactly what I did.

"What's the next book about?" she asks. "Without spoiling anything for me."

Chuckling, I get up from the counter and head to the fridge, grabbing a bottle of water that Savannah was kind enough to stock for me. "Much of the same… my hero Max will have a new problem to quell in the streets of New York. And he'll fuck his way through a bevy of beauties while he's at it."

"Of course he will," she says drily. "Any other hints?"

I stare at her a moment, and it hits me hard that she is really quite gorgeous. While she's a little too saccharine for my proclivities, I can't deny that she's actually pretty fucking hot. She's a little too thin and probably would bruise easily, but her dark hair and amber eyes, along with her smooth skin, begs my attention. Unfortunately, she'd probably break too easy under my rough ministrations so I dismiss the thought of fucking her, even though my cock seems to sigh in frustration over said banishment.

"I wrote a new character into my book yesterday," I tell her. "I'm basing her off you."

Savannah's eyebrows shoot sky high, and she gives me a lopsided grin. "You mean I'm going to be a heroine in your book?"

"Sadly, no. You're more like an anti-heroine," I tell her truthfully.

"What does that mean?"

"It's like an important figure in the book, but they don't possess the conventional heroine traits."

"Oh," she says matter-of-factly. "So, no red cape and superhuman powers to help Max battle evil?"

"Sorry, babe," I tell her as I walk back over to my seat. "You just don't have what it takes. In fact, I think you're going to meet quite the gruesome ending."

"Bummer," she says while toying with her food.

"If it's any consolation, Max is going to give you a few great orgasms before you meet your demise."

"Well, that's something, I guess," she says, and then sets her fork down. "So, exactly how did you paint me in your novel?"

I scoop up a bite of rice and vegetables, pop it in my mouth, and chew. After I swallow, I set my fork back down. "No offense, but you're kind of timid. You're the type of woman that takes whatever is handed to her, and tries to make the best of it. You're not very proactive, with no real gumption to take your fate into your own hands. That's how I'm developing the character. I mean, she'll have the best of intentions, but she's always going to wait for Max to save her, rather than try to save herself."

She just stares at me. Her face is impassive at first, but then I see a kernel of heat start to glow. "That is so not me," she huffs.

"Yes, it is. You're a passive woman."

Savannah grips the edge of the counter. "You don't know me at all."

"I know enough."

"Give me one example," she dares me.

"Okay… earlier today, when I told you that you were making too much noise with the hoover, and then I told you to use the broom, you just took it from me. You didn't lay into me for manhandling you, you apologized even though I was the ass, and you just accepted what I told you to do. And I may appear to be a slob, but even I know that you can't use a broom on the area rugs. You have to use the hoover to clean those. Yet, you never stood up for yourself."

Savannah's mouth falls open. She starts to say something, and then snaps it shut while her gaze darts down to her plate. Pushing her stool backward from the counter, she raises her gaze to mine again. "I was just trying to be a good employee," she argues.

"A good employee would have shown a little gumption and told me what you really needed to clean properly. See… you're passive."

"I called you an asshole," she points out.

I can't help myself but throw my head back and laugh. "Ah, yes, you did. But you wouldn't have done that had you not had a flash of temper run through you. That was all involuntary. You'd never have the guts to stand up for yourself like that in calmer times."

"Okay… that caught me off guard, but that's just one example," she says.

"I could give you dozens, Savannah. How about when you showed up at my house last week. You were so intimidated by me being in my boxers that you would have given up this job you say you so desperately need. You got intimidated when I asked you about your feelings for Brody the other night. Now, I'm not saying there's anything wrong with being that way... I'm just saying you have anti-heroine traits that I'm going to exploit in my book."

Her eyes narrow at me, and I can tell she's pissed. I'm betting she's going to push out of her shell again with me in three, two, one...

"You really are an asshole," she exclaims hotly, and then takes a deep breath that she lets out in a rush. "And yes, I realize I'm calling you that in another bout of anger, but I vow to you... I'm going to call you that one day without any provocation. Mark my words."

I can't help but grin at her.

Savannah scoots the stool back further and steps away from the counter, leaving the rest of her meal uneaten. She turns and heads for the door.

"Running away?" I taunt her. "So very anti-heroine." I'm not sure why I'm goading her, but I'm enjoying this moment.

"Not at all," she replies smoothly as she picks up her purse. Her voice is even and without anger. "As it so happens, I have a job to get to that starts in about half an hour. Thank you for dinner. It was… enlightening."

"What job are you going to?" I ask curiously, because all of a sudden, I kind of don't want her to leave.

"I work part time for a photographer as an assistant," she says as she turns to look back at me.

"Have an interest in photography?"

"That's actually my main job. I have a BA from Carnegie Mellon with a minor in photography and digital imaging. Unfortunately, I just got laid off from my job as the photographer for the local newspaper, so I'm taking whatever kind of work I can find right now."

"You're kidding?" I ask, absolutely surprised for some reason.

"What… blowing your image of the passive, little house cleaner? Didn't think someone of my mettle could finish college? Have a real career?"

"No, that's not what I think at all," I tell her, although… if I'm honest, I probably assumed she didn't have much ambition.

"Well… sorry if that puts a kink in the anti-heroine character you're writing. If it's any help to you, I haven't started looking for another photography job yet. That should keep me firmly in your narrow little box you have formed around me for the time being."

Okay, I deserved that.

"Why haven't you looked?" I ask, because I'm stalling so she'll stay for maybe just a moment more and continue to fascinate me. "Clearly, you didn't go to college to clean houses or be someone's assistant?"

"Because… I'm probably going to have to relocate to find something, and I haven't decided where I want to go yet. So, I'm just surviving right now."

It seems sweet Savannah, who is definitely still on the shy and timid side, may have a bit more to her than I originally suspected. Before I can say anything though, she turns to the door. "I need to go, so I'm not late. Thanks again for dinner, and if you don't mind rinsing the plates when you're done, that would make my job a little easier on Friday."

She's out the door before I can even say goodbye.

I finish my meal, ruminating on our conversation. It hits me hard that it was probably the longest conversation, sober anyway, that I've had with someone in a long time. I didn't think Savannah Shepherd held much interest for me, but I'm finding she has layers that I had overlooked.

Maybe she's not quite the Milquetoast I thought she was.

This, of course, does not bode well for the character I just introduced. My muse apparently has a bit more resolve than I originally thought, and my mind starts spinning on how I can work this into my story.

EIGHT

Savannah

I fumble putting the key in Gavin's front doorknob, blinking my eyes to clear my vision. I'm so exhausted I'm practically asleep on my feet, and I'm not sure the last time I ate. I'm going to have to sneak a few veggies out of his fridge or something just to stop the rumbling of my stomach.

I've gone twenty-six hours now with no sleep. Yesterday, I cleaned two houses, and then hit the road for a contract assignment for the newspaper. It was in Charlotte for the opening of a new restaurant by an Outer Banks local who has a sister restaurant in Nags Head. That turned into a twelve-hour trip, ten of which was driving in one day. I got back to the Outer Banks less than thirty minutes ago and headed straight here to clean Gavin's house. When I'm done with his cleaning, I'm going home, where I'm going to collapse into a coma and sleep until tomorrow morning when I'm scheduled to volunteer at The Haven.

Finally, the key slides home and I open the front door. I can hear Gavin moving around in the kitchen. When I walk in, he's pulling a bottle of water out of the fridge. As he straightens and closes the door, my stomach gives a little flip because holy hell, he's standing there without his shirt on and his chest is just as magnificent as I remembered it. He's wearing nothing but a pair of track pants and silver and black running shoes. His chest and face are covered with sweat, his hair plastered to his head, and it's clear he just worked out or something.

Twisting the cap off the water bottle, he gives me a smile and says, "Good morning."

"You're an asshole," I tell him with a straight face, fulfilling my promise to call him that without any provocation. I stifle the yawn that wants to burst out of my mouth, which would totally dilute the power of my message.

He smirks at me briefly, and then starts drinking his water. The way his throat moves is freakin' sexy as hell, and I use the opportunity to stare at him unnoticed.

When he finishes the entire bottle, he sets it on the counter. "I just got done with my run, and I'm going to hit the shower before I start writing. Can you go ahead and start with the vacuuming so it doesn't interfere with me later?"

I roll my eyes at his thoughtful gesture and walk to the counter to pick up his empty water bottle. Pulling open one of the bottom cupboards, I toss it in the recycle bin. "Sure. Anything else special today?"

"Um… maybe a sandwich at lunch?" he asks.

"Be glad to," I say as I notice that the sink is full of dishes again, but at least they all appear to have been rinsed off. Geez… why can't he just put the damn things in the dishwasher?

"Are you still mad at me?" he asks.

I jerk in surprise. "No, why would you think that? Because I called you an asshole?"

"No," he says chuckling. "You gave me fair warning you were going to do that. Bonus points for that, by the way. It's just... you seem kind of quiet today."

Cocking an eyebrow at him, I grab my vacuum cleaner and head for the staircase. "Just trying to stay within the bounds of your stereotype of me," I quip, but truthfully, I'm too freakin' tired to muster up the brainpower to hold conversation.

When I reach the bottom of the stairs, I feel a pull on the vacuum cleaner. I turn to see Gavin pulling it out of my hands. "I'll carry that up for you."

"Thanks," I murmur, not quite sure how to handle this nicer, more gentlemanly Gavin Cooke.

"My pleasure, Sweet," he says and then bounds up the steps ahead of me.

"Sweet?" I ask, dumbfounded by this apparent nickname he's given me.

"Yeah... 'sweet'... because you're... well, sweet."

"For a writer, you're not very original," I mutter, and he laughs in response.

When I reach the top of the stairs, I see the vacuum cleaner waiting there and Gavin disappearing into his room. I go ahead and get started on the three spare bedrooms first, which will give Gavin plenty of time to get showered and vacated before I vacuum the large area rug in his bedroom.

Unfortunately, the normal lull that I find so peaceful with the vacuuming about sends me into a deep sleep while I'm standing, so I make my movements a little shorter in stride to bust up my rhythm. Glancing at my watch, I see I've only been at it for five minutes, and I'm about ready to topple over. God, I can't wait for this day to be over.

When I finish with the spare bedrooms, I cautiously walk into Gavin's. His bathroom door is still shut, so I plug in the machine and start to move it across the huge rug. I try to make quick work of it so I can get out of the privacy of his room, but within just moments of me starting, the bathroom door opens and a wave of steam pours out.

And yeah… Gavin walks out with nothing but a towel around his narrow waist.

I sneak a quick glance at him, and shit… that memory will be seared into my brain forever. He's a pretty ripped guy, but my eyes were helplessly drawn to that dark line of hair that went due south from just below his navel. It brought back memories of the way he was exposed outside of his boxers when I first met him. I had a guilty curiosity course through me, wondering how big he would be if he were fully erect.

Gavin doesn't say a word, although I probably wouldn't hear him over the hum of the vacuum. I turn my back on him, moving my way around the other side of his bed. Just as I'm about finished with that side, I jump as something goes sailing past my shoulder and lands on the floor beside me. Glancing down, I see it's the towel he was wearing. My skin prickles with awareness that I'm standing in the same room with a very naked, and very sexy, British author.

I know this is a test. He's testing me to see how anti-heroine I can be. I'm sure he expects me to blush deeply—which, okay, I am—but I'm sure he expects me to stiffen up in mortification and ignore his taunt due to extreme embarrassment.

It's time to show Mr. Cooke my heroine traits.

Holding the vacuum handle in one hand, I bend over and grab the towel, throwing it over my shoulder. I turn my head, look straight at him, and will myself to maintain eye contact and not look at anything below his chin.

"Thanks," I call out loud enough that he can hear me over the vacuum. I even give him a quick wink before turning back around.

Holy hell... he was completely naked. While it was a brief glance and I definitely sought out just his eyes, my surrounding vision took in his nude form in all its glory. I'm sadly disappointed I didn't get a better look at the rest of him, and my cheeks burn with the realization that I am undeniably, one-hundred percent, completely attracted to this strange and frustrating man.

But God... look at him. What's not to be attracted to?

I go back to finishing a few more swipes of the rug. Turning the vacuum off, I push it out of his room. I have the distinct feeling he's smirking at me. I wish I were brave enough to do something that would leave him confounded, wondering if Savannah "Sweet" Shepherd isn't quite the demure little creature he has me pegged to be.

But truly... I don't have that in me. Especially not with the lack of sleep I'm functioning under. I'd probably end up doing something completely lame and cheesy, and my new nickname from him would be "Dork."

When I reach the hallway, as an afterthought, I can't help but turn back around to ask him, "Do you want me to clean your office really quick since I didn't get it last week?"

Damn... he has a pair of jeans on already, but his chest is still yummy and bared to me. He nods his head while reaching in a drawer for a T-shirt. "Just give it a quick dusting. You can do the floor next week. I have to make a few calls before I start writing."

I quickly run downstairs and grab my bucket of supplies, trudging up to the third floor. The last flight of stairs leaves me winded, and I'm betting that has everything to do with lack of food energy.

His office is nice with dark hardwoods and burgundy walls. It holds nothing but an ornate wooden desk in the middle of the room that faces the floor-to-ceiling glass windows that overlook the ocean. His desk is well organized with a laptop in the middle, a stack of legal pads, and a few pens. To the right of the laptop sits a small frame, and I creep forward to get a closer look.

I'm surprised to see it's a picture of a little boy sitting on the steps outside of a house. He's adorable, with brown hair and bright blue eyes. He's showing a semi-toothless grin at the camera, and I have to wonder who it is.

I hear Gavin coming up the stairs so I quickly get to work dusting his desk, making a quick pass over the framed photo but steering clear of his laptop. I also wipe down the doors and windowsills, deciding against cleaning the windows because they look to be in good shape and I know Gavin wants to get to work.

By the time Gavin sits at his desk and boots up his computer, I'm backing out of his office. Just before I leave, he reminds me, "A sandwich and some chips if you don't mind around noon."

"Sure thing, boss man," I tell him and shut the door behind me.

"Sweet... wake up," I hear a voice say, sounding like it's way off in the distance. I push mentally against it and sink back down into slumber.

Something touches my shoulder lightly and shakes me. "Come on, Sweet... get up."

"Stop," I say grouchily, swatting at the offending thing that's shaking me.

I hear a chuckling sound, and it gets louder. "Savannah... wake up. You're going to get a kink in your neck in that position."

What?

I lift my head up and blearily open my eyes. Looking around in confusion, I'm in a place I don't immediately recognize, and then Gavin's face comes into focus. Then I see that I'm in his kitchen.

Why in the hell am I in Gavin's kitchen?

"Gavin?" I ask as I sit up straighter and rub my eyes.

"You fell asleep on the counter," I hear him say, and awareness starts to filter in.

I finished cleaning but had miscalculated the timing of his laundry, still waiting on the last load to dry. I went ahead and fixed him a sandwich, put it in the fridge, and then sat on one of the stools at the kitchen island. I vaguely remember laying my arms on the counter, resting my head there for just a second. I intended to close my eyes for just a moment, hoping to get some relief from the blistering headache that had started about an hour before.

A huge yawn courses through me and I arch my back, stretching my arms skyward, and yup... my neck is sore from the position I was in. No clue how long I was out.

"Tsk, tsk, tsk," Gavin says. "Sleeping on the job. What's a stern employer to do?"

"Sorry," I mutter, rubbing my eyes again. "I didn't mean to fall asleep."

"No worries," he says as he leans a hip against the corner beside where I'm sitting. Crossing his arms over his chest, he looks down at me. "No offense, though. You kind of look like crap. Rough night of sleep?"

"Try no sleep at all," I tell him with another yawn. "I had a job for the newspaper over in

Charlotte yesterday and when I got back in to town, I came straight here to clean your house."

"What the fuck, Sweet?" I hear him growl, and I focus my weary gaze on him. He looks angry but for the first time, it doesn't cause a frisson of unease to course through me. I think I'm too tired to be intimidated by him. "You didn't have to come today. You could have just gone home and slept."

Pushing myself up from the stool, I stand a little wobbly. "Well, yeah… sorry, but the poor have to work when they can so it wasn't an option for me to ditch my job."

"Go lie down on my couch and get some more sleep," he commands me, and I don't even bother looking at him. Instead, I head into the laundry room, where I can still hear the machine whirring. The timer says it has twenty more minutes.

Just great.

Walking back into the kitchen, Gavin appraises me while standing in the same position.

"I made you a sandwich. It's in the fridge," I tell him and sit back down on the stool again, resting my chin on my hand. "I still have twenty minutes before your last load of laundry is done, and then I'll get out of your hair."

"Go lie down on the couch and sleep for twenty minutes then," he demands of me again.

"No, thanks," I say, refusing to look at him, even as my eyes start to droop.

"For fuck's sake," I hear him grumble. The next thing I know, one of his arms is sliding under my legs, the other behind my back, and he's lifting me from the stool.

"Gavin," I yelp in surprise as he carries me into the living room, I'm sure to deposit me on the couch. "I don't need to sleep. I can do that when I get home."

"Just shut up, Savannah. For once, your mouth isn't so sweet," he growls at me, and then bends over to lay me on the couch with surprising tenderness.

I start to sit up the minute his arms release me, but he does nothing more than put his large hand in the center of my chest and push me back down. Whereas ten seconds ago, I felt bone weary with exhaustion, the warmth of his hand through my T-shirt causes my pulse to speed up. I struggle for just a moment, attempting to continue my rise, but his brute force wins out and he pushes me all the way back down.

"If you don't lie down, I'm going to lie down on top of you and pin you there. Now which do you want?"

"Fine," I huff out just to get him to leave, because there's nothing appealing about him laying his body over mine, right? "Just until the laundry is done. Now go eat your sandwich and get back to work. I'll see you next week, okay?"

He stares at me a moment, his lips curved up in amusement. "Sure thing, Sweet. See you next week."

Gavin turns away and heads back into the kitchen. I close my eyes, and I'm immediately out.

NINE

Gavin

What the fuck are you doing, Cooke? I ask myself for about the hundredth time as I watch Savannah sleeping on my couch. The sun has gone down, and she's been out for a solid nine hours. I've never seen anyone sleep that hard before. She hasn't moved a muscle... at least not as far as I can tell.

After I deposited her on the couch, I ate my sandwich and went back to work, banging out another three thousand words before dinnertime. I came back downstairs, expecting to see the couch vacated, but she was still flat on her back, one arm resting over her stomach where her T-shirt had ridden up just enough to give me a tiny peek at the smooth flesh. Her long legs were bare as she was wearing a pair of denim shorts today because the weather is quite mild. My fucking fingers itched to touch her, but I shook my head to clear it of such ludicrous thoughts and went into the kitchen to heat the Mexican casserole she left me.

I vowed to myself if the smell of the food woke her up, I'd offer her some and send her on her way. When that didn't work, I figured the banging around in the kitchen while I ate and then rinsed my dishes would wake her up, and then I'd send her on her way. She stayed soundly asleep.

Only after I grabbed a bottle of scotch and a glass, this one a plastic tumbler with a brown and green palm tree on it, and poured my first drink, did I sit on the loveseat opposite of her and vow to myself I'd wake her up after I finished my first one.

Now, two glasses of scotch later, she still hasn't stirred. I don't know why I'm not waking her up and making her leave. Staring at her in the dim light cast from the one lamp I have turned on, my thoughts take a dark turn. Why is this slip of a girl causing me so much fascination? She's not like my usual brand of tramp that I like to fuck and then tell them to get the fuck out of dodge. I'm attracted to her... sure. But it scares me to think that the attraction is because I can't quite figure her out. I normally steer clear of any type of situation that takes me out of my comfort zone, and she definitely makes me uncomfortable.

I'm pleasurably warmed by the scotch, yet I hesitate to pour another glass. Just weeks ago, I only survived my life by drinking myself into a stupor most nights. Sometimes I'd really launch myself into oblivion by taking some coke, desperate to escape my past.

But now, I don't have that compulsion. I'm drinking my scotch tonight and enjoying the smoky, sweet flavor... relishing the slow burn when it hits my stomach. I'm not burning my taste buds out by gulping it down, but rather taking small sips to appreciate the fine art of single malt chemistry.

It's definitely an appreciation tonight, not a compulsion.

Sitting in the semi-dark, sipping my liquor and watching a woman sleep. Some would find that romantically sweet. I find it to be macabre, because no matter the fascination sweet Savannah holds for me, when it boils right down to it, deep down I want to break her. I want to prove to myself that she's nothing special… that she's exactly as I imagine her to be. An uninteresting sort of woman who thinks more of herself than she actually is, and in the grand scheme of things, she'll never amount to more.

It's why I haven't changed the plot line of her character. Yeah… she called me an asshole, and yeah, she's asserting herself with me more, but she'd never have done those things if I hadn't practically dared her to do them. She doesn't have it in her… not for the long haul anyway, to really push at me.

Demand of me.

Demand of anyone, for that matter.

No, she doesn't have the strength of character that would be deserving of heroine status in my book, so I'm not changing a damn thing I've written just because she's shown a little gumption of late.

Savannah lets out a soft sigh from the couch, and I watch her intently. The hand across her stomach moves up, and she stretches both of them over her head, arching her back off the couch in a sleepy stretch. It pulls her T-shirt up higher, exposing more of her stomach and thrusting her breasts out.

The two glasses of scotch I've had haven't mellowed me enough that my dick doesn't take notice of the unintentional, but sexy move. It thumps against the zipper of my jeans with interest.

I wonder if I could seduce her... right now? I wonder if I gave into this attraction... this lust that's brewing for her, could the pounding of my cock between her legs drive her right out of my thoughts for good? Maybe that's what I need... just to fuck her, with raw, primal energy... enough to scare her away for good. Maybe then, I could quit thinking about her. She'd run away crying, her dignity shredded, and I could hire a new cleaning service and be done with her.

Savannah takes a deep breath, lets it out, and then goes still. I can't see if her eyes are open in the shadows where she lies, but by the measured movement of her chest, I think she's gone back down under.

Setting my empty tumbler on the table beside me, I stand up and walk over to the couch. I stare down at her, her face so serene and peaceful. I wonder if she's dreaming.

Without a second thought, I sit down on the edge of the couch, in a small area available to me by her left hip. Taking my finger, I stroke it over the skin of her stomach and say, "Sweet... it's time to wake up?"

She gives a soft moan in her sleep and arches her back off the cushions again.

And fuck, that's sexy.

And yeah, I definitely want to fuck her.

"Savannah," I call out to her softly and bring my hand up to her face, grazing my fingers over her temple. "You need to wake up."

Her eyes flutter open, immediately making contact with mine, and I let my hand drop away.

"She's alive," I murmur as she stares at me with dark eyes.

"What time is it?" she rasps out, turning her head to the left to look out the back glass door.

"Just after nine PM," I tell her. "You slept like a rock. I could have had my way with you, and you would have never known."

"Oh, yeah?" she asks skeptically, and with sleep still heavy in her voice. "Like what?"

Oh, little girl, the things I could have done to you.

I go for the shock factor to see what she does. Reaching my left arm behind me, I place my fingers on her calf. Her skin is warm and silky, and her breath hitches at the slight touch. "I could have skimmed my fingers up your leg, right past your knee… up your thigh," I tell her, moving my fingers up that same path I'm describing. When I get to the edge of her shorts, I halt my progress. "I could have inched my way right under these short little shorts… found the edge of your damp panties just to prove that you were having a sexy little dream while you were sleeping."

A tiny moan comes out of her mouth, and her eyes glitter back at me from the ambient light of the lamp reflecting in them. "You didn't do that," she says without any type of conviction at all… and is that a bit of longing I hear?

I finger the edge of her shorts. "I've done all kinds of dark and dirty things that your limited imagination could never fully appreciate. It would have been nothing for me to do that to you."

"Maybe so," she breathes out in a rush, "but you wouldn't have done that without my consent."

"Hmmm," I say thoughtfully, releasing the denim material and placing my fingers on her hot skin, feeling her muscles jump underneath my touch. "I'm wondering… would you give me your consent right now? Would you let me tunnel my fingers inside just a bit, let me see if your panties are damp because what I'm saying to you now is turning you on?"

She doesn't move a muscle… holds her breath and watches to see what I'll do. But that doesn't work for me, because she's going to need to be a little more forceful if she wants what I'm offering. I can see what she wants in her eyes, but yes… I want more.

"Tell me, Sweet," I taunt her as my fingers stroke back and forth underneath the hem of her shorts, just a mere inch from the edge of her panties. "Do you have it in you to ask for my fingers, or would you rather leap off this couch and flee away?"

Savannah inhales sharply, and I tense as I wait for her to choose the latter option. I'm so fucking turned on right now by trying to dare her into letting me seduce her, that I'd probably hold her down and not let her up. She pulls her lower lip in between her teeth and chews on it thoughtfully while she weighs her options.

"Come on, Sweet," I encourage her, my voice rough with need. "Show me what you got inside of you… deep down inside. Take a walk on the wild side… you know you want to."

Fuck me standing. Savannah flexes her hips upward, a silent demand that I move my hand. It's clear to me now that she wants it, but she's still too afraid to demand it out loud.

Moving my hand away from her leg, I shake my head and chastise her. "Not good enough, Sweet. You need to demand of it of me."

Savannah gives a tiny cry of frustration, and I can see the warring within her eyes. I've taken her so far out of her comfort zone that her natural inclination is going to be withdrawal, but her body is reactive to me and it's battling with her common sense.

"I know what you want," I tell her softly. "You know what you want. But prove to me you have it in you to demand it."

Blowing out a breath, she says, "I want you to…"

"Tell me," I urge her on.

"Touch me," she says softly.

"Where?"

Her eyes squeeze closed, her brow furrowing inward. When she opens them again, she gives another frustrated sigh. "Between my legs."

"Uh-uh," I chide her. "Dirtier. Make it dirty for me."

Savannah opens her mouth… she's on the verge of telling me what I want to hear, and my cock swells in anticipation. She's going to push past her barriers and restraints, show me her dark side, and then it will be okay if I fuck her.

I can finally fuck her.

"I can't," she exclaims and surges off the couch. I rear backward, surprised by her move as she tries to push past me.

My arm snakes out and grabs her around the waist, pulling her back down onto my lap, right onto my aching erection.

"No," she cries out, struggling against me.

"Shh," I whisper against her ear, but I don't tighten my hold on her. She's upset, and I don't want to frighten her. Fuck… I want to console her for some insane reason, which is not a part of my DNA.

"Shh," I whisper again as I gently rub her back in broad strokes to calm her down. "I'm sorry."

"You're an asshole," she practically whimpers with her face pressed into my shoulder.

Sighing, I push her back from me so I can look her in the face. "Yes, I am. I shouldn't have pushed that way. I thought you could take it."

"I'm not some sort of sick game for you to play with," she says, her voice sounding stronger.

"I know," I agree with her, because it was the sickest of games. But fuck… she wanted me. For a moment, she was all in, and had I just accepted it when she said she wanted me to touch her between her legs, my fingers would be buried deep within her right now. But I let my own darkness and need for control dictate to me the way it would be played out. So I could make the terms and force her to abide by them.

Pushing Savannah off my lap, I wait until she's standing steady and say, "You should go."

She walks on shaky legs into the kitchen, and I stand from the couch to face her while she gathers her purse and keys. Dragging my fingers through my hair, I sigh in frustration.

Sexual frustration, but also mental frustration. What the fuck was I just doing?

When Savannah reaches the door, she hesitates and then says without turning to look back at me, "I don't understand what just happened."

"Fuck if I know," I mutter.

Savannah then turns to look at me, cocking her head to the side. "I'm curious, Gavin. Did you want me too, or was that just a way to try to break me out of the mold you wanted to put me in?"

Her words floor me and shame me all at once. In five long strides, I'm standing before her, cupping her by the back of her head with my hand. Leaning down close, I tell her, "I fucking wanted you. Don't doubt that. But you're right… I wanted to break you first."

"Why?" she whispers, her eyes cautious.

"Because I'm dark that way. I'm way too bitter for your brand of sweet."

"I find that to be sad," she consoles me.

"Very," I agree with her as I release my hold and turn away from her. "I'll see you next week."

I hear Savannah open the door as I start to walk back into the kitchen.

"Gavin?" she asks hesitantly.

"What's up?" I ask, struggling for seeming nonchalance as I turn to look at her.

"Want to take a break from your writing? Do something to get you out of this house tomorrow? It might do you good."

"Excuse me?" I'm bewildered by this absolute change of subject.

"I um... well, I volunteer at this no-kill animal shelter called The Haven. Want to come help me?"

I stare at her like she's a phenom from another planet. Her face is earnest, her intentions pure. She's saddened by my darkness and wants to pull me out of it.

Oh, Sweet... not going to happen.

"No, thanks," I tell her. "Not my sort of thing."

"Oh... okay. Well, if you change your mind, just call me."

"I won't," I assure her. "But thanks for the offer."

"Sure," she says with a smile. "See you next week."

TEN

Savannah

Oh my God! I think I may be absolutely and completely obsessed with Gavin Cooke. I hate myself for it, but it's completely true. I feel like a completely different person when I'm around him.

When he's taunting me.

Goading me.

Seducing me.

I'm so far out of my league that my natural inclination is to turn tail and run, but there is a dark part to me... way deep down, that wants to explore the feelings he's conjuring up inside of me with his voodoo magic.

Last night... oh God, last night!

I have never... ever... been so turned on, so sexually aware, as I was when he was speaking dirty words to me with his fingers on my leg.

He pushed and pushed at me, and I wanted to roll over and give in. I wanted to tell him the dirty word he was looking for so he could push those fingers into me. I wanted it so bad I could taste it, and yet I let my fear and common sense prevail.

When he pulled me back down onto his lap, and I could feel that huge erection pushing into my leg, I wanted to rub up and down on it and beg him to do something to me. I want to change time right now, go back, and demand it of him, like he wanted and I refused.

I obsessed about it for an hour after I got home, still exhausted, yet too wired to sleep. I even sent him a lame ass text, giving him the address of The Haven and telling him, *Just in case you change your mind. I'll be there all day.*

He never responded, but that wasn't a surprise to me. Gavin is so closed off in his own world that I don't think he bothers with societal conventions.

Pushing the wheelbarrow back into the supply room of the main kennel, I check my watch and see it's only nine AM. It's taken me just a little over an hour to feed all the dogs and cats. I make my way back through the kennel, making note that most of the dogs have left their runs because it's nice and cool out. It should warm up a bit, which will make it perfect for me to start bathing them outside.

Heading over to the stable, I mentally go over the rest of the chores I need to do today. After I finish feeding the horses and clean out their stalls, I have to bathe the dogs, clean out the cats' litter boxes, and re-stock the indoor supply room from the small shed that houses the bulk feed supply. Then Brody asked me to run a few errands, which should still give me plenty of time to get back for the evening feeding.

It's a tough day of work, and I only do a full Saturday once a month, but it's my pleasure to do so to give Alyssa and Brody some time together away from The Haven. They devote their entire life to their work here, so their Saturday's off are well deserved.

Just as I finish cleaning out the stalls, I hear a vehicle pulling up behind the kennel. I decide to leave the horses out a bit to stretch their legs in the small paddock, and head out to see who it is.

Possibly Gavin?

As soon as I step outside of the stable, I see, with utter disappointment, that it's Brody pulling up. Not that I'm not happy to see him, because, hello... it's Brody, but because I had been hoping—in my heart of hearts—that Gavin would come and spend the day with me.

I wanted to get to know him better, because his dark allure was pulling at me hard. He also has me fascinated by this concept of how he views me, and I feel the burning need to make him see that I'm so much more.

Brody gets out of his car as I walk across the grass that is just starting to turn brown with the cooler weather. "What are you doing here?" I call out to him.

"Alyssa's getting girlie shit done to her nails with Gabby and Casey, so thought I'd come hang out here today," he says with a smile.

I follow him into the kennel and he heads for the office he and Alyssa share at the front of the building. "Come on, Brody. It's your day off. You should be out having fun."

"Yeah, like what?" he asks as he sits down at the desk and fires up the computer.

"Oh, I don't know... get your brother and go surfing."

"Yeah… sorry, but when it gets chilly enough you have to wear a wetsuit, I don't go in the water anymore."

"Wuss," I tease him.

"Absolutely," he affirms, clicking on the Outlook button to pull up his mail. "So what all still needs to be done today?"

"Most everything. I just got the animals fed and the stalls cleaned."

He browses the emails for a moment, and then turns to me with a serious look. "Go ahead and clean the litter boxes and then run those errands for me. I'll handle washing the dogs."

"No freakin' way, dude," I tell him with a stern look. "I'm volunteering my precious time here, and you are not taking away the one fun thing I look forward to all week."

Brody gives a bark of a laugh and stands up from the desk. Chucking me under the chin with his knuckles, he says, "Fair enough. Didn't think I'd be able to pull that one over on you. Let's go split the work, and then I'll take you out to lunch before we run our errands."

I follow Brody out of the office, back through the kennel, and out a side door that takes us to the cats' building. "We need to stop by the feed supply store and pick up some probiotics," I tell him. "That new lab mix, Nelly, has some loose stools."

"Got it. And we need to hit the lumber supply store. I saw one of the fence posts on the paddock is cracked near the bottom. I think one of the horses kicked it."

We start to work cleaning out the litter boxes, and yeah, I get sidetracked playing with the five new kittens that came in last week. It takes so little to amuse them, nothing more than the string from my hoodie that I wave in front of their fuzzy little faces.

"So, what was the deal with that English dude you were talking to at the bar last week? He said something that pissed you off."

Picking up one of the kittens, I hold it above my face and watch its little paws try to swipe at me. "That's Gavin Cooke. I clean his house, and he can be a bit prickly."

"What did he say to you that made you practically run out of the bar?"

"I didn't practically run out," I grumble, although I did have an insane urge that night to flee from his sexual innuendos. "He just asked if you and I were lovers."

"No way," Brody exclaims as he dumps fresh litter into on one of the boxes. "Why would he think that?"

"I don't think he really did. I think he was just trying to get under my skin, which is something he apparently enjoys doing."

"Maybe he was trying to get under your skirt and was checking to see if you were single," he muses.

"Not his style," I tell Brody adamantly, and I'm amazed I know Gavin well enough to know exactly what his style is. If he wanted to get under my skirt, he would have said something like, *I want to fuck you, and I could care less if you're fucking someone else.*

Yes, that was Gavin's style.

"Well, he seems kind of full of himself," Brody says casually. "Besides… he got under Tanya Stokes' skirt that night, so I'm sure he was a happy camper."

I spin toward Brody fast, bringing the kitten down to my chest to cuddle. "How do you know that?"

"Because she was hitting on him pretty hard prior to that. He bought her a few drinks. They left together that night. Pretty obvious, right?"

"I guess," I mutter as I put the kitten back in his cage.

Man, that bothers me. I mean, I sort of figured Gavin was a player, but he's kind of a grumpy recluse, so I never figured him to hit a local establishment and then hit the local talent so quickly. I know deep down that there's really nothing special he sees in me. He's a man with certain proclivities. I fascinate him for some reason, and he wants to exercise those proclivities because I was opportune. And I have no right to a feeling of betrayal, because we have no relationship… no exclusivity… no expectations to be broken. In fact, I'm betting if anything were to ever happen with Gavin, it would only be on the terms that there was no relationship… no exclusivity… no expectations.

Not that I'm expecting anything with him.

But still… the prospect of a hot, one-night stand with him is a thrilling prospect. It's so not me… the anti-heroine.

Do I have the daring to do it? It's something I need to consider, but one thing is for sure, if I do… I'll have to do the pursuing, because he made it clear that I had to voice what I wanted. The thought of doing something so outrageous, so beyond the limits of my comfort, makes me slightly nauseated.

Oh, who am I kidding? I don't have it in me. He's exactly right. I'm always going to be the woman that waits for the guy to make the move… to save me… to give me an orgasm. I don't have it in me to be the seducer.

Sighing in frustration, I open up the last cage and reach in past a sleeping black and orange tabby to pull the litter box closer to me.

"What's with the dramatic sigh?" Brody asks.

"Nothing," I say absently, and then I change my mind. Brody has hard life experiences, and from those experiences, untold amounts of wisdom which I intend to tap into. "Actually... have you ever felt like you were just stagnating... just running in place without any idea of where you'd go if you could ever get off your hamster wheel?"

"I'm happy to say 'no' to that answer," Brody says as he closes the last cage that he was working on. Turning to me, he leans up against the metal housing and shoves his hands in his pockets as he waits for me to enlighten him.

"Never?" I ask in slight disbelief. "Not even after you got out of prison?"

"Not even then," he confirms. "I didn't have any ambitions or goals at that point, so there wasn't anything to stagnate. I was satisfied with just *being*, if you know what I mean."

I don't know what he means, but I could imagine. Brody's charmed life of medical school and a prosperous future were ripped away when he went to prison. Since getting out last spring, he was absolutely content to just sling drinks at Last Call and hide himself away from the rest of the world. Thank God Alyssa reached through to him... got him to want to live life again to the fullest. Now he runs The Haven with her and couldn't be happier.

It's what I want.

To be absolutely happy with my profession... my life... my world. I want to get off the freakin' hamster wheel of mediocrity.

"So I take it you feel like you're stagnating?" Brody asks as he pins me with his eyes.

"Think about it," I tell him in a rush. "I have a degree that's practically useless, I got laid off from my job with which I had hope to put said degree to use, I clean houses for a living now, and oh, yeah, I work for a sleazy photographer who comes on to me every chance he can, and I have to put up with it because I need the job too damn bad. On top of that, I haven't even started looking for something else, because I don't know what the hell to do with my life. No fortitude... no drive. I'm an anti-heroine."

Brody's eyebrows rise high, and he gives me a smirk. "That's a mouthful. Got anything else?"

"I'm done," I mutter quietly, feeling dejected over the lameness of my life. We both walk out of the cats' housing and head to the large supply shed so we can load up on restocking supplies in the kennel room.

As we reach the door, Brody reaches out and touches my shoulder to stop me. "Savannah... you have more fortitude and spine than most people I know. Don't forget what you did… one of the bravest things I've ever heard of in my life," he murmurs.

My skin prickles at his pointed reminder to me of a past that is filled with fear, pain, humiliation, and oddly… achievement.

"That was so long ago," I protest as I turn to step inside the supply shed.

"Not so long ago," he argues softly. "It speaks of who you are at the fundamental core of things."

His words press in upon me. Really? Is he right? Do I have more resolve and moxie than even I give myself credit for?

He's talking about a secret I once shared with him and Alyssa… that's really not a secret, because it was splashed all through the newspapers back in Indiana. I went through hell during my senior year of high school, taking on a predatory monster and his super wealthy, socially connected family. I was bullied, berated, and mocked for my actions. I lost my closest friends and caused my parents' untold anguish what with the eggs being thrown at our house and the late night, threatening phone calls. I was called a whore, a liar, and made into a public spectacle.

But in the end, I stuck to my guns and I won. I was vindicated, and I went through untold torture to get to the finish line. I stuck my chin out, stiffened my spine, and I never gave up.

Yeah, Brody is right... that was definitely my shining moment in life. I had something within me to battle against evil, and I never gave up. I never waited for someone to save me. I saved myself.

Gavin Cooke doesn't know what he's talking about.

Anti-heroine my ass.

ELEVEN

Gavin

I hear something... a creak maybe... down on the first floor, and my ears perk up. Glancing at the time on my laptop, I see it's getting close to ten o'clock and I'm on fucking pins and needles waiting for Savannah to get here. I even left my office door open this morning so I could hear when she arrived. So I could, by chance as far as she knew, go down into the kitchen to get something—a bottle of water maybe—and see her.

Fuck, I need to see her, because I've spent the last three days obsessing about the woman. Ever since I pushed her off my raging erection and right out the door last Friday night, said raging erection has become positively monstrous. Jacking off doesn't seem to help, because all I can think about is how her skin felt when I slid my fingers up her leg, or how her eyes darkened when she told me to touch her between the legs, or how frustrated she looked when I wouldn't.

I'm frustrated as hell that she wouldn't go that extra step and give in to me. I'm frustrated at myself that I let a golden opportunity get away, because had I just given up a minutia of control, I could have had her. I could have fucked my brains out and then been done with her.

I had to stop myself probably five times on Saturday from going to help her at that animal shelter, just so I could get another whiff of her scent, maybe brush up against that warm skin. I feel like a boy with an insane crush or something. Frankly, it's buggering me.

Leaning forward in my chair, I read the last few lines of my manuscript and sigh. It's not flowing the way I want it to. I started a scene this weekend, writing it almost word for word exactly how my Friday night turned out on the couch with Savannah. My hero, Max, demanded she give him the words he wanted to hear. He wanted to hear her beg, *I want you to touch my pussy, Max.*

And just as it happened in real life, my little anti-heroine, who I named Honey—because, yeah… honey is sweet—pushed away from him in embarrassment and shyness, refusing him.

I wrote it that way because I have no intention of changing the plot line regarding this character. Max is ultimately going to have her, but he'll discard her as well. And he won't be able to save her from evil, and she sure as hell won't save herself.

Yup… needs to stay that way… true to my muse.

Staring at the screen, I wait for further inspiration to hit, but it never comes. I read my last paragraphs over and over again, now doubting whether Honey should really deny my hero.

My fingers twitch.

What the fuck… the scene definitely needs tweaked.

Max inched her skirt up her leg, letting his fingers glide along her skin. "You know what I want to do to you? I want you to let me touch you… see if your panties are as wet as I suspect they'd be. Then I want to finger fuck you... let you ride my hand a bit. Just to start..."

Honey's breath turned ragged, but she remained absolutely still other than her fingers, which dug into his shoulders.

"Tell me, sweet girl," Max crooned at her in a velvety voice. "Tell me you want it too... tell me what you want me to do to you."

Honey's eyelids drooped, and she licked at her lips. Max's fingers stroked along the edge of her panties, causing her to jerk slightly in his arms. He was so fucking hard at that moment he could probably jackhammer a sidewalk with his cock.

"Come on, baby," Max murmured near her ear, easing just the tip of his finger under the elastic edge. "Show me that raw craving I know you have."

Honey gave a soft cry and tilted her hips in a vain attempt to move his hand closer to her core.

"That's a bad girl," Max said with censure and, just to punish her a little, pulled his hand away. "I need the words, Honey. Give them to me."

"I want you to..."

"Tell me," he demanded harshly.

"Touch me," she said in a frustrated rush.

"Where?"

Honey's eyes darkened and the pulse in her neck was leaping. "Between my legs."

"Not good enough," he sneered. "Dirtier. If you want it, make it fucking filthy for me."

Honey gnashed her teeth, and her eyes sparked with determination. She leaned in close to Max, putting her lips just a hair's breath away from his, and snarled, "I want you to touch my pussy, Max. I want you to finger fuck my pussy."

Max chuckled as he brought his hand between her legs, stroking the damp cotton of her panties. "Good girl. I'm going to hit you hard with my fingers, then I'm going to bend you over and fuck you hard from behind."

Yes! I yell out in victory inside my own head as I type out those last few words. That is fucking perfect. Exactly the way it should be.

Pushing back in my chair, I let the elation of a well-written scene course through me as I stare at the computer screen. It's how it should be. Well... it's how it should have been the other night. How I wanted it to turn out. How I wanted Savannah to demand me to pleasure her.

But fuck if that happened.

The thrill of the great scene wanes as I realize I'm not keeping Honey true to my muse. I'm making her into something I want Savannah to be, and it's sick, sick, sick. It's sick, because I've decided I want Savannah badly even though she represents so much of what I don't like in a woman, so I'm trying to plump her up into something she's not… in a fucking work of fiction.

I'm quite possibly the world's biggest wanker.

I hear the faint click of the front door closing and know that Savannah has arrived. My pulse leaps with the knowledge, and I push out of my chair.

As I hit the bottom landing that abuts the kitchen, I see her laying her purse and keys on my counter. She darts her eyes at me, and then turns to lift her bucket of supplies up. "Good morning," she says softly.

I stare at her, my mouth unable to form any words, because I'm not the type to exchange pleasantries. What I really want to do is crowd in to her, push her back against the refrigerator, and get all up in her space, so we can maybe go back to that intimate interlude that got destroyed by her skittishness. But in the bright light of day, that doesn't seem plausible. She's not coming out of a deep sleep, with a foggy brain and sluggish reactions. No, she's standing there, seeing me with clear eyes and probably a jaundiced mind.

So, I don't say anything, and I just walk to the refrigerator to get a bottle of water. I do, however, walk between her and the back counter, taking care to walk close enough by her that my arm brushes against hers. I can see her actually push herself into the counter to give me space, and that doesn't set well with me. Normally, just knowing that I was affecting her that way would give me a rush, but it's not what I had intended to occur. I want her to step in closer to me, not shy away.

"Do you want me to vacuum right now?"

"You can do it whenever," I tell her as I twist the cap off the water bottle. "It's fairly warm out today... I think I'll write on the back deck."

"Okay," is all she says as she starts loading the dishwasher with the huge pile of plates and silverware I've accumulated.

I wait for her to say something more but she doesn't, soundly ignoring me as I stand there. I don't like it, and I don't know what to do about it because I suck at normal conversation. When it's clear that she's not going to give me the time of day, I give a silent sigh and head back toward the stairs to grab my laptop.

Just as I hit the bottom step, I'm struck with inspiration and turn toward her. "I'd like to hire you for the full day tomorrow."

Savannah jumps in surprise and turns to face me. "I'm sorry... I can't. I have two houses plus a photo shoot to attend."

"Cancel them," I tell her. "I'll pay you more than whatever they're paying you."

She huffs at my demand and turns back to the dishwasher. "Sorry, Gavin, but I can't cancel. That would be unprofessional."

"Who cares?" I throw out. "I'm paying you more than they would."

"And, I'd probably lose those jobs for good, so that's still not going to work for me," she says with exasperation as she closes the dishwasher.

"Then I'll hire you full time," I say... maybe a tad too desperately.

She turns back to me with a bit of a softer look. "Um... no thanks. But what is it you needed me for tomorrow? Can it wait until Thursday as I can swing it that day?"

My brain fuzzes for a minute, because I have no clue why I'm hiring her. I don't need a damn thing.

Think, Cooke. Think.

Finally, I blurt out, "I need to go to Raleigh to pick up a car I'm buying. I want you to drive me so I can work the entire time."

F-u-u-u-ck.

Looks like I'm buying a damn car so I can spend a few hours with this woman.

"Seriously?" she asks. "Why can't you just buy a car here?"

Fuck, oh fuck.

"Um... because they don't sell the type of car that I want in this area. The closest dealership is Raleigh."

I hope to God there's a dealership that has foreign imports or something unusual in Raleigh, because I am so fucking flying by the seat of my pants at this point.

"Well, if you can do it Thursday, I'll be glad to drive you," she says and then starts scrubbing the counters.

"That works for me," I tell her. "I'll just go up now and call them to let them know I'll be there Thursday instead."

"Cool," she says, never lifting her head to look up at me again.

Her indifference to me is pushing all my buttons, and I feel the insane need to get her attention. Except, the way that I want to get it is by stalking up to her and kissing her hard... maybe with my hand between her legs. But that won't do, because it will send her scurrying like a frightened mouse, and I'm not ready to send her totally packing just yet.

So for now, I'll have to bide my time and play according to the rules she's silently laying out.

After I get back into my office, I quickly do a Google search and find there's a Maserati and a Rolls Royce dealership in Raleigh, breathing a quick sigh of relief my impromptu trip didn't get cancelled before it started. I unplug my laptop to take it outside to do some writing when my phone rings.

Pulling it out of my pocket, I see it's my father calling and as much as I don't want to talk to him, I know it's probably important, so I answer.

"Hi, Dad," I say as I connect.

"Gavin," he says cautiously and I cringe, because his pain is my pain and I've had enough of both for now. "How have you been?"

"Fine. Good. Settled in and writing nicely. You?"

"I'm good," he says, but his voice is sad. "We're doing the best we can."

I close my eyes against hurt and take a deep breath. "So, what's up?"

My dad is silent for a moment, and then he clears his throat. "Listen… you got an offer on the house. It's way more than what you're asking for, so I accepted it."

Pressure squeezes my chest, strangling every nerve, muscle, vein, and artery within. I open my mouth to tell my dad, *That's great. Awesome.*

But not a fucking sound comes out.

"It will all be settled within the next month," he continues, and I feel dizzy so I sit down in the squeaky office chair I haven't been able to replace yet.

"So... um... listen, buddy. We're going to have to clean it out," he says sadly, and I grip the edge of my desk as darkness clouds my vision. "What do you want me to do with Charlie's stuff?"

My eyes flick to the photo of Charlie on my desk, and his smile fails to warm me. I think about all of Charlie's things in his room. His octopus stuffed animal and his little red fire engine hat that had a light and siren on top that he loved to wear wherever we went. His little tennis shoes with Velcro straps and purple dinosaurs on them.

"Son?" my dad says gently. "What do you want me to do?"

I blink hard, trying to focus. Giving a little cough, I try to clear the emotion from my throat, but it doesn't work. "Pack it up... give it all away to a charity or something," I rasp out.

My dad is silent for a brief moment, and then he murmurs, "Okay. I'll call you again in a few days to check in on you."

"Okay," I say absently, my mind already shutting down from this conversation. "Cheers."

But then I abruptly call out to him, "Wait."

"Gavin?"

"Just wait... don't give it away. Hold it at your house if you don't mind. I'm not ready..." I start to say, but then my voice cracks.

"I understand," my dad says with only the grace that a parent can show to a child in pain. "Don't worry about it, okay?"

"Okay," I tell him.

We talk for a few more minutes, then my mum jumps on the phone to say hello. We carefully skirt around talking about Charlie, and when we disconnect, I'm relieved the conversation is over.

Setting my phone down on the desk, I scrub my hands over my face, and then through my hair, where I scratch at my scalp. I feel itchy all over and resist the urge to scratch at the skin on my arms. I wait for sadness to seep in, but as I look back over at Charlie's photo, I feel anger surge through me.

Hot, acidic, burning, lava-like anger builds, roiling and racing through my body. I want to hurt someone... lash out at them. Make them feel what I feel, so maybe if by sharing the burden, it will hurt me less.

I briefly think about Savannah downstairs, obliviously immersed in her own little world, and the urge to break her cleanly in half to alleviate some of my own misery takes root. I could walk downstairs right now and with a few seductive words have her begging me for it. I could bend her over the couch, fuck her hard, and then tell her to get the hell out of my house because she wasn't any good.

Yeah, that would crush her… demoralize her beyond repair probably.

And I'd feel good for a few minutes after, I'm sure.

But then I think about having to see the pain in those soft, brown eyes and the anger turns directly inward at me, punching me in my stomach with the force of a nuclear bomb.

Hurtling out of my chair, I grab the edge of my desk and pull upward as hard as I can, toppling it over and sending my laptop and Charlie's photo crashing to the floor. I don't give a moment's thought to neither the laptop nor the precious manuscript I had been working on, but immediately run around the overturned desk and grab the frame that holds Charlie's picture. The glass is shattered, causing dark, fractured spiderwebs to obscure his smiling face.

A knock sounds at my door, as I pull the picture in tight to my chest.

"Gavin… is everything okay?" I hear Savannah call out.

"It's fine," I tell her, and my voice catches. Clearing my throat, I call out again. "It's fine. Go away."

"Are you sure?" she asks hesitantly.

The anger flashes hot, and I yell, "Sod off already. I said I'm fine."

She doesn't answer me, and I can hear her footsteps fall softly away from the door. Leaning back against the wall, I bang my head against it once.

Fuck… when will this ever end?

TWELVE

Savannah

It's amazing the way people will fawn all over you when you're paying $140,000 in cash for a car.

Here's your Perrier, Mr. Cooke, with a slice of lime.

Can we run out and get you some lunch, Mr. Cooke?

Is it warm enough in here for you, Mr. Cooke?

Can I strip you naked and ride you hard, Mr. Cooke?

Okay, that last one didn't happen, but the receptionist that sits behind her black, lacquered desk and gushed over him for ten minutes before asking for an autograph most certainly was asking that in her mind. I could see it in her eyes.

To give him credit, Gavin takes it all in stride, waving most of them away with an impatient hand. He gave the autograph to the bleached-blonde receptionist, but barely spared her a glance and assured everyone he didn't need anything but his car.

I watch as Gavin goes through the paperwork, signing and initialing wherever the salesman points his finger. I can't fathom what it's like to have that much money, yet he never acts entitled or better than everyone else. Sure, his house is huge, but he told me on the drive up here that he would prefer something small like the little two-bedroom flat he had in London, but that he didn't want anyone near him. He didn't tell me why he felt the need to buy a brand new Maserati Quattroporte, especially when he never goes anywhere, but I didn't think to question him on that.

Besides, he worked most of the way up here as he said he would—laptop propped on his lap—and I listened to my music through my ear buds so as not to disturb him. There really wasn't any opportunity to do much talking.

Gavin had sent me a text Wednesday night, telling me what time to be at his house. When I showed up this morning, he met me out on his front porch and barely grunted a hello, but he did order me out of my car, insisting we'd take his rental to Raleigh so we could leave it there.

I wanted to ask him so badly about the noise I heard in his office on Tuesday. It was a massive crash, and I'm guessing it was his desk. Those things don't just topple over on their own, so I have to assume he upended it. When I went to check on him, he was clearly upset… I could hear it in the tone of his voice, before he snarled at me to leave him alone.

His tone scared me… vicious and pain filled all at the same time. I hesitated for just a moment, feeling like I should push the door open and see what I could do to help, then I remembered that Gavin Cooke is nothing more than my employer. A darkly compelling and extremely sexy employer… but nothing more.

"You ready to go?" Gavin says to me as he stands from the salesman's desk. He looks so amazing, wearing a pair of charcoal-gray slacks and a long-sleeved, lightweight black sweater. The temperature was supremely brisk this morning, and we both dressed accordingly. I chose to wear a light, wool skirt in brown-and-red plaid with brown tights, paired with a pair of brown Mary Janes and a cream sweater. Living on the sunny beaches of North Carolina, I tend to dress in shorts and tank tops for a good chunk of the year, but when I feel the nip of cold weather, I'm all over the appropriate fashions… wool, tights, boots, and trendy scarves. I only get to experience it for a few months a year.

I follow Gavin outside, the salesman hot on his heels. "Are you sure you don't want me to take you out on a drive first, to show you all the features?"

Shaking his head, Gavin heads to the passenger side of the shiny black car, that I have to admit, is one of the most beautiful vehicles I've ever seen with its gently curved, sleek lines and polished chrome accents. He opens the door and motions me inside. "No thanks. I think I can figure it out."

"But I need to show you how to transition between automatic and manual," the salesman practically whines as I slide onto the butter-soft, white leather seat. I'm sure he's never had someone buy a car completely untested before.

I don't hear Gavin's response because he closes the door once my legs are securely in and walks around the front of the car with the salesman trailing behind. When he opens the driver's door, I hear him say, "Here are the keys to my rental. Someone will be by to pick it up later today."

He tosses the keys to the salesman, who fumbles them briefly, looking utterly put out at not being able to show off the car.

Gavin slides into the driver's seat, and he looks so natural doing it. "Thanks for your help," he tells the salesman, who looks completely flummoxed, and shuts the door in his face. Starting the car, he revs the engine hard, causing the salesman to jump backward a step.

I cover my mouth with my hand so as not to laugh, and Gavin shoots me a sideways grin. Putting his seatbelt on, he says, "Ready to see what this puppy can do?"

"I can see it already put a dent in your wallet," I quip as I pull my seatbelt on.

He puts the car in reverse, backs it away from the salesman, who gives us a small wave, with a smile now on his face as I'm sure he's calculating the commission he just made. "It's just money," Gavin says.

"Says the person who has it oozing out of his pores," I say with a snort.

Putting the car in drive, Gavin pulls away from the sales lot and out on to Capital Boulevard. "You sound like you begrudge me my newly earned wealth."

"Not at all. I think if I had as much money as you, I'd buy this car too. And one for each of my friends."

Gavin gives a short laugh but it's genuine, and I realize I don't think I've heard such an easy sound come from him before. It's nice.

"So, tell me about your friends," he says casually as we make our way south down Capital back to the beltline. "I've already deduced you're friends with that bartender at Last Call. Not lovers, by the way."

"Not lovers," I agree. "That's Brody, and he's not a bartender. He was just filling in that night. He actually runs The Haven with his fiancée, Alyssa."

"You have a lot of respect for them," he deduces from the tone of my voice.

"A ton. Alyssa is like a saint. She started The Haven a few years back and was working her fingers to the bone to keep it going. Brody has been working with her full time for a few months now."

"What did he do before that?" Gavin asks inquisitively.

"He was in prison," I say softly, wondering if whenever I think of Brody being locked away for something he didn't do will ever not cause me pain.

"You're kidding," Gavin says with disbelief.

"No. Drunk driving accident and someone died."

"That's awful," he says in commiseration. "How long was he away for?"

"Five long years."

We're silent for a few moments, and I have no clue if Gavin wants to ask me more about Brody or not. It's a morbid story, which would hold fascination for even the most disinterested person, but he instead asks, "What about your other friends? The group of girls you were with the other night."

"You know Casey already, but Alyssa was there, and the other woman is Gabby. Her fiancé, Hunter, is Brody's twin brother and he also owns Last Call."

"Twin brothers, both engaged to girls that are close friends," Gavin ruminates. "Will there be a double wedding?"

"No clue," I say with a grin. "But it was a double engagement. The boys pulled it off and proposed at the same time."

"Quite the tight little circle you have there," he muses.

"Not really. I mean… they've all known each other for years. I'm new to the group and not as close to them. Well, I am to Brody, but we tend to work a lot together at The Haven."

"And Alyssa doesn't get jealous," Gavin teases.

I snort. "If you knew Alyssa... and if you knew the relationship she and Brody have together, you'd never ask that."

"So, Brody is like your best friend?"

"No. I don't have one of those, but he's probably my closest."

"The one that knows all your secrets?" Gavin asks as he turns to me for a brief glance.

"He knows one," I tell him mysteriously.

"Hmmm," Gavin says as he strokes a finger over his chin. "Are you going to share with me?"

"Maybe one day... but not today," I tell him firmly.

We reach the 440 beltline and I point to Gavin to take the second exit that will have us heading back east. Traffic is light, and he smoothly transitions onto the highway. I watch as he flicks the gearshift. As he speeds up, he uses his fingers to pull at a paddle behind the steering wheel.

"What are you doing?" I ask with interest, because the engine revs louder with each pull on the paddle.

"I'm in manual mode now. These paddles are gear shifters," he says as the car leaps forward when he shifts again.

I can feel the vibration of the engine through the creamy, leather seats and hear it scream in abandon as the car surges forward. He moves us into the far left lane and we fly past the other traffic that seems to be standing still.

"Why use the paddles to shift if the car does it automatically for you?" I ask as I watch him shift up and then down again when he slows to a more reasonable speed.

He turns his head to look at me, rolling his eyes in the process. "You're a woman. What could you possibly understand about a V8 Ferrari-built engine that goes zero to sixty in five seconds flat?"

Laughing, I tell him, "Considering that just sounded like gibberish to me, clearly I don't understand a thing."

"Exactly," he says as he exits onto US 264, a four-lane highway that's practically deserted. "But I have an idea."

Gavin starts to slow the car and pulls off onto the right shoulder. When he puts it in park, he undoes his seatbelt. "Get out."

"Excuse me?"

"Get out. You're going to drive so you can feel what real power is like underneath you."

"No way," I protest.

"Chicken," he counters.

I glare at him.

"Anti-heroine," he says with a sly grin.

"Fine," I grumble, throwing off my seatbelt.

Gavin and I switch places. After I get the seat adjusted and my seatbelt back on, he points out some of the basic features.

"What about the paddles?"

"I'll let you try those later. Right now, we'll just leave it in automatic."

After I put the car in drive and check my side mirror to see that no traffic is coming up on me, I gingerly push on the gas pedal and the engine screams as it leaps forward. I immediately hit the breaks in surprise, which causes the car to slam to a stop, throwing Gavin forward, his hands slapping hard on the dashboard.

"Holy shit," I exclaim.

Gavin busts out laughing and pats me on the leg. "The accelerator is very responsive. Give it a gentler push."

I try again, softer this time, and the engine hums for me as the car creeps forward. I put on my blinker and slowly merge onto the highway, gradually accelerating up to the speed limit.

My hands grip the steering wheel with white knuckles as I realize all of a sudden that I'm driving a $140,000 vehicle.

Then they start to sweat.

"Relax," Gavin croons at me. "You're doing fine."

"I don't want to wreck your car. It would take me a lifetime to pay it off," I mutter.

"That's what insurance is for," he says casually. Then he demands, "Go faster."

I push a little more firmly on the accelerator and the Maserati leaps under my request, the engine growling sexily at me. I can't help the smile that comes to my face.

"Nice, right?" Gavin says.

"Oh, yeah," I agree, and my smile goes wider.

"You're fucking sexy as hell," Gavin says so softly that I almost doubt I heard him right.

I turn to spare him a glance... and his eyes are pinned on me, the gray irises darkened, even with the noon sun sparkling bright. I swallow hard, because it's the same look he gave me the other night, when I told him to touch me between my legs.

A tingling sensation spreads out from the back of my neck and my thighs involuntarily clench together, as I turn my eyes back to the road.

Gavin's left arm raises up and his fingers skim along the back of my neck, pushing upward over the base of my skull and sifting through my hair. "Have you thought about the other night?" he murmurs.

My hands grip the steering wheel harder and my foot eases up off the accelerator a tiny bit, but words are stuck in my throat. I'm afraid to say anything.

"I have," he admits softly as he shifts in the seat and leans closer to me. "I've thought about it a lot. About what I could have done differently."

"Gavin—" I croak, but he cuts me off.

Bringing his right hand across, he places it on my knee and starts sliding it up my thigh. My pulse skyrockets and my foot actually falls off the gas pedal, as it's almost impossible for me to concentrate on driving while he's touching me.

"Speed back up, Sweet," he whispers as he leans closer and sticks his nose under my ear. "Don't want a cop to pull you over for going too slow."

"I can't—"

"You can," he insists quietly, and his hand travels higher. I blink hard and push the gas pedal, getting my speed back up to within a normal range.

My legs fall open a bit to give him easier access and within just a moment, his fingers sit at my hipbone. His index finger strokes back and forth over my brown tights, but I can feel the burn of his touch all the way through to my soul.

"Let's do this a little differently," Gavin says with his finger moving softly against the inside of my thigh. "I really want to touch you and all I want from you is to say 'yes'."

"Oh, God," I gasp out as his finger drifts over to press up against my center.

"Say 'yes,'" he urges, his lips now against my ear, and I'm helpless.

"Yes," I moan.

Gavin sits up suddenly and pushes my skirt all the way up so it bunches around my hips. "Lift yourself up a bit," he growls.

I do as he commands, my foot pushing down on the accelerator inadvertently, causing the car to jump forward.

"Easy," he chuckles, and I let up off the gas a bit.

Taking both of his hands, he pinches at my tights with his fingertips and with a grunt, jerks at the material, causing it to rip right at the inside of my thigh where it meets my hip.

"Fuck yeah," he groans, and I glance down to see him pulling one edge of the tights away from my skin with his left hand while his right hand tunnels in.

"White lace panties," he murmurs as his finger slips under the edge. "And they're damp. My favorite kind."

I can't help the half sob, half moan that comes out of my mouth, and he tries to comfort me by leaning forward and kissing me on my lower jaw. "Easy, Sweet. We're just getting started."

That's what scares me. I can barely control the raging of my blood and nonsensical sounds that want to pour forth from my mouth. I'm for sure going to wreck this car.

Softly inching his finger closer, he makes contact with my center and swipes his finger up and down. The move parts my swollen lips, and I can feel the slickness of my response coating his path. My hips flex up, trying to push his finger closer, and he doesn't wait.

His finger sinks deep inside of me. I groan hard from within my chest, and tears prick at my eyes because this is the most erotic thing that's ever happened to me in my life. Gavin pulls his finger back, slightly constrained by the material of my panties and tights, and pushes back in a bit rougher.

When he pulls back out again, he moves the tip of his finger and starts circling my clit. His breathing becomes harsher, his lips pressed against my neck, and his breath fanning out gives me additional shivers. He moves faster against me, because we don't have time to drag this out, and I find I wouldn't want it any other way.

I'm driving an Italian sports car on a lonely highway with an insanely gorgeous and carnally sinful man with his hand between my legs. There's no other way for this to go but hard and fast.

"Need you to come for me, Sweet." Gavin's words pour out rough across my skin and my foot presses down hard on the accelerator. The needle on the speedometer climbs higher, and the engine cries out for me to give it even more reign.

Gavin's finger circles, rubs, and presses against me, and I can feel the wetness of my desire slicked all around.

"I'm going to—"

"Fuck yes, you are," Gavin growls.

"I'm—"

"Come on, Sweet… give it to me," he urges and stops his rubbing to jam two of his fingers inside of me, hitting me deep and just at the right spot.

"Give it to me, Savannah," he pants again.

He pulls his fingers out to press down hard on my clit.

"Fucking. Give. It. To. Me," he practically snarls. And I do.

Bursting apart from the inside out with a long moan, I give it all to him.

THIRTEEN

Gavin

I can hear Savannah moving around downstairs as she cleans, and I'm bound and determined to ignore her. Kind of like the way she ignored me on the ride home yesterday after I made her orgasm all over my hand. I had pulled my hand from between her legs and stuck my index finger in my mouth, licking her off me.

"Delicious," I said, and she groaned again while her breath came out in sharp, little pants. I wanted to demand she pull the car over to the side of the road, pull her across my lap, and slam her down on my cock. I badly wanted her to ride me there, on the side of Highway 264 in the bright light of day, while other cars whizzed by, but I could tell by the shyness in her eyes and the way she refused to meet my gaze that it wasn't going to happen.

So I suffered the ride in silence, ultimately pulling out my laptop and fleshing out a new scene between Honey and Max. One where they were in a car together and after the finger fucking was over, she did, in fact, ride his cock hard on the side of the road. The unfortunate by product to writing that scene with the smell of Savannah still wafting up from my fingers as they moved across the keyboard was that I had a raging hard-on the entire time.

Yes, I want to ignore her, the way she ignored me after, but the monster in my pants perked up eager the minute I heard her walk in. Reaching down, I palm my dick through the rough material of my jeans and squeeze it. I close my eyes and groan as I imagine it's Savannah's hand on me.

Just that thought... just the thought of her small hand stroking my cock raises so much lust within me; I stand up abruptly from my desk and mutter a curse. Never... in all those months I visited sex clubs and fucked my way through London have I ever been this worked up over a woman.

And a woman that shouldn't even hold any appeal to me. She represents everything that's the antithesis to my darkness. She represents the possibility of moving myself out of that darkness, and allowing a little bit of bright back into my life.

That thought makes me shudder, not in a very good way, and my erection wanes.

That's better.

I head out of my office and down the stairs, determined to be able to confront her. To prove to myself that I can be around her and still be me.

I find her in the living room, dusting the furniture. She's wearing a pair of faded, but well-fitting jeans and a long-sleeved T-shirt. Her dark hair is pulled up into a high ponytail, and she's humming to herself while she works.

It makes me want to drag her down to the couch, strip her, and fuck her with my mouth.

Spinning away, I walk into the kitchen, my hands balled into fists and my cock hard again.

Opening the refrigerator, I stare blindly at the contents, not really wanting anything but not sure what to do at this point. My well-laid plans to confront Savannah having been blown all to hell.

"Hungry?" she asks behind me, and my cock leaps.

She has no idea just how hungry I am.

Closing the refrigerator door, I turn to stare at her. She looks uncomfortable, as well she should be. I fingered her in the car yesterday, and we barely said two words to each other after. I want to do it to her again, and so much more. Normally, the Gavin Cooke I've become would just move in and take what he wanted.

But as she stands there, uncertainty in her eyes, I can't bring myself to make a move.

I've become the anti-hero now.

Max would be disgusted by me.

"No," I finally say to her. "Not hungry."

Not for food, anyway.

"Okay," she says, and I think I see a small level of disappointment in her eyes. She starts to move past me, on her way to the laundry room, I suppose, and I catch a whiff of her perfume. It's sweet… flowery… innocent. Just like her.

Before I can stop myself, my hand jets out and grabs her by the wrist. "Go to dinner with me tonight?"

She jerks in surprise, and her eyes widen. "Dinner?"

"Yes. It's this concept where two people sit down at a table and other people serve them food."

The corners of her mouth tilt skyward, but she asks again, "You want to take me to dinner?"

No, Sweet... I want to ravage you, strip you bare, burrow into you, and pound this compulsion out of me.

"Yes... I want to take you out to dinner." Which is so fucking weird, because I don't wine and dine women. Never needed to before.

"Why?" she asks skeptically.

"Why not? I find I like your company, I don't know anyone else here, and I'm bored sitting around by myself all the time."

"Oh," she says softly as she casts her eyes downward, and I'm surprised by her lack of enthusiasm over my invitation.

Lifting her head up by putting my fingers under her chin, I peer down to look at her. "What's with the uncertainty?"

She shakes her head as if denying me. "It's nothing. I mean... I just didn't think you were the type... never mind."

"What? That I wasn't the type to take a woman on a date?" I tell her in a chastising tone.

Her eyes harden a tiny bit, and she smirks at me. "No, you seem like the type to pick a woman up in a bar and then leave with her so you can bang the hell out of her."

My hand falls from her face as dismay fills me. She clearly heard about the blonde woman I left the bar with the other night. No sense in hiding it though, so I tell it to her straight. "I'm not a saint, Savannah. I like to fuck. I like to give in to those base urges. So what?"

"Exactly," she says as she brushes past me. "So what?"

"Wait a minute," I say as I turn and grab her again. Spinning her around by the arm, I pull her in closer to me. Her breath hitches and her eyes dilate a little, and it's clear to me… she's definitely attracted to me in such a way that maybe I don't have to expend any further energy in seducing her. "Are you saying that you're okay with just a fuck between us? You don't need a romantic dinner and candlelight? Soft words… slow seduction?"

She snorts at me. "I think we completely bypassed that step yesterday, don't you agree? We went right to the after-dinner dessert."

"That we did," I murmur as I pull her in closer, flush up against my body so she can feel how much I want her.

As much as her words seem like a bold statement to me that she doesn't need the softer side of Gavin, I don't believe it for a second. Savannah may even be trying to prove to me, at this very minute, that she can play the confident role of a heroine. A woman that knows what she wants and goes for it, no matter what the cost.

Even though that would be a dream come true for me right now, I'm bound and determined to prove she's not that type of woman.

Bringing my hands up, I cup her under her jawline, my hands circling around her throat. I give a soft squeeze and use my thumbs to stroke just under her chin. "So, I'm getting the feeling from you that maybe you want to finish what we started in the car yesterday?"

Her eyes flare and her tongue comes out to swipe at her lower lip, but she doesn't affirm or deny my words.

I decide to push harder, because one way or the other, I'm going to make her prove me right.

Releasing her face, I drop my hands to her hips, pulling her up hard against my erection. I dip my legs and tilt my hips up, grinding it against her pussy.

A soft moan filters across her lips, and her eyes close.

"Want me to fuck you, Sweet? Want my cock between your legs? Or do you just want to go out to dinner with me tonight? Your choice."

I hold myself still, waiting for her to just accept my damn dinner invitation and prove me right.

"I want you to fuck me," she whispers as she slowly opens her eyes. "Right here... standing up, on the floor... I don't care."

My body jerks in surprise, and I almost glare at her with skepticism. She returns my stare levelly, without a hint of hesitation or doubt.

Part of me... a small part, for sure... wants me to deny her and insist we go out tonight. But the vast majority of my body, my brain, my cock... it's screaming at me to take her.

"Where did my little anti-heroine go?" I ask her in wonder.

"She's decided to take a walk on the wild side," she tells me evenly.

"Are you ready for my brand of filth?" I ask, and I can see a kernel of doubt in her eyes.

But she stiffens her spine, raises her chin, and says, "I'm ready."

I close my eyes, take a deep breath in, and release it out slowly. When I open them up again, I pin her with a dark smile. "You asked for it, Sweet."

As I drop to my knees before her, she gives a soft gasp when my fingers deftly start working at the button to her jeans and tug the fly open. I don't even hesitate to push my hands into the waistband, pulling her jeans... snagging her panties along the way... dragging them down to mid-thigh. Grabbing her behind her legs and leaning forward, I stick my nose right between the juncture of her thighs and inhale deeply.

"You smell fucking intoxicating," I murmur before dragging my tongue right up her center.

Savannah cries out in surprise, and her hands slam down on my shoulders to grip me hard. Yeah, she fucking smells great, and tastes even better.

Leaning back slightly, I look up at her to find her eyes squeezed shut tightly, her lower lip gripped hard between her teeth. I reach up and grab her hands from my shoulder, bringing them down to her pussy while I watch her face.

"Hold yourself open for me, baby," I whisper. Her eyes fly open, staring at me in bewilderment. Pushing her hands back toward her body, I give them a soft squeeze while I stare her in the eyes. "Do it. Spread yourself for me."

A strangled sound comes out of Savannah's throat.

"Do it," I order, my voice hoarse with desire as I release her hands.

Lowering my gaze, I watch as her slender fingers press against herself, pulling herself open... showing me all of her beautiful secrets. My cock hardens to painful proportions.

My hands come back up and grab her by the hips. I lean forward while she stands there, her legs constrained by her jeans and underwear, but fully exposed to me as her hands clear the path for my tongue.

Pressing my mouth against her, I flick the end of my tongue against her clit, and she cries out. I give her a long, hard lick, and she cries again. She so fucking responsive that I bet I could make her come in a nanosecond, but I'm thinking I might save that pleasure for a rainy day. Moving my right hand over, I push it between her legs and slide my middle finger into her. She's fucking dripping for me. Lust rages through my body, almost making me dizzy.

I can't wait.

I jump to my feet, pull one of Savannah's hands away, and mash it up against my cock, which is straining hard against my zipper. "See what you do to me?" I growl.

She gives me a glazed nod and tentatively squeezes, causing my hips to jam forward, seeking more contact from her.

Taking Savannah by the shoulders, I spin her around and then grab her around the waist, lifting her from the floor because her legs are encumbered by her jeans. I step forward just two paces, until I'm pressing her into the edge of the kitchen table. Thankfully, it's huge and sturdy, and I'm not worried about it supporting our weight.

Gripping her by the back of the neck with one hand, I push her facedown onto the table. With the other hand, I bring it up between her legs from the back. I slip two fingers in her this time and feel her muscles contract around me, even as she shoves her ass backward, seeking more.

I feel frenzied... needful, and this is going way faster than I had imagined. I give her an out. "Are you okay? Want me to stop?"

Her head thrashes back and forth on the table, but I need to make sure. "Tell me to stop, Sweet."

"No," she practically yells. "Don't you dare."

Oh, fuck. No stopping this runaway freight train now.

I release my hold on her and undo my jeans, pushing them down and pulling my cock out. Pushing in closer to her, I rub it as best I can against the back of her pussy, not getting easy access because her legs are practically glued together by her jeans.

But I don't have time to get her clothes off. My body is demanding relief... the type that I can only get from Savannah... at this very moment.

Not a moment longer.

I pick her up by the hips, lifting her off the floor, and dip my knees. My cock, which is hard as a rock and tilted upward, gets the perfect angle and I push in against her, past the silky skin of her thighs, and right to her wetness.

I hit the mark on the first try, feeling her slick warmth open up to me.

Lowering her back to the ground, I swiftly pump my hips up, slamming into her in one hard move, causing her to scream out.

Her voice is hoarse and raw. I thought for a minute I hurt her, were it not for the soft, "Yes," she lets out at the end. But she proves to me she's okay... more than... when she gyrates her hips, causing her internal muscles to massage my dick in an almost excruciatingly sensual way.

She is exquisite.

Beyond.

I can't control myself, having never felt this burning need to push myself beyond all barriers. I pull back and slam back in, relishing in her cries as the kitchen table scoots forward a few inches. I do it again, and again, vaguely noting the way her fingernails scrabble against the wood of the table as she tries to claw at something.

My moans turn into grunts, my ass muscles contracting hard on every thrust into her. My fingers dig into her hips, and she cries out the sweetest words ever.

"More."

"Oh, God, Sweet… what are you doing to me?" I ask as I slam into her over and over again.

Her orgasm hits her fast and hard. I'm unprepared when her hands unclench, her palms lie flat on the table, and she pushes her chest up. Arching her back deeply, she throws her head back and groans as I feel her body stiffen and her pussy clamp down hard on my cock.

And fuck… then I'm coming, so hard… so long.

I push into her one last time, grit my teeth, and unload every bit of depravity into her body, and then I come some more.

My body shudders from head to foot, and another wave of pleasure hits me as I continue to jet into her.

Savannah slumps to the table, and I realize my knees are shaking. I unclench my death grip from her hips, wincing when I see the red marks I've left behind. I bend over her, pressing against her body, and rest my chin on the back of her head.

We lay like that for what seems an eternity, our mutual breaths that were raging just a moment ago now starting to calm.

Lifting my head up, I kiss her on the back of the head, and then nuzzle into the hair at the back of her neck. "You okay?"

"Mmmm. Hmmm," she moans softly. I can't see it, but I can hear the smile on her face.

"Will you go out to dinner with me tonight?" I ask her.

"Mmmm. Hmmm," she responds, and I smile back.

FOURTEEN

Savannah

What in the hell am I doing? Agreeing to go out to dinner with Gavin?

Earlier today—in his house—the *way* he took me.

That was it. It was supposed to be done, over. My itch scratched, his itch scratched. I could show him that I was so much more than what he thought and perhaps by doing so, I could prove to myself I had more grit than he gave me credit for.

What I didn't count on was all of these emotions to swell through me. From the moment I told him I wanted him to fuck me—and yes, I'm still blushing red over that—to this moment, now, that I stand before my mirror, checking my hair and makeup before Gavin arrives to pick me up, I've been inundated with fears, insecurities, and doubts. What I did… with him… was absolutely not me.

I'm not that type of girl.

Never have been.

But I can't deny that experience with Gavin was singularly the most thrilling thing that has ever happened to me in my life. I felt free, beautiful, desired, and sexy. I felt like I held power, even as I was slammed with apprehension when I gave him the go-ahead. It was scintillatingly delicious, and even as I sit here and tell myself that I'm not that type of woman… I want to do it again.

When Gavin finally lifted off my body, pulled away… pulled out, I felt loneliness. Then I felt the product of his desire sliding down my legs, and I was mortified and terrified that we had unprotected sex. I couldn't believe that I never gave it a single thought. Not once during the entire time he was making love to… no, *fucking* me. I didn't care. I kind of still don't care, because had he taken the time to stop… put on a condom, the moment probably would have been broken. It would have been like a raging river slamming against a dam, and we would have most likely stopped once we regained our senses.

The fear of not feeling Gavin—of not giving into those desires and lust—outweighs my fear over having unprotected sex, and I want to bang my head against the sink for ever being so foolish. So stupid.

I had stood up quickly from the table and, even with shaky legs, managed to pull my underwear and jeans up, practically running into the bathroom to clean up. I stared in the mirror above his guest bathroom sink, admiring the flush in my face and the redness on my neck leftover from the most powerful orgasm I've ever felt in my life. And I didn't feel too much regret.

When I walked out of the bathroom, feeling like I had more control over my feelings, Gavin was standing in the kitchen, drinking a bottle of water and watching me like a hawk. Whereas I felt a bit nervous and unsure, he looked like he wanted to eat me up, causing a low throb to start between my legs. He had held the bottle out to me, asking silently if I wanted a drink, but I shook my head and started for the laundry room.

"I'll pick you up at seven tonight," he said. "Text me your address."

I nodded and didn't say anything in response, but rather went and folded his laundry. When I was done and came back into the kitchen, he was gone, and I didn't see him the rest of the time I was there cleaning his house.

My front doorbell rings, bringing me out of my memories, and I stare at myself in the mirror. What is this evening going to hold? Is this a "thank you" dinner? A "thanks for letting me fuck you" type of thing? Or does Gavin want something more from me?

Do I want something more from him?

I don't know the answer to that, but I do know my heart is racing with fear and excitement.

When I open the door, he's standing there with his hands casually tucked in the pockets of his dark-washed jeans. He's got on a dark gray sweater and a black leather jacket, making him look edgy and sinful as hell. His eyes rake down me and back up again, appreciation clear. "You look beautiful," he says, and I try not to preen under his gaze.

He had said to dress casual for the night and I took him at his word, choosing a pair of boot-cut, dark denim jeans paired with a deep purple turtleneck. I matched a camel-colored, short-waisted, leather blazer along with matching boots in the same color. The finishing touch was a scarf of melded colors of purple, blue, green, and brown that I tied twice, but loosely, around my neck, so it draped about a quarter ways down my chest.

"Thank you," I say with a smile, and then I try for a little cheekiness. "You look pretty hot yourself."

He steps forward, across the threshold, and invades every bit of my personal space. Running a finger along my jaw, he murmurs, "Not as hot as you bent over my kitchen table this morning."

Oh, geez.

My insides instantly melt, my bones liquefy, and I have to take a step back to clear the fog from my brain. Gavin is all too aware of the effect he has on me because he laughs softly and then grabs my hand. "Come on. I'm starved."

We've been making small talk, and I think it's because we're both nervous. Well, because I'm nervous. I don't think Gavin has an apprehensive bone in his body. He exudes confidence and control. He humors me when I ask question after question about his writing career, even admitting that he's changing the character he based on me in his manuscript. He named her Honey, which is a stupid name in my opinion, but he said he wanted it to be clear she was "sweet" ...like me.

I thought that was kind of sweet, so then the name Honey grew on me a bit.

We're eating at one of the better seafood restaurants in Nags Head, and I just ordered the fried oyster platter. Gavin wrinkles his nose and says, "Why do you North Carolinians fry all your seafood?"

I shrug my shoulders and say, "Everything tastes better fried."

Gavin disagrees and orders a baked sea bass entree with a grilled veggie mix on the side.

When the waiter leaves, I decide a change of subject is absolutely necessary. "We had unprotected sex."

Sighing, Gavin takes a sip of his water and sets it back down. "I know. It hit me the minute I slammed home but fuck if I could stop."

His words... his dirty, filthy words that remind me of how unbridled his passion was, shock me for a moment, and then fill me with a weird warmth. Because it speaks to the fact that he wanted me so badly, that he was out of control. I never thought I'd incite such desire in a man... let alone a man like Gavin Cooke.

"You don't have to worry about me," Gavin continues. "I swear I'm clean."

"Always kept it wrapped up?" I quip nervously.

"Always," he says firmly, his eyes boring into mine. "I've done a lot of stuff that would put a permanent blush on those pretty cheeks, but I've always been careful."

"What kind of stuff?" I ask, naïvely... jealously.

"You really want to know?" he asks.

No. "Yes."

"Let's just say... over the six months I was writing *Killing the Tides*, I did a lot of experimenting. You can call it research if you want."

I give a nervous laugh. "Like bondage or something."

He never drops his eyes from mine, and his voice is hard when he admits, "BDSM, multiple partners, orgies, anal, voyeurism, sex in public. You name it... I probably tried it. Does that turn you on or off, Sweet?"

My mouth falls open in disbelief, and a strange feeling takes hold. I'm slightly disgusted by this, but at the same time, a little bit turned on. I realize without a doubt that I'm completely out of my league with him, and that what we did this morning... while it was the most erotic thing that's ever happened to me... it's probably on the tame side for him.

Sadness overwhelms me as I realize and think to myself, *How could I ever be enough for him?*

"What about you?" Gavin asks, not bothering to wait for my answer. Not that I'd ever admit that what he said turned me on or off.

I blink at him. "What about me?"

"The unprotected sex," he says with a smirk. "I've assured you, now you assure me."

My face burns hot, and my eyes lower to the table. I fiddle with my napkin on my lap, because how presumptuous of me not to have immediately put his mind at ease.

"Sweet?" he calls to me softly. "I can tell you don't have much experience, so I'm not too worried about catching anything from you. Am I right?"

My eyes lift to him, and I nod in assent.

"But—"

"And I'm on the pill," I say hastily.

Gavin's breath comes out in a rush of relief, and he says, "Thank God." I find it interesting that he was clearly more worried about me getting pregnant than getting a dose of the clap, although both seem equally disconcerting to me.

He smiles at me then, and it's the most brilliant smile I've seen on his face yet. He reaches his hand across the table at me, and I release my napkin to take it. "Now that that's out of the way, tell me your secret."

"My secret?" I ask in confusion.

"The secret you said you would tell me maybe someday," he reminds me while stroking his thumb over the back of my hand.

"Oh, that," I say with immediate understanding. "It's not all that interesting."

"It must be if it's a secret," he prompts.

"It's not really a secret. It's public knowledge, just not something I talk about."

"Yet, you told Brody about it."

"He's my friend… my closest."

"I'm betting Brody was never as close to you as I was this morning… when I was deep inside your body."

I pull my hand away and glare at him. "Why do you always try to shock me with your sexual innuendos?"

"Love," Gavin drawls in that sexy, English accent. "That wasn't innuendo. That was pure fact… I was deep inside your body this morning, feeling every inch of your sweet pussy surrounding me."

"Stop it," I hiss at him across the table.

He leans back in his chair slowly, giving me a calculated smile. Drumming his fingers on the table, he says, "It's time for you to stop being shy with me, Sweet. I know you inside and out now."

"You don't know anything about me," I counter.

"I know plenty. I know you're unbelievably sweet, kind, and caring. I know you have an amazing work ethic. I know you're smart and funny, and you're fucking sexy as hell. I also know that you're a risk taker and that you are *nothing* like I first thought you were. I know you're private and timid, but when you get angry, you stand up for yourself. I know your body feels amazing wrapped around me, and I know that I want to feel it again… tonight as a matter of fact. I know that I love to hear you scream in pleasure, and I know my cock is aching for you right this very minute. If I thought you'd let me, I'd pull you into the bathroom right now and fuck you standing in one of the stalls, hopefully while someone came in, and we'd have to be very quiet so as not to get caught. And I know… without a doubt, you'd scream anyway, regardless of the danger."

Heat courses through my body, along with gratification that he does know quite a bit about me already. That means he was looking at far more than just my tits and ass, and he has found appreciation outside of those things that normally a man would notice about a woman.

"Now, tell me your secret," he commands.

Sighing, I pick up my glass of water and take a sip. When I set it back down, I decide to tell Gavin about the hardest thing I've ever done in my life. Because then… maybe then… he'd understand that I'm truly not the meek little kitten he takes me for.

At least, I haven't always been.

"I was almost raped in high school," I say without preamble, deciding just to go ahead and blitz him with the information.

"What the fuck?" he says as he jolts upright in his seat and then leans forward to grab my hand again.

"By my boyfriend," I continue while never letting my gaze drop from his. "We had been dating for a few months, and he was pressuring me to have sex. I wasn't ready… I wasn't in love with him, and I was a virgin. I didn't want to give it up to him."

Gavin grits his teeth hard, his eyes blazing. "What happened?"

"We were at a party… a bonfire, everyone was drinking. He was drunk, and I was drunk. He tried again, and I said 'no.' He apparently thought 'no' meant 'yes' and wouldn't stop."

"But he did stop," Gavin demands with menace in his voice. He knows he stopped because I told him I was "almost" raped.

"Yes… only after someone heard me scream and interrupted him. He immediately jumped off me and left."

"What did you do?"

"I went straight to the police and reported it," I tell him sadly, because while it was the right thing to do, it caused so much more strife in my life than if I had just stayed silent.

"Good for you," he says with a smile, squeezing my hand.

"No, not good for me," I tell him as I pull my hand free from his grasp. "Going forward with my allegation was the worst thing that ever happened to me."

Gavin blinks at me, confused. "What do you mean?"

"I mean Kevin... my boyfriend... my attacker, was captain of the football team and the most popular guy in high school. His father was our small town's beloved, local doctor. His mother was on the church choir. Kevin denied it happened, and no one believed me. He was my boyfriend after all. Everyone was of the mindset that a man can't rape his girlfriend."

"Tell me you're joking. What about the person that saw it happening?"

"A friend of Kevin's that wasn't willing to testify to what he saw."

"So what did you do?" he asks with trepidation.

"I did the only thing I could do. I told the truth and stuck to my guns. There was physical evidence.

My clothes were torn, Kevin had choked me so I had bruises on my throat, and I had scratched him across the face. Coupled with my testimony, that was enough for the DA to press charges."

"Was there a trial?"

"Yes. It was many months later, and I went through a living hell to get there. I lost all my friends because no one would believe me. I was bullied... physically pushed around by girls who all had a crush on Kevin and wouldn't believe it of their popular sports star. Guys would grab at me, thinking I was loose. Adults in the community shunned me because I was bringing disgrace to our sleepy town. Even the local paper wrote editorial opinions taking his side. My parents were the only ones that stood by me."

"You're fucking kidding? Who does stuff like that?"

"The town of Clearview, Indiana," I tell him evenly.

Gavin swallows hard, and I can see a bit of fear in his eyes. "How did it end?"

I shrug my shoulders. "Justice prevailed. He was convicted of sexual battery. Got a year and a half in prison, but was out in nine months."

"How is that justice?" Gavin asks angrily.

I give him a soft look of assurance... letting him know that I'm okay. "It's justice because the jury agreed with me that Kevin tried to rape me. After everything I went through… that was the most important thing that could happen for me. Didn't matter to me what his sentence was—it was that I proved everyone in that fucking town wrong."

Gavin is quiet a moment, digesting my story. He pushes slowly out of his chair and walks to the opposite side of the table, dropping to his knees beside me. He grabs my face in his hands and leans in to kiss me on my lips. It's our first kiss, and it's soft and sweet, filled with care. I realize… that Gavin and I had sex today, and he never even kissed me on the lips until now.

How very strange.

How very naughty and thrillingly bad.

When he pulls away, Gavin says, "Oh, Sweet… after hearing that story, you are, without a doubt, the strongest heroine I've ever known."

FIFTEEN

Gavin

My words are coming faster than they ever have as I bang out page after page on my manuscript. Honey has been transformed completely. After she takes it upon herself to give Max a stellar blow job while he's driving his royal blue, Shelby Mustang GT500 with white racing stripes down the hood, she informs him that she's going to fight by his side. The only thing she asks in return is that he fuck her hard and never leave her. No... she doesn't ask... she *demands* it of him.

I'll never leave you, Max vows.

Who would have thought that Max would ever entertain the thought of monogamy?

My phone rings, startling me and completely fucking up my concentration. Sighing, I grab it and see it's Lindie calling from New York.

"You're disturbing me," I grumble into the phone when I connect.

"Well, if you'd return a call, text, or email once in a while, I wouldn't be forced to perform such a dastardly deed," she throws back at me. "So how are things going?"

"They're fine," I tell her, my eyes glancing over the last few paragraphs I just wrote. "I'm going to need another few weeks though."

"No can do," she tells me. "Your editor said no more extensions."

"Well, if they want a completed manuscript, they're going to have to fucking wait," I snarl, having no time to argue about this shit. God, I long for the days of self-publishing.

"Are you drinking?" Lindie asks suspiciously.

"Not at the moment," I tell her as I stand from my desk, walking over to the glass doors that lead out on to the deck. The sun is hanging bright this morning, casting silver sparkles on the blue-green of the Atlantic. They twinkle merrily; sometimes a strong ray of light causes a sharp burst of brightness that hits me in my eyes and dazzles me.

"Tell me you got your shit together, Gavin," she implores. "That you do not need this extra time because you're sunk deep in the bottle."

Rubbing the bridge of my nose, I reassure her. "I'm fine. I've just added a new character to the book and it's taking me a bit longer."

"Wait a minute… you can't do that. They're expecting a very specific story line."

"And they'll get the same story line," I placate. "Just with a little bit more added."

"Don't fuck this up, Gavin," she tells me straight, and that's why I pay her. To keep me straight.

"Stop worrying. Get me two weeks and you'll have a masterpiece," I promise.

We talk some more about the publishing schedule, another manuscript she wants to pitch for me, and updates me on the status of her negotiating a movie deal for the trilogy. It all goes in one ear and out the other, because all I can think about now that I've stepped five feet away from my laptop is Savannah.

The anti-heroine who would be heroine. She's the reason I need the extra few weeks on my manuscript. Not only has she thrown my story for a loop, but she also has me wanting another taste of her. And I don't think just one more taste is going to satisfy me for some reason.

I had always figured I'd head back to London when I was finished with this manuscript, but now I'm not sure if I'm ready to give up her brand of sweet just yet.

"Are you listening to me, Gavin?" Lindie asks in exasperation.

"Not a word," I tell her honestly. "I need to get back to writing."

"Don't forget... you have a book signing in Chicago next month."

Fuck... I did forget. The last thing I want to do is go sit at a table while a long line of people wait to meet me. "Email me the details so I can put it all on my calendar."

After I hang up with Lindie, I stare at my phone for a moment. I look back to my laptop and the manuscript that is begging for me to massage it, and then look back to my phone. Before I can stop myself, I text Savannah.

What are you doing right now?

Slipping my phone in my pocket, I decide to go downstairs for a snack, but I get an immediate chime and pull my phone back up. She responded.

Reading your book. You?

My thumb grazes over the screen… over Savannah's words, and I think about our dinner last night. Her story—about how she was nearly raped and the hell she went through to get vindicated—amazes me. It made me realize that I had truly misjudged her. I didn't give her credit for this calm, inner strength that she seems to possess. Over the last several months, I had let myself refuse to believe that any woman could possess those traits.

And yet, here was a woman that was absolutely gorgeous, sweetly innocent, yet with a backbone of steel who made my cock hard all the time. My attraction to her went through the roof after she shared her "secret" with me, yet at the end of the night, when I took her back home and walked her to the door, I did so with the absolute conviction I was not going to be fucking her that night.

Before she even had a chance to unlock her door, I bent down and with one hand cupping her face, gave her a very short, very chaste kiss before I said, "Goodnight, Sweet."

Confusion filled those beautiful eyes, and she said, "I don't understand."

"I'm saying goodnight," I affirmed. "And I'll see you next Tuesday."

I turned to leave her, because if I looked at her another moment, I was going to drag her down to the wooden porch and fuck the hell out of her. And that wouldn't have been right... not after she just told me about getting attacked and mauled by a man that clearly felt he had the right to take what he wanted.

Just like me half the time. I take without any regard to the consequences I would leave behind. I've already done it once with Savannah and, if I did it again, it would almost make me feel like I was no better than that monster Kevin.

"Did I do something wrong?" Savannah had asked before I could make my way off her porch.

Turning back to her, I took her face in my hands. I leaned down and kissed her again. This time not so sweet, not so chaste, and my dick got all excited for what it thought might be coming. But I pulled away, kissed her nose, and said, "No, Sweet... you happen to do everything just right."

Then I left her standing by her door. I tried to forget her for a while. In the two hours I was working on my manuscript, completely lost in my writing zone, I had indeed pushed her away. But for almost every other minute of my conscious time, she's been plaguing my mind. I laid in bed last night, thinking of how badly I needed her yesterday... how I wasn't going to let anything stop me from fucking her on the top of my kitchen table, and I thought about how hard I had indeed fucked her and how fucking mind-blowing the orgasm I had was. Then I jacked off to the memory and was satisfied for a while.

Then that passed, and I was left wanting again.

I text her back. *Let's go for a ride.*

She responds immediately. *Shouldn't you be writing?*

I need a break. I'll pick you up in fifteen minutes.

The only thing she wrote back was, *Okay.*

Savannah opens her door, smiling at me shyly. I stand there a moment... drinking her in. She's wearing her long, dark hair loose, spilling over her shoulders and down her back. Another pair of tight, faded jeans, a heavy cream, cable-knit sweater, and black riding boots with brown leather trim completes the look of a woman that's set to go on a lazy car ride with me down the coast.

Which was my original intention. Just to get out for a bit... spend some time with her. See what other surprises she can hit me over the head with. See if maybe I can figure her out, look for cracks or falsehoods. Maybe even expose her for a flash in the pan, and maybe not a woman deserving of what may be growing into an obsession for me.

Instead, I'm overwhelmed with desire for her.

Desire, not lust.

Because they are two different things.

Lust suggests a carnal need to slake oneself until there is no further need.

Desire suggests a craving... something that is pervasive and without end. Something that slowly pulls at you... warms you from the inside out and fogs your senses entirely.

This is what I feel for Savannah at this very moment, as she stands before me all sweetly naïve as to what I really want. It's the first time that I want something that I don't think I deserve in the slightest, and the selfish part of me... the part of me that doesn't give a fuck if I end up shredding her in the process, decides to take it.

Stepping into her house, I crowd into her, causing her to step back a few feet so I can I follow her in. I shut the door behind me and bend down, lifting her up and wrapping her legs around my waist. Her arms automatically come up to grip my shoulders, and I take the opportunity when her mouth opens in surprise to kiss her, slipping my tongue inside.

This is the third time I've kissed her.

But the brotherly kiss I first gave her last night, and the slightly hotter kiss that I followed up with on the heels of the first one, shouldn't even count.

No, this is truly our first kiss and I go in deep and possessing, demanding she yield to me.

She does… immediately, her fingers digging into the muscles at my shoulder. Her mouth moves against mine, her tongue battling… tasting oh so sweet, feeling divinely warm. A tiny little moan slithers up from her throat and coats my tongue with her own desire, and I start walking through her living room.

I pull my mouth slightly away, but I leave my lips resting lightly against hers. "Where's your bedroom, Sweet?"

She leans in and runs her lips up my neck, one hand going up to the back of my head to grip my hair tightly. "Straight back, second door on the left."

Savannah's fingers tighten in my hair, and she tugs my head to the side as I walk down her hallway. Her tongue flicks against my earlobe and then she bites it, causing me to groan at her boldness. I may have to change her nickname to Spicy, because she's not all sweet I'm finding.

I make it through her bedroom door, briefly taking note of the pale, yellow walls and white eyelet and lace comforter on her bed, complimented with a slew of white-and-yellow little pillows with lace trim and silk bows.

So sweet.

So Savannah.

I walk to the end of the bed, lift a knee up to crawl on it with her still clinging to me, and then bend forward until her back hits the mattress. She releases her hold on me, laying her head back and looking up at me with hot eyes.

"I thought we were going for a ride," she teases me, and I find I like being teased.

"Change of plans," I tell her as I sit back on my haunches, studying her loveliness. Prior to this moment, I was trying to lump Savannah into a category based on my experiences and hurts. She was either the heroine or anti-heroine type, and now I'm not sure what she is.

She's just something... else.

I think about what she told me last night... about the hell she went through after nearly being raped. I wonder if the horror of that moment... when she had no control over her situation, when she was clawing at her would-be rapist with a fevered desire to protect her innocence… I wonder if those memories come back to her when another man touches her.

It makes me doubt what I'm about to do to her, and my selfishness takes a back seat.

"Do you want me to do this?" I ask her hesitantly.

"It depends… what are you about to do?" she asks coyly, and without her saying another word, I can tell by the look on her face, by her shy words that are tinged with longing, that she wants whatever I give her.

But I need to make sure. Lifting my hand, I skim my fingers up her neck and wrap my hand around her throat lightly. I use my thumb to stroke her jawline for a moment, then lift my hand and trail my fingers back down her neck and to her collarbone just peeking out from her sweater. "I'm going to possess you, Sweet. I'm going to take my time doing it. I'm not going to let you up out of this bed until I've had my fill of you, and honestly… I'm not sure how long that will take. I'm going to control your body… make you scream… make you writhe against the bed, love. I want you to beg me for it… and only if your words are sweet enough for my ears, will I give it to you. So, I ask again… do you want me to do this?"

She never hesitates… not even for the half second it takes her to suck in air between her teeth. "God, yes."

Her complete surrender slays me. Leaning forward, I place my hands on the bed at her shoulders and kiss her again. For the fourth time, and it's even better. Her lips are so soft, her breath tasting of mint and sugared coffee. Her tongue is at turns bold, then shy, and as I move my mouth over hers insistently, I find it doesn't take much for her to submit to me wholly.

Pulling back from her once again, I scoot off the bed. "You have way too many clothes on for what I have planned."

"Better remedy that," she says with a grin and sits up to start pulling her sweater over her head.

Placing my hand at the center of her chest, I push her back down on the bed. "Uh-uh. Let me do this. Let me unwrap you in my own way."

She immediately lies back on the bed, bringing one hand to rest across her stomach and the other thrown over her head. She watches me with curious eyes filled with soft yearning. "Okay," she whispers. "But will you undress first?"

"I thought I was in control," I chastise her gently with a warning look.

"Please."

Just one word. *Please.* And I give into her immediately.

Kicking my tennis shoes off, I reach down and quickly remove my socks. I've never stripped for a woman before... not at her request, and sadly, I find there's no sexy way to remove one's socks and shoes. But once they're out of the way, she gives me a soft command. "Your shirt... take it off."

Smiling darkly at her, I lift the hem of my dark gray Henley and lift it slowly up my torso. For the first time ever, I'm glad that I work out. I'm glad that she'll watch me as I reveal myself to her, and I hope she finds pleasure in looking at my body.

I'm temporarily blinded when I pull the shirt over my head, but I hear her loud and clear when she sighs in pleasure. As I toss the shirt aside, I find her eyes pinned to my chest. I stand there... absolutely still, and watch her watch me. Her eyes roam... over my stomach, my ribs, my chest... my shoulders, my arms, then back to my stomach again, before dropping down a bit lower where she looks hungrily at my hard-on straining against my jeans.

My hands come up and pop the button, and she stares at me harder. When I hesitate, she never gives me a moment of respite and says, "Hurry."

Oh, fuck... she's seducing the shit out of me and has no clue. The fact that my sweetly timid Savannah is demanding me to undress... so she can see my straining cock, causes my head to fill with a thick fog of primal lust.

Taking a deep breath to control my raging pulse, I unzip my fly and push my jeans and underwear all the way down. The elastic snags momentarily over my erection, and then it's freed where it stands up tall under her gaze. I clumsily kick my jeans off and away from me, and then stand up straight before her with my hands loose at my side.

Savannah just stares at my cock, her eyes wide, and I realize even though I fucked her brilliantly yesterday, she's never had a clear look at my completely nude form before. I can tell by the look on her face that she likes it, and I have to restrain myself not to fall on top of her.

"You're stunning," she says reverently, and my knees almost buckle from her praise.

"Will you touch yourself?" she whispers. Even though her words are barely audible, they are delivered with command. I have no clue where Savannah learned how to say these things, or where this boldness is coming from, but I'm becoming powerless against it. I think I may do anything she asks of me.

My hand almost rises to do her bidding, then I shake my head and blink away the fog. I give her a dark smile and reach down to one of her booted feet. Squeezing her calf underneath the soft leather, I tell her, "Not another word out of that beautiful mouth of yours. I'm in control."

"But—"

"Not another word," I tell her with a hard stare and squeeze her leg. "If you do, I'm going to stuff my cock in your mouth to keep you quiet."

Savannah's eyes close and her body shudders in pleasure over the thought. I have to bite the inside of my cheek until I almost draw blood to stop myself from crawling up her body and doing just what I threatened.

When her eyes open back up, she just nods at me and keeps her lips sealed firmly shut.

SIXTEEN

Savannah

All I can think about, at this very moment, is sucking on Gavin's cock. His threat to shut me up by putting it in my mouth causes lust to course through me, and I can feel heavy wetness between my legs. I've never given a man a blow job before... never wanted to. Not until this very moment. I briefly think about pushing up off the bed and latching my mouth on to him.

That would show the supremely confident Gavin Cooke, who seems content to put me in a narrow category, what he's dealing with.

The only thing that stops me is the promise in his eyes that he is going to deliver something to me that is going to probably shatter me to pieces. I'm quite sure... when we're both done and spent... I won't ever be the same.

So I hold my tongue, hopeful that it will have a chance to lash at that beautiful piece of velvet and steel at some time in the future.

I feel so beautiful... so wanton... so free, as I lay here on the bed, fully clothed while the most gorgeous man I've ever laid eyes on stands before me utterly naked. He's almost blinding in his magnificence, and the darkness that seems to coat a good portion of his character attracts me as much as his physique and beautiful face.

I was so confused last night when he left me. I was sure he wanted me... wanted to make love... fuck me again, whatever you call it. A man like Gavin has urges that I know he gives in to over and over again.

It was almost demoralizing when he stepped away, but when he told me I was doing everything right, it made sense to me. I was being me, and Gavin was attracted to that. It didn't matter if I was a heroine or not. There was something about me that had caught his eye, and I was going to see where it took us both.

Gavin unzips one boot and pulls it off, before doing the same to the other. He quickly takes off the thick, wool socks I'm wearing and tosses them casually aside.

His gaze comes to mine and his gray eyes are so dark, they almost seem black.

"You can't imagine the things I want to do to you, Savannah."

He says my name... not Sweet, and it's almost like a prayer. I sigh with contentment.

Leaning over the bed, he slips a finger under the waistband of my jeans and strokes my skin. "So soft," he murmurs.

I wait for him to take my pants off but instead, his hand comes up and grips my sweater at the center of my chest. He pulls on the material, bringing my upper body off the bed. He slowly lifts me up until I'm sitting straight, and then he keeps pulling me toward his face.

He kisses me again, hard and rough, and when our tongues touch, he groans in my mouth. I groan back.

His hands swiftly pull my sweater up and over my head, my brain mentally calculating the lingerie I chose to wear. I don't have much in the way of sexy, but I'm relieved when I remember I put on a pretty, matching set... taupe lace bra and bikini panties.

He tosses my sweater aside and stares at the swells of my breast as they heave within my bra. His fingers come to the edge, and he slowly pulls the lace down until my nipples pop free. The material scraping causes them to form into hard, little knots, and I moan over the sensation.

"Christ, your breasts are perfect," Gavin growls. Then his hands are under my armpits, lifting me straight off the bed and up into the air. My own hands come to rest on his biceps as he lifts me, bringing one breast to his mouth where he latches on and sucks at a nipple so hard that I cry out in desperation.

Gavin groans as he sucks at me, and then softly licks his tongue over the hard pebble to alleviate the sting. He turns his face to my other breast, holding me up in his powerful arms, and my head falls backward weakly.

He licks at my other nipple, sometimes sucking softly, sometimes hard, and then he bites at me gently, causing my whole body to jerk as I'm suspended above the bed in his hold.

"Need to taste you more," Gavin murmurs as he lowers me back down. "Need my face between your legs. Need you on my tongue. Have you ever had a man's tongue inside of you, Sweet?"

Oh, God. His words… his filthy, filthy words. They cause my body to shudder, my head to go dizzy, and my legs to clamp tightly together.

"Have you, Sweet?" he asks gently as he unzips my jeans and pulls them off my legs. My head shakes side to side, even as my eyes stray to his erection, which, impossibly, seems even larger than before. I note the pearly liquid seeping from the end, and my mouth waters to taste it. I actually start to sit up off the bed, but Gavin's hand pushes against my chest again to keep me pinned down. "Don't even think about it, love. Not before I get my chance."

Gavin's fingers hook into the edges of my panties at my hipbones and he drags the lace down my legs, tossing them to the floor. He never makes a move to undo my bra, the cups still folded below the swells of my aching breasts.

Lowering his hands to the inside of my legs, Gavin spreads them apart, and I can't help but be a little shy under his bold gaze. His fingers drag up my inner thighs until they reach my center, and he carefully spreads me apart for his perusal. His thumbs move inward to stroke me softly, spreading my wetness around. Cocking one wrist, he slips a thumb inside of me, arching it downward and pressing against my inner walls. My hips shoot off the bed, and he laughs at me softly.

He removes his thumb and brings it to his mouth, licking me off the pad and closing his eyes in pleasure. "Fuck, you taste good... sweet. Like honey."

I can't help the laugh that bubbles out of me, knowing without a doubt he's making a play on words with his new book heroine. Or is she an anti-heroine? I can't remember at this point.

Reaching down to my ankles, Gavin steps slightly away from the bed and drags me with him, so that my butt rests on the edge. He then kneels down on my carpet, his face so close to me that I can feel his warm breath as it rushes over and cools the wetness between my legs.

His hands push my legs further apart, and then his hands come up to spread me open again. He blows softly over me, and I shiver.

"You're glistening for me, Sweet," he says reverently. "Going to drink up every bit of you."

"Yes, please." I sigh, and then my eyes snap to his because he told me to keep my mouth shut.

Images of him lifting me up and pushing my face over his cock fill me, and then I shudder.

He laughs at me softly again and says, "It's okay, love. I want to hear you now. Don't hold back."

Gavin then dips his face down and softly covers me with his mouth. His tongue pushes at my center, straight into me, and my hands practically slam against his head to hold him in place. He moves his face side to side, sliding his tongue in opposite directions, massaging me all over.

"Mmmm," he groans against my warm flesh. "I could do this all day, Sweet. Fucking gorge myself on you."

His words rumble over my sensitive skin, and he pushes his entire mouth against me harder. I cry out, the pleasure rippling through me. I've never felt anything like it before and my hips circle and gyrate, demanding more.

He gives it to me. Long, slow licks alternated with quick flicks against my clit. He pushes his tongue in and out of me, even raising his face and rubbing me with his chin. My entire body is on fire, my muscles clenched so hard I feel like the tendons will snap, and then he puts his mouth right over my clit and pulses his tongue over it. Faster, and faster, and harder. He adds one finger, then two... then, oh, God... three, pumping them in and out while his tongue flutters over me with speed and determination.

My lower back tightens, a molten throb starts between my legs, and then it spirals up my spine. The pressure inside of me builds. I squeeze my eyes shut, and it hums with fever. Then it releases... bursting so hot and hard that my entire body bucks off the mattress and a scream tears out of my throat. It goes on and on... the orgasm... my scream... and Gavin never stops moving his tongue against me. I raise my legs up wildly even as another burst of pleasure pulses through me, then I dig my heels into the mattress and cry out again as another orgasm rips me open.

But Gavin doesn't stop. He presses his face into me harder and groans, lashing at me with his tongue, his fingers still tunneling in and out of me. He raises his mouth up just a tad, just enough to growl against me, "One more, Savannah. Give me one more."

He's relentless, frantically moving his lips and tongue over me, in me, out of me... raising his mouth every so often to urge me onward... upward. "Come again, Sweet. I fucking need you to come again. I want you destroyed by my tongue."

And he destroys me again, this time a slower burst but no less powerful. My entire body quakes and tears spill warmly down my cheeks, as a long moan pours out of my mouth. My fingers are latched onto his head. I flex and swivel my hips, mashing myself against his mouth to draw out every last bit of pleasure he's dealing me.

When one last, but strong shudder works its way through me, Gavin finally lifts his mouth. It's glistening wet, and his eyes are heavy and languid. He stares at me, almost in fascination, and his lips curve upward. "That was the hottest thing I've ever seen," he says quietly, his hands going to my legs and stroking me softly.

I'm utterly spent... boneless... not an ounce of strength left in me.

Gavin slowly stands, wiping his mouth with the back of his hand. Bending over me slightly, he cups the back of my thighs with his big hands and lifts my legs up. Then he pulls them open wide while I just watch him in fascination. He stares at me between my legs and leans forward a bit. My ass is still hanging on the edge of the bed, and I start to scoot backward to give him some room to come up here with me.

He just shakes his head and says, "Don't move."

Leaning forward a bit more, Gavin pushes on the backs of my thighs, pushing them closer to my chest until my ass raises up just a tiny bit. He steps in closer, releasing one leg and grabbing his cock. His eyes never leave my pussy as he guides himself to me.

Dipping his legs a bit, he angles his hips and places himself at my core. I can feel just how wet I am when he rubs the head of his erection against me. When he taps his cock against my clit, a mini burst of pleasure courses through me, and I groan.

"Going to fuck you now, Sweet," he warns me, but it's not needed. I'm aching with the need for him to take me, and I answer by tilting my hips so I rub against him.

Gavin hisses between his teeth and then leans over me, pushing inside of me just an inch. He's huge… a wide, long, lovely hardness that feels so silky soft at the same time. His eyes close briefly, then open again, and he pushes in just a bit more.

"Christ, you're tight. So wet, hot, and tight, and I think I'm going to die," he says.

For all the carnal rage that has been happening these past several minutes, his words are so solemn that I get the feeling he's experiencing something that is solitary and foreign.

Of course, this is all solitary and foreign to me, but I wouldn't want it any other way.

His eyes lift to mine and we stare at each other, a silent understanding between us that after he pushes all the way in—after he completes his possession— that things aren't going to be the same for either one of us. Whether we are together or apart, whether this never happens again, this will be an amazingly, unique experience for both of us.

My hand reaches up and, for the first time, I touch him. On his lower abdomen, just below his navel. I trail my fingers lightly over his skin, fingering the coarse hair that starts there and moves down in a blazing glory to the massive erection that's a quarter sunk between my legs.

"Give it all to me," I tell him... in a soft command, but a command nonetheless. "All of it."

Gavin groans and then pushes all the way into me, all the way down, down, down until his pelvis is mashed against mine. His chest heaves in and out, but his eyes never leave me.

"Do you feel that, Sweet?"

"Yes," I murmur, because I feel every inch of him.

"Did you feel that exact moment?" he asks, almost urgently.

"I felt it," I reassure him.

Because I felt it to the absolute center of my soul. The moment that he just completely possessed me, when his body grabbed ahold of mine and laid claim to it. When he just ruined me for anything else.

I felt it. He felt it.

It was beautiful and scorching, and I'm terrified over what it all means.

Gavin starts moving inside of me, luxurious strokes, and I can feel him branding every inch of me. He holds my legs spread, still standing flat-footed on the floor but leaning over me to get just the right angle. He hits me deep, over and over again. His movements are measured, his pace quickening. I note the way the muscles on the side of his neck strain and the lines of tension around his mouth tighten. His brow furrows inward, but his eyes look pained with the need to release.

He fucks me harder... faster, angling his body over me so he's tunneling down and in, back out again, then oh so deep once more.

It's beautiful, it's freeing, it's everything I ever wanted from a man before, but never really knew existed.

Gavin surprises me by moving his arms under my lower back, raising a knee to the bed, and lifting me slightly. He moves his entire body, cradling mine with it, and laying me back down into the middle of my mattress. His hips never miss a beat, continuing his rhythm. His hands come to my face, and he kisses me while he fucks me. His tongue moves slower than the beat of his cock within me, and I'm so overwhelmed by sensation that I miss the rumbling climax start in my center once again.

It pulses over me, through my body, and my legs come up to wrap around Gavin's hips. He goes harder... impossibly hard, and I cry out as I become lost in a sea of pleasurable release.

Gavin thrusts forcefully into me... one last time, raising his body up, supported by his palms flat on the mattress. He looks directly at me, goes absolutely still, and whispers, "I'm coming, Sweet. I'm coming just for you."

Then he shudders hard and squeezes his eyes shut. His arms give away and he falls on top of me, his hips now shallowly pumping between my legs as he groans into the hair on the side of my head.

"Just for you," he whispers again before he goes completely still and lets out a huge breath of air against me.

SEVENTEEN

Gavin

Savannah drives the Jeep a little uncertainly… timidly, and I'm convinced we're going to get stuck in the soft sand as she maneuvers the vehicle onto the beach. We had borrowed Casey's Jeep, and I was shocked to learn that she had been in her bedroom the entire time I was fucking Savannah, who was apparently not concerned with screaming the house down.

I smile as I watch the way she tentatively hits the gas, urging the Jeep along a path of tire tracks that had been laid before us. When we were in her bed together, her boldness came through. The second time we went at it, she surprised me by taking the lead, coaxing me back to life with her soft hands and equally soft lips on my skin. She pushed me onto my back, rose above me... settled down over me, and I was in heaven. She led the entire way and as I looked up at her while she pumped me to nirvana, I was amazed by the sexy confidence that shone in her eyes.

Yet, Savannah is still softy sweet and unassuming in other aspects of her life. When we were finished, and our heart rates came back under control, I suggested we go for that drive. She hesitantly asked me, "Can I take you to see the wild horses on Corolla?"

"Why so shy?" I asked her with a grin as I nipped at her lip and ran my hands over her breasts.

She moaned lightly and didn't say anything.

I lifted my head and looked down at her. "Why wouldn't I want to go see the wild horses with you?"

She shrugged and lowered her gaze. "I just figured maybe you had other things to do."

Oh, sweet Savannah. She fucked me like there was no tomorrow, milking me dry while she gyrated with abandonment on top of me. She forced me to come, even though I tried to hold back so I could prolong the exquisite pleasure, and when she finished me off, she turned shy on me.

It was fucking adorable.

"Let's go see your wild horses," I told her and kissed her softly. "Then we'll go eat lunch, then I'm going to take you back to my place, and I'm going to fuck you again... and again."

She blushed prettily, and then we got dressed.

"You see the fencing that extends into the ocean?" She points out to the right as the Jeep lurches and groans over the quickening sand.

I look over to see thick, wooden logs—a foot in diameter—rising up vertically, extending out into the ocean. The waves crash against them, and I see the flash of metal rungs hung in between them to make a barrier through the water.

"It's so the horses can't leave this protected area," she says and then points back over her shoulder to the road we just left. "There is cattle grating behind us. They won't walk over it, so they keep contained to this part of the island."

I'll admit... I'm excited about seeing these horses that live on the beach, eat the wild sea oats, and drink puddled rainwater. She told me all about the little beauties as we got dressed, but I struggled to pay attention to what she was saying as she shimmied into her underwear. I had to restrain myself from tearing them off her and pushing my tongue between her legs again.

As we were leaving Savannah's house, I noticed some framed photos on the wall in her living room. They were framed in whitewashed wood... four of them mounted side by side. They were of the exact horses we were on our way to see, and I had never seen anything more beautiful. The pictures were taken at sunrise, as the sun was halfway lifted from the depths of the Atlantic horizon. The sky was a beautiful pink and orange, with dusky blue clouds that hung low on the water's edge. Four horses stood knee deep in waves that repetitively rolled onto the beach, three adults and a tiny foal. Three of the photos showcased all the horses, but the last photo was just of the baby horse as it frolicked in the surf. She caught it perfectly, kicking its spindly legs out behind its awkward body.

"Are these the Corolla horses?" I asked.

"Yeah. The herd is much larger though."

"These are amazing," I commented as I studied them. "Where did you get them?"

"Oh, I took those a few years ago. One of the lucky times I got to see the horses in the surf. That's a rarity."

I turned to look at her in disbelief. "You took these?"

I was astounded. The lighting was perfect, the angle and composition flawless. It was the type of work you'd see hung in an art gallery.

She just smiled at me shyly, and I said, "I want to buy these from you."

She blinked at me once and said, "I'll make you some prints and give them to you."

Shaking my head, I insisted. "No… I want these. Exactly as they're framed. How much?"

Savannah looked at me as if I was an oddity she had never beheld before. "I'll give them to you," she insisted.

"No, I'll buy them."

"Then you won't get them," she said and turned to walk out the door.

Gone was the shy woman of five minutes ago, and in her place was a woman in command.

Utterly fucking fascinating.

Savannah turns the Jeep to the left, onto hard-packed sand where we're not in danger of getting stuck, heading north up the beach. It's absolutely deserted, as she said it would be in the dead of winter, but several rows of tire tracks lets me know that other vehicles have been down this route today.

We drive for a few hundred yards and come up on a truck parked in the middle of the wide stretch of sand. I see a man and a woman, bundled up in winter gear, fishing in the surf. Savannah waves at them as we drive slowly past, and they wave back.

She keenly searches the distance in front of us, vainly seeking the elusive horses.

"I don't come here that much, but it's really hard to catch them on the beach. They mostly stay on the other side of the dunes, back among the houses over there," she says as she points out. "We'll definitely see some once we turn off."

We drive for a while, not seeing a single horse, so Savannah makes a left hand turn through a break in the sand dunes. We lurch over some more loose sand before she hits a hard-packed dirt road that winds in and out of a small neighborhood of beach homes.

As we turn a corner, we see some of the horses... just a pair of them as they graze on the short grass yard of a red-stained house that sits on stilts.

Savannah puts the Jeep in park, and we watch them for a bit. They're really small, and they look like they'd buckle underneath me if I tried to ride one. Not that I'd want to. I'm not overly fond of horses, having been nipped by one when I was little. They're dark brown with long, shaggy hair and kind of cute.

"It's against the law to approach or touch the horses, and you can't feed them either."

"Why's that?" I ask as we watch another horse come from around the side of the house and join the other two.

"They're diet is very specific. If you were to feed something to them that they weren't used to, it could make them really sick. Plus, they can be dangerous. You don't want one to take a bite out of you."

Fuck yeah, I don't want that.

After a few moments, Savannah puts the Jeep in drive, and we meander through the dirt streets of Corolla. Pushing further away from the ocean, there are fewer houses and the dirt roads wind among a thicket of trees that Savannah tells me consist of wild persimmon, yaupon, myrtle, and red cedar. The trees are shaped and molded by the ocean winds, creating thick canopies and heavy shade as we drive along. We see several more horses and spend a good hour just driving around and watching.

Finally, Savannah heads us back to the beach, which is the only way to make our way back to

Highway 12. Unless you know how to drive a vehicle on the beach, you don't come to Corolla.

When we make our way back over the dunes and onto the harder sand, the ocean is revealed before us and my breath catches in my throat. Right before us stand five horses on the edge of the water, the incoming waves lapping around their lower legs. Savannah immediate stops the Jeep and puts it in park.

"Come on," she says as she jumps out of the vehicle. As I exit, I watch as she reaches in the back seat, grabbing her camera bag that she had tucked in there earlier.

We walk around to the front of the Jeep and I lean back against the front grill, watching as she pulls her camera out. She removes the lens cover with deft fingers, flips a button, and makes a few adjustments to the settings. Savannah then walks a few feet forward, still a good thirty yards from the horses, and drops to her knees in the cold sand.

Camera to her face, she silently shoots picture after picture, her form still and gentle. The horses meander north, wading in a bit further until the cold water rolls in just under their fat little stomachs that Savannah told me earlier were often swollen because they will sometimes drink the saltwater.

Every few minutes, Savannah stands, walks a few feet down the beach—away from me—and continues to take photos. I sit back against the front of the Jeep, still warm from the engine, and listen to it making ticking sounds.

She's so fucking beautiful right now. Solely focused, enraptured with the beauty of the ponies walking through the frigid surf. The wind blows, lifting her dark hair all around, causing her to reach a delicate hand up to push at it time and again. I could watch her forever, I realize, and that thought causes my stomach to tighten in almost disbelief. Savannah is a pretty package, in some regards, like many of the other women I've used and then forgotten.

But she's also more, and the more is something that pulls me to her. It's her ever-changing seasons of personality, her bold moves and shy smiles. I want her desperately but, *For how long?* I ask myself.

Savannah finally rises from her last kneeling position, stretching the kinks from her back from holding said position for a long time. Turning to face me, she starts walking back. She has a well-satisfied smile on her face, and her eyes are sparkling as she gets closer.

With her camera in one hand, she walks straight up to me, never pausing in her stride, and my legs open up when she's a foot away. She walks right in between them, lays her small hands on my chest, and stands on her tiptoes to kiss me.

Pulling away laughing, she asks, "Wasn't that incredible?"

"Incredible," I agree as I stare down at her, wanting more than anything to see that look on her face over and over again, from here to eternity.

Savannah lays asleep in my arms. Glancing at the clock beside my bed, I see it's just short of ten o'clock at night. After our outing on the beach, I took Savannah out to lunch in Duck and then back to her little beach house, where I ordered her inside and told her to get a bag with few days of clothing.

She cocked her eyebrow at me in question.

"I have plans for you," I told her simply.

"Like what?" she asked with a grin.

"They involve a bed, a couch, a bathroom counter, the back deck of my house, and probably the driver's seat of my car. You'll be occupied for a while."

"Don't you have work to do?"

"Yes, but I could use a break," I told her, even as my mind calculated the hours I'd have to buckle down once I got my fill of her so I could get back to my writing.

"Well, I have work," she said primly and didn't move from the seat of the Jeep.

"Of course you do," I said sarcastically. "But that doesn't mean you can't sleep at my house, right?"

"Oh, so we'll sleep on the bed, the couch, the bathroom counter, the back deck of your house, and in the front seat of your Maserati?" she asked playfully.

"No," I had told her. "We most definitely won't be sleeping on any of those surfaces... except perhaps the bed."

Savannah had scrambled out of the Jeep and within fifteen minutes, was back and crawling in my Maserati so we could go get started on my checklist of places I wanted to fuck her.

Leaning over her as she sleeps, I can make out the planes of her face in the moonlight coming through the windows of my bedroom. She's naked with the sheet and comforter pulled up to her chin, her mouth slightly parted as she silently breathes. I bend down and rub my lips against hers. She sighs into my mouth, so I kiss her.

By the time my tongue slips inside, her arms are around my neck and she gives a sleepy moan. My hand goes between her legs, and I know she's fully awake by the time my first finger is joined by another.

"Gavin," she pants against my mouth.

It's all the invitation I need. I pull the bed covers back, sliding my body down hers. Pushing her legs apart, I bring my mouth to her pussy, laving at her like a starved man and she's the only food that will sustain. After she comes beautifully, I crawl back up her pliantly soft body and enter her with a single thrust, fucking loving the way she calls out my name when I hit her deep.

Then I fuck her slowly, twining my fingers among hers and finally groaning from the bottom of my chest when I come deeply inside of her.

I find Savannah downstairs the next morning, standing at the counter, watching the coffee as it brews. She hears me, turning to give me that shy smile over her shoulder, and says, "Good morning."

"Would have been better if you were in my bed when I had woken up," I tell her as I come to stand beside her. Her cheeks fire red over my compliment, so I reward her by threading my fingers through her hair, to the back of her head, and pull her upward for a kiss.

When I release her, she gives a tiny sigh of contentment and pulls away to grab two coffee cups. After she pours for both of us, doctoring hers up with milk and sugar, I take her hand and lead her into the living room. I sit on one end of the couch, and she curls her legs up underneath her on the other end.

She's so fucking sexy, wearing nothing but a T-shirt and pale blue panties that I can see sticking out from under the hem.

"I have a proposition for you," I tell her after I take my first sip of coffee.

"If it involves us naked and with you giving me a big, fat orgasm, then I accept," she says with a grin.

Laughing… laughing, and it feels so good. Foreign, but good.

"Funny girl. I think I can manage that… but later. I want to talk business with you."

Her eyes go serious, and she takes another sip of coffee. "What's up?"

"I want to hire you to be my assistant," I tell her and wait for her reaction.

I have no clue what it will be, but this is an idea I started harboring yesterday as I watched her take photos the wild horses in the ocean. I thought about it some more, once while I was plunged deep inside of her, and again as I watched her in the moonlight last night. I came to the realization that I wanted more of her, and seeing her a few times a week after she cleaned my house wasn't enough. It wasn't going to be enough, even if she stayed over with me every night.

No, I wanted her in my house... while I worked, knowing she was nothing but a flight of stairs away from me, so I could have her whenever I wanted.

Simply put... she had become an obsession for me, and while I wondered about the lunacy of my thoughts, I really decided that I didn't give a flying fuck if I was going crazy. In the short time I'd known her, I had become addicted to her brand of sweet.

"Your assistant?" she asked in confusion. "What do you need an assistant for?"

Indeed... what do I need one for?

"Lots of things," I blurt out, my mind racing to come up with ideas. "Errands... I have errands to run. I have fan mail to go through, correspondence to answer. I have a schedule I need to maintain. I have a book signing in Chicago week after next, and I need help with research and proofreading. I have phone calls to return, dry cleaning to pick up, Facebook and Twitter posts to respond to, and a blog to maintain. I need to buckle down on this manuscript, and I don't have time for all of that."

"Why do I feel like there's more to it than that?" she asks skeptically, holding the rim of her coffee cup just below her nose so she can breathe in the fragrance.

"You caught me," I say with a grin. "I just want you around twenty-four-seven, so I can fuck you whenever I want."

That's so much closer to the truth than she'll ever know, but I'm not about to admit that to her. That, all of a sudden, she's become my weakness.

Luckily, Savannah takes it as a joke and snorts at me before taking another sip of coffee.

"So, what do you think?" I ask her. "I'll pay you twenty dollars an hour and you can give up breaking your back cleaning houses and having weird photographers grope at you. You can also take the time to find another photography job… one that will be perfect for you when I'm done here and ready to leave."

"And when might you be ready to leave?" she asks quietly.

Shrugging my shoulders, I hedge. "A few months probably."

I know I promised my manuscript would be done in two weeks, but no way is that happening. I'm going to drag it out just a bit further, so there is no real need for me to leave the islands just yet.

No need to leave Savannah just yet.

"Let me think about it," she says thoughtfully.

EIGHTEEN

Savannah

It took me all of eighteen hours to think about it, then I accepted Gavin's offer. I gladly called Eric and gave him my notice... effective immediately. I also called the two women whose houses I cleaned in addition to Gavin's and told them I had to quit because I was accepting a full-time job. They were sad to see me go, but mollified when I recommended a good cleaning service that Casey had told me about.

When I wake up for my first day on the job as his assistant, Gavin's breath is hot on the back of my neck and his hand is working between my legs, two fingers deep.

"About time you woke up, love," he murmurs, and then kisses me on the side of my neck. "I thought we'd start our first workday together right."

"I insist we start every workday this way," I pant as he strokes me in just the right way.

"And weekends?" he teases as his index finger circles my clit and causes my back to arch away from him. .

"And weekends," I agree as I feel my impending orgasm start to crash through me.

Abruptly, Gavin's hand is gone, and I am thrown violently backward from the precipice of pleasure. "Why'd you stop?" I practically shriek.

Rolling from the bed, Gavin gives a soft chuckle and makes his way over to the dresser. "I have something in mind."

I lift my head and shoulders from the bed, propped on my elbows, and watch his amazingly sculpted ass and chiseled shoulders as he rummages through one of his drawers. When he turns to face me, he has a silk tie in his hands, pale yellow with light blue stripes running diagonally across it. I watch, mesmerized, as he walks back toward the bed, winding the very ends around each of his hands until there's only about half a foot left in between. He gives a snap outward, drawing the material taut.

"Wanna play?" he asks me deviously.

I swallow past the immediate dryness he's caused in my throat and nod my head, even as a small twist of fear snakes up my spine. I've never been tied up before, and it's clear the intent deep within his gray eyes.

"Come here," he commands me, and I don't hesitate before throwing the covers off and rolling out of bed. His eyes run up and down my body appreciatively as I walk toward him, and Gavin never fails to make me feel anything less than the most beautiful creature in the world when I'm in his presence.

When I stop just a foot away, he tells me, "Turn around. Put your hands behind your back."

I do as he asks, trying to control the trembling of my body. Gavin bends over and places a soft kiss on my shoulder.

"I won't hurt you, Sweet," he tells me gently. "Not unless you beg me to."

I groan at the thought of all the ways in which I may beg him to make it hurt. Images of his open palm smacking my ass pour through my mind, and I can feel desire building between my legs.

Gavin starts to wrap the tie around my hands as my wrists rest against each other behind my back. As he works, he murmurs in my ear, "You know… I've experimented with all types of bondage. I've used cuffs, gags, shackles, and crotch ropes."

When I shudder, he licks the shell of my ear and taunts me. "That's right, sweet girl… crotch ropes. I'm betting you would love that, having me wrap you in soft rope, over your breasts, binding you at the elbows, then running it right down in between your legs… right up the center of your—"

The moan that tears out of my throat is unexpected, and my head falls backward as if my neck has no strength to support it in the face of such filthy imagery. Gavin laughs softly, pulling tighter on the tie around my wrists. "I'm teasing you, Savannah. I'd never want to dirty up my sweet that way."

Disappointment sweeps through me in a rolling wave, but then he says, "Not unless you begged me to."

I don't even have a chance to groan out a response because Gavin gives a slight tug to the material binding my hands behind me and turns me around by my shoulders.

He peers down at me, his eyes searching mine. "You okay?"

I nod at him, giving him a sure smile. "Peachy."

"Good," he says, almost with pride, and strokes a finger down my cheek. "Now... get down on your knees for me, Sweet. I want to see what you can do with just your mouth alone."

Now I can't help the groan that tears up out of me, and Gavin's eyes fill with heat from my response. I hold his gaze, even as I lower myself to the soft rug that covers a good chunk of his bedroom's hardwoods. When I come eye level with his cock, I let my eyes slide down his body and look at the massive erection standing straight up just inches from my face. It's so beautiful... dusky rose with a thick, fat vein running underneath.

Gavin's hands gently cup the sides of my face. "Open your mouth, love."

I lick my lips once and then open my mouth, raising my eyes to meet his once more. He looks down at me with such intensity that I feel burned from the inside out.

"Fuck... you are so beautiful, kneeling there in front of me, utterly submissive and helpless. Tell me, Sweet... are you going to swallow me down?"

I nod at him, refusing to say the words aloud because I'm afraid they'll come out in a helpless squeak of desire, which would not be sexy at all.

"That's my girl," he says softly, pulling my face toward him.

Gently, he guides me forward until the head of his cock brushes against my lips. I circle my tongue briefly around the head before pushing forward and taking him all the way in.

Gavin grunts loudly in pleasure and the knowledge that I just pulled forth that ubiquitous sound from deep within him floods me with power.

His fingers thread through my hair and grip me by the back of my head. I pull back, dragging my tongue down the length of him and pulling forth an equally sexy groan from him, before sucking on the tip. I start to go down on him again, but Gavin applies pressure to my head to stop me.

His voice sounds strangled when he says in wonderment, "You're a little too good at that. Tell you what... hold still, beautiful girl, and let me just fuck your mouth for a minute."

I have no clue what that means, but then he shows me as he holds my head tightly and starts to move his hips. In and out of my mouth, his cock moves, not too deep, stopping just before hitting the back of my throat. I curve my tongue along him, sucking in my jaws slightly on every other beat to give him more friction.

"Fuck, Sweet... where did you learn to do that?" He moans and pumps in and out of my mouth a bit faster.

Frustration hits me out of left field, because all of a sudden, I have an insane desire to touch Gavin. I absolutely need to put my hands on him, to touch his exposed cock as it moves out of my mouth, to roll his balls with my fingers. I pull hard at the bonds on my wrist and feel utterly helpless while he moves in and out of my mouth, once going a little too deep, causing me to gag.

"Sorry, baby," he mutters, dialing it down a notch.

I kneel there, helpless before him, knowing that he could do whatever he wanted if given the urge. My eyes slide to the left and widen when I see the full-length mahogany mirror that sits in the corner his room. As is typical, Gavin has a T-shirt draped over the top of it, too lazy to throw it in the hamper, but there's enough mirror exposed that I can see Gavin move his hips back and forth, his thick cock tunneling in and out of my mouth. My breasts are thrust forward, my fingers flexing helplessly behind my arched back, and Gavin stares down at me while he works himself in and out of me.

He must notice my eyes are averted because slowly his head turns. He looks at me in the mirror, watching as I helplessly blow him with my hands tied behind my back.

When our eyes meet in the reflection, his hands grip my head tighter and he moans, "Fuck, Savannah... that's sexy as shit. Watching you, watch us in the mirror. Hot, right?"

I nod my head as best as I can, because words are prohibited by the glorious length of Gavin that is in my mouth.

I'm surprised when Gavin rears back, tearing himself free of my mouth. The emptiness causes my jaw to sag, and I immediately notice it's sore from the pounding he just gave it.

My gaze moves from the mirror and up toward Gavin, whose chest is rising and falling in rapid motions, a light sheet of sweat on his forehead.

"Why did you stop?" I ask uncertainly.

"Because I was getting ready to come," he says, almost in agony as he pants hard, and his hand goes around the base of his cock. He squeezes hard... almost as if to quash his impending orgasm. "Wasn't ready to come just yet."

"Oh," is all I manage to say before Gavin is lifting me from the floor and onto the bed. He puts me on my knees and then with his hand at the back of my head, pushes me down to the mattress until my cheek is resting there.

His hand releases me but slides backward down the middle of my back, straight down to where he drags his finger down the middle of my ass cheeks. I moan at the forbidden touch he gives me. "I'd love to fuck your ass one day, Sweet. Think you'd let me do that?"

A strangled sound comes out of my throat, and I involuntarily start to rise from the bed. Would I let him do that? I have no clue, but his hand comes back up to the middle of my back and he pushes me back down.

"Don't move," he says, and then I can feel him step away from the bed. I have no clue what he's doing, but then I hear him across the room. "This mirror will come in handy."

Gavin comes back into my line of view and sets the full-length mirror up on its stand so it's right beside the bed. I blush warmly when I see my naked body, on my knees, breasts flatted on the mattress, my face flushed and my lips swollen from the workout he just gave my mouth. Gavin comes up to stand behind me, his hands caressing my butt.

We stare at each other in the mirror again, and he says, "You see how beautiful you are? Bound, helpless, bent to my will. You'd take anything I gave you, wouldn't you, Sweet?"

I don't even bother nodding my head in agreement, because he knows the answer.

I would, indeed, take anything he asked me to.

Caressing one hand down my ass, he slides it down between my legs and pushes a finger in. It slides silky smooth through my wetness, and I start panting as he pumps it in and out a few times.

My eyes watch him, and then slide from the action of his hands to his rigid erection, which seems to be straining upward, just behind me. I want him inside of me so bad that I ache all over.

"What are you looking at, love?"

My eyes slowly slide from his cock to his gaze as he watches me in the mirror. "I'm looking at you."

His fingers move inside me, tortuously slow, and he smiles at me lewdly. "You were looking at my cock. Your eyes were all over my cock, thinking of me sliding it inside of you, right?"

"Yes," I whisper.

"Is that what you want?"

I nod, but he just keeps working his finger inside of me. He waits, going back full circle when he first intimately touched me on the couch that day last week. He's waiting for me to say the exact words to tell him what I want.

Taking in a deep breath, I make sure my eyes are directly connected to his. "Gavin… I want you to fuck me with your cock. Is that clear enough for you?"

"Crystal," he says with a smile, white teeth flashing against his dark, stubbled face.

He moves behind me, taking his erection with one hand to guide it inside. I'm so slick with pent-up lust and desire, he slides in easily even as I feel the slight burn from the way he stretches me.

We both groan loudly. It melds together, sounding like one harmonious and erotic vibration throughout the room.

"I wish I were a poet," Gavin murmurs as he starts moving in and out of me. "I wish I were a poet because then… and only then, would I have the words that would be salient enough to describe the way you feel to me. I'd fucking be a best seller every time if I could just describe how I feel… at this very moment, when I'm lodged deep inside of you."

Oh, Gavin. His words… they *are* poetry, and it's not just in the humble consonants and vowels that pour out of his mouth. It's in his tone… with utter worship in his emotion. It speaks deeply to me, and while Gavin has made every part of my body tremble with pleasure, for the first time, my heart gives a bit of a squeeze as I realize that we both have feelings that are starting to get deep.

He moves with tenderness and care within my body. Yes, he's taking me from behind with my hands bound behind my back. My shoulders ache and my thighs tremble, and I know this should feel impersonal, but it doesn't. I'm giving something to Gavin that he very much enjoys, and I'm finding that I, myself, enjoy this different bit of sex as well.

But nothing about our positioning—with him at my back so our lips never meet and my pose completely subservient—speaks of an impersonal nature. No, on the contrary, as Gavin and I stare at each other in the mirror, our breath quickening even though he's moving oh so slowly within me… I can feel a connection to him at this very moment that buries deep into my soul and sinks its claws permanently into me.

NINETEEN

Gavin

Savannah has been my personal assistant for a week and, unfortunately, she's doing too damned good of a job. With her taking off my plate every little annoyance and administrative task I always had to handle on my own, I'm freed up to do nothing but write. My productivity skyrocketed, even with me taking breaks during the day to come downstairs and molest my Sweet. Those tend to be the best parts of my day.

At night… we spend hours exploring each other's body, and after having known each other for just under two weeks, I'm finding it neither odd nor weird that I'm liking her available to me at all hours of the day and night.

I had asked her just yesterday, "Does Casey think it's weird that you're sleeping over here every night?"

Savannah laughed at me, full throated and husky. "No. She said she was just glad that I was finally *getting some.*"

I laughed in return, kissed her hard, and then made love to her on my bathroom vanity, knocking one place I had promised she'd be fucked off my list.

Yes, Savannah is the most efficient personal assistant ever. Hell, even her research is quick and spot-on, further speeding up the process of finishing my manuscript. At this rate, I will definitely be done within a week. I had vainly hoped to stretch it longer just to give myself some more time with her. At least I'm taking her to Chicago with me on Wednesday, and we'll be gone a few days. Maybe I can extend my trip there, lengthening the time frame within which I can complete the manuscript, and thus prolonging my time with her.

Lindie called me again yesterday, reminding me that I had a deadline, and I told her to fuck off... that I'd take another month to write the damn thing if I felt that is what was needed. She responded with her ever-present question, "Are you drinking, Gavin?"

Deeply... from between Savannah's thighs, I thought to myself. *And oh, the intoxicating rush of it all.*

I assured her I was fine, but that you could not rush creativity. That must be a standard response from her other authors because she got quiet and didn't push at me anymore. I then gave her the power punch and reminded her that the book wasn't set to be published until the following year, so we had plenty of time. I had the sneaking suspicion that my editor had set a deadline on me with plenty of cushion in case I couldn't meet the original schedule.

My manuscript was changing in flavor, and those changes would often spill from laptop to real flesh. It happened on more than one occasion this week. I'd be writing an intensely erotic scene between Honey and Max—Max, by the way, having given up his philandering ways—and I would be so immersed in the scene that I'd get a massive erection.

I didn't need Freud to point out to me that the sex scenes between Honey and Max were nothing more than my own subconscious desires for the depraved things I wanted to do to Savannah being played out across my laptop screen.

I'd come out of my writing haze, read back over the intense eroticism I had just written, and would be struck with a massive yearning and a raging hard-on for Savannah. I'd merely push back from my desk, stalk around my house until I found her, and then I'd play out that scene for real.

Once I took her out on the back deck, with the frigid, late January wind blowing around us, and the beach thankfully deserted. Pulled her pants off, left the rest of our clothes on, and set her ass on the deck rail. I did nothing more than free my cock from my zipper and fucked her fast and furiously. I immediately carried her inside afterward, her nipples erect from the cold, and put us in a hot shower, where I went down on her with the warm water pelting my body.

Another time, I found her sitting at my kitchen table, her nose practically plastered to her own laptop while she did research for me on Jack the Ripper. I had a sub-plot where one of the demons in my fantasy universe was actually a reincarnation of Jack, who liked to shred his victims from the inside out. I merely walked up to her, grabbed her by the ponytail she had ensnared her beautiful hair in, and tilted her head back to look at me.

"I want you," I told her simply, and her eyes burned like the setting sun.

I pulled her up from the chair, sat myself on the warmed seat, and ordered her to strip. She didn't hesitate. When she was completely naked, I told her to ride me. My cock was already hard, but I let her do the rest of the work. Her hands were slightly shaking and her breath was already shallow by the time she freed me from my jeans and climbed onto my lap. Just before she lowered herself to me, I told her to wait, and I brought my hand between her legs. She was already damp—I'm sure she started to glisten the moment I pulled on her ponytail—but I worked her with my fingers for a while until she came close to climax. Then I dropped my hands and let her finish us both off while she rode me with abandon.

She had me groaning like a ravenous animal when I came, gripping her hips and grinding her down hard on me as I unloaded.

"Sweet," I had growled.

When we both stopped shuddering, she nuzzled my neck and whispered, "I'm going to call you Filthy."

She leaned back and looked down at me with tenderness and humor wrapped up in a pretty bow, and I felt my heart turn over in my chest.

"I'm the filthy to your sweet?"

"You're many things to me," she murmured before kissing my lips. "But filthy is my favorite."

I took Savannah whenever I wanted, and she never once said no. On the contrary, her eyes always fired hot and she gave in to my every desire. And yes, I was playing out all my desires from laptop to flesh, but I'd be ten times the fool if I didn't admit to myself that there was something more going on inside of my not-so-fictitious manuscript.

Honey and Max were transforming. His eyes no longer hungrily roamed over every piece of womanly flesh that came his way. No, they stayed glued to Honey the entire time, and hers to his. They developed a bond, which stretched, forged, and ultimately cemented through their darkest days together. In the worst of times, they were each other's anchors. In the best of times, they became each other's light.

My own sanity worried over this change, because it was an absolute divergence from the plot that I had promised my publisher. Max was a stud... most of his appeal centered in the loner, alpha tendencies displayed throughout my first novel. Men wanted to be him because he fucked his way across the United States. Women wanted just one crack at the pleasures he promised.

But now… now he was monogamous and entrusting his heart to just one woman, and it worried me to no end that perhaps my own heart was becoming too deeply immersed in the sweet beauty of Savannah Shepherd. For the first time, in a long time, I yearn to walk away from the bitterness and pain of my past life, and move into something that was good, sweet, and without tarnish. I crave the light that Savannah shines on me.

Her smile calms, her soft touch unmans. Her laugh fortifies, and her brazen look overwhelms me.

I'm falling in deep with her, and rather than trying to claw my way out, I find myself wanting to tie anchors to my feet so that I can submerge in just a little further.

This was something I promised myself I'd never do again, so brutal was the hurt I suffered from Amanda's hands. Yet even as I repetitively warn myself that I'm treading on thin ice by laying my heart on the line, I can't help but seek her out over and over again.

Standing up from my desk, I roll my neck from side to side, loosening the tension that took hold from my thoughts and worries. Glancing at my watch, I decide to go for a run. Savannah is out at the grocery store and picking up my mail from the post office. I have time to get a run in and a shower before she returns, and then I think I'll sit in the kitchen and ogle her while she cooks us dinner.

When I return from my run, Savannah is in the kitchen, a vision of domesticity as she mixes a red sauce on the stove. She lifts the lid of another pot and gives it a stir.

"Hey," she says cheerfully. "You had a ton of mail at the post office, but I'll sort if after dinner. I probably need to check it every day just to stay on top of it."

I walk up behind her and slip my arms around her waist. Nuzzling her neck, I tell her, "You're not working after dinner."

Savannah tries to wriggle out of my grasp. "You're all sweaty, Gavin. Gross."

"Come take a shower with me then," I urge her.

"Can't. Pasta will be done in about five minutes. Go take a quick shower and then come eat," she tells me firmly, managing to slip free. I think briefly about pulling her to the floor and getting her sweaty with me but instead, I swat her on the ass and jog up the stairs.

After a quick shower where I ignore my aching cock, because just being pressed up against Savannah is enough to get me massively turned on, I return down to the kitchen in a pair of old sweatpants and a T-shirt. She's straining the pasta and humming to herself.

"Want some wine with our dinner, Filthy-boy?"

I grin at her nickname and walk over to my wine rack. Pulling out a bottle of Cab, I open the drawer for the corkscrew. Savannah pulls two plates out of the cupboard and dishes up a heaping pile for me that she drizzles with a garlicky tomato sauce. She then serves up a much smaller plate for herself, and I pour two glasses of wine.

We sit beside each other, making small talk, our knees bumping companionably against each other. I find I like her in my kitchen, in my house, sitting next to me, slurping noodles. It's so simple, yet so complex, because my meals have all been enjoyed in solitary fashion for so long. Yet I can't deny the feeling of peace and fulfillment I get just by having her here.

"I've been meaning to ask you," Savannah says as she twirls pasta around her fork. "Who is that adorable little boy in the photo on your desk?"

My own hand freezes mid-twirl, and my head spins slightly. I wasn't prepared for Savannah to ask me about Charlie, yet my beautiful little boy isn't exactly a secret. While it's true he sits in my office with me day in and day out, the only reason he's secluded there is because that's the only photo I have of him and I want him near me while I work. All the other photos of his smiling face are now sitting in dusty boxes at my dad's house in London.

I remember Lindie once asked me about Charlie, and I snarled at her so viciously that she turned pale and immediately started yammering apologies. I told her to mind her own fucking business and stormed out of her office.

Charlie is to me what pain, regret, and misery are to a broken man, and sharing his story with Savannah could spiral me down a hole that has taken me months to climb out of. Yet, Charlie is also sunshine, toothless smiles, and warm baby kisses. He holds the largest chunk of my heart and that should be celebrated.

There's no denying that Savannah has a piece of my heart as well. She squirmed her way in, set up residence, and has no chance of leaving any time soon. Maybe it's time for both pieces of my heart to get to know one another.

Clearing my throat, I set my fork down and turn to face her. "That's Charlie... my son."

Savannah's face lights up in a smile, and she pushes at my shoulder with her hand. "You have a son? No way. I can't believe you never told me." She turns all the way on her stool to face me and leans forward with excitement, her dinner completely forgotten. "Tell me all about him and spare me no detail."

Oh, Sweet… you don't want these details, but I'm going to give them to you anyway.

And because I know what I'm getting ready to tell her is going to wipe that smile right off her face, I raise my hand and stroke her cheek, even as I say, "He's dead, Sweet."

Savannah's face pales and her beautiful brown eyes fill with crystalline tears. Her hand comes up to cover her mouth, and she lets out a half sob. "Oh, Gavin. No. No. Please no."

My heart twists painfully, not only because it still hurts to say my beautiful baby boy is dead, but also because I see Savannah has taken on all of my agony onto her delicate shoulders. I nod my head at her, giving her the only thing I can… a sad smile.

"Oh, baby," she breathes out as tears stream down her face.

She launches off her stool and scrambles onto my lap. My arms come around her to hold her in place, and she cups her hands to my face. "Oh, no, no, no," she murmurs as her lips touch my forehead. Then my eyes, then my cheeks. She nuzzles her face into my neck, placing warm kisses along my skin that are immediately drenched in her tears, and then she buries her face against my collarbone and cries.

My heart swells with her suffering for me, and the bitter ash of telling her that Charlie is dead is replaced by an immense need on my part to help alleviate her own suffering.

Standing up from the stool, I carry her into the living room and sit on the couch, cradling her on my lap. "Shhh," I croon to her and let her cry herself out while I stroke her back and her hair.

While she pours out her sadness on to my shirt, my gaze travels over to the fireplace. I look at the four framed photos of the Corolla horses that she hung the other day. I had come down from my office to eat some lunch and immediately noticed them. She gave me a shy smile, and I kissed her deeply to show my appreciation.

Studying them now, I find I like them very much in my house. Because Savannah gave me something of hers that was personal. Just as I just gave her something of mine that was personal.

Savannah shifts in my arms and pulls back. She looks at me with tears still swimming in her eyes and says, "I'm so sorry. I shouldn't have asked."

I lift my hand and place my fingers against her lips. "It's okay you asked. He's not a secret. What happened to him isn't a secret."

She kisses the pads on my fingers, then grabs my hand and kisses my palm... my wrist, before placing her hand against the beating heart in her chest. "I can't even imagine."

I lean forward and touch my mouth softly to hers, and she takes in a stuttering breath. "I'm glad you asked. It's something I want to share with you. I want to share him... with you."

"You don't have to—"

"Savannah," I say as I cut her off. "You've turned my world upside down in the few weeks I've come to know you. There's never been anyone that I've wanted to share Charlie with. Only you."

Savannah settles on my lap, places her cheek to my chest, and strokes my arm. "Tell me then. Tell me about your sweet boy. Tell me how he lit up your world, and then left you in darkness. Share it with me and let it unburden you."

"Oh, God," I whisper as I lean down to kiss her on the head, squeezing her tight. "How do you always know what to say to me?"

Her hand slides up my chest and rubs me over my heart. "Because I've seen what's inside of here.

I've felt it… beating true and strong. I feel it when you make love to me, and when you're fucking me, and when you're everything to me in between."

"So sweet," I murmur with my lips against her head.

I decide to tell her every bit of it, starting from the beginning… starting with Amanda.

The woman that killed my son.

TWENTY

Savannah

My heart is breaking. Literally breaking in half, then the two massive pieces are toppling over within my chest, where they fracture further and throb with pain for Gavin. My lungs feel constricted and my head is pounding as fearful blood surges through me.

"I met Amanda during my last year of university. It wasn't love at first sight, but it was certainly complete and utter fascination for me. She was a poet... you know, one of those dark types that dressed in black from head to toe, smoked cigarettes, and quoted from Poe and Donne in her normal conversation. Her eyes were perpetually sad, and I used to think it was because she wrote sad poetry all the time."

I listen to his story intently, noticing that there's no fondness in his voice, but no bitterness either. It's as if he's telling me a simple story about a ship sailing past the shore one night.

"At any rate, we dated... fell in love, lived our lives together. Amanda eventually moved out of her Goth phase but she continued to be morose, even when she wasn't writing her dark poetry. After I graduated, I got a job as a technical writer for a company that developed training manuals for large corporations. By day, I'd work my job putting dry and boring words on paper, and at night, I tried to make Amanda happy."

"Why was she so sad?" I ask, my fingers lightly stroking his chest while my face is pressed against his heart, so I can hear the thrum of his life.

"She was depressed... or so we came to find out when I insisted she see a doctor. We were living together, and I was thinking about asking her to marry me, but I wanted her to be well. I wanted her to be happy and in love with me the way I was with her. They tried her on various medications, she seemed to get better for a while, and our lives marched on."

"Did you marry?" I ask hesitantly.

"No. But she got pregnant. We were just using condoms, and I guess one must of have broken. It was a surprise to both of us, but we were happy with the news. Nine months later, Charlie was born." Gavin pauses, clears his throat, and says in a raspy voice. "He was so beautiful. So perfect."

"He looks just like you," I say.

"Except he had Amanda's eyes," he adds on. "At any rate, I was brimming with happiness, but Amanda seemed to become more depressed again. Her doctors tweaked her medication, but nothing seemed to be working as a permanent fix. Postpartum depression, they said, and that it would get better if we just gave it time."

"But it didn't?" I guess.

"No, it didn't. Amanda seemed to drift further and further away. I had to urge her to do simple things to take care of herself, like bathe and eat. I couldn't trust Charlie with her, so my mum would watch him while I was at work. But I chose to ignore it, because Charlie was well cared for during the day, and at night I had him all to myself while Amanda would sit in front of the telly and watch game shows."

"You must have felt so lonely," I say quietly.

"Sometimes… but mostly I wasn't because I had Charlie. And he had me, and really… that's all I cared about. However, there were times that Amanda seemed okay. She'd take an interest in Charlie and me, and I could almost pretend that things were going to get better. She even had times where she was perfectly normal and was able to care for Charlie just fine."

Gavin shifts on the couch, pulling my body up tighter to his. He takes a deep breath in and lets it out slowly.

"One weekend, I got a call on a Saturday that a project I was working on needed some changes made before it was going to be presented for review on Monday. I had to go into the office. I tried to call my mum to watch Charlie, but she was out. Amanda seemed okay that day… had even gotten up that morning and made us breakfast. She assured me she would be fine with Charlie and urged me out the door. I was hesitant, but I looked at her as she smiled at me with reassurance, and I figured it was only a few hours. What could possibly happen? So I kissed her, kissed Charlie, and I left."

My heartbeat is pounding madly within the weak walls of my chest, and I almost beg Gavin to stop the story. But I hold my tongue while he continues.

"I was gone for two hours and twenty-three minutes. When I walked back in the house, I found Amanda sleeping on our bed. I couldn't find Charlie anywhere."

My stomach cramps as I imagine Gavin's rising panic while he searched for his son.

"I ran out the door... through the yard, calling his name. One of the neighbors heard me and came out to help me search. We went from yard to yard, until we reached the end of our street, which butted up against a small embankment that rolled down to a tiny creek at the bottom of the hill. We found Charlie there... in the water. He had a bruise on his head. The coroner thinks he must have fallen and hit his head, landing face first in the shallow water. He drowned. He was two years old."

My fingers clutch desperately to Gavin's shirt, clawing deeply and biting into his skin. My tears start up again, and I let them silently fall down my cheeks. He holds me while I hold him, burrowing my face in tighter to his chest while my tears wet his shirt.

After several minutes, I lift my head and look up at Gavin with sad eyes. His own are swimming in the memories of his dead son, and I touch my fingers to his cheek. "How did you ever survive something like that?"

"I didn't," he says simply. "I tried as hard as I could to kill myself with drugs and alcohol. I don't even remember the first few months after his death, because all I could do was blame myself for leaving him with Amanda."

I jolt upward and out of his arms. Turning my body, I straddle his lap and hold his face firmly in my hands. "No," I practically shout at him. "That was not your fault. That was all on Amanda. She failed Charlie, not you."

Gavin takes one of my hands in his and kisses my wrist. He leans forward, grazes his lips over mine, and gives me a sad smile. "It was on both of us, Savannah. I've accepted my role in his death, and I'll always bear that cross."

"What happened to Amanda?"

"She had a breakdown. The police investigated, but no charges were filed against her. She had a legitimately documented medical condition of depression, and besides... I didn't want her to go to jail for it. She couldn't help her illness... that was beyond her control."

"Weren't you angry with her though? I don't even know her and I'm angry at her, and I don't care that she was sick." My voice is rageful and so unkind. So not me.

"I wanted to kill her," Gavin admits to me. "I wanted to drag her down to that little creek and hold her facedown in the water, so she could feel the water saturate her lungs and know what it was like to suffer that slow death."

My body shudders over the violence in his voice, but then he takes another deep breath and lets it out slowly. "But I found another outlet for my anger. Outside of the drinking and drugs, I expressed my frustrations in other ways."

Gavin doesn't elaborate, and I have a feeling I wouldn't like to know those other ways. But I think I really *do* know, because he has hinted at it before. "With sex?"

"With everything," he tells me honestly. "I did everything to the extreme, and much of that involved sex. I immersed myself in the dodgy underbelly of London, and I learned all the ways I could hurt a woman so exquisitely she'd orgasm multiple times. I took pleasure whenever it was offered to me, sometimes even paying for the privilege to forget my shitty existence while a woman would suck me down. I did things that would so thoroughly disgust you, Sweet, that I really have no right to even let you sit here on my lap and let you comfort me."

His head hangs low with shame and dejection, and I didn't think my heart could break further.

With shaking hands, I grip his face tighter and lift it so his eyes meet mine. "You could never disgust me. Those things you did… they were but a moment in your life. Just a tiny, incomprehensible moment, and you did what you had to do to survive. And you did survive. Just look at you now… you more than survived. You flourished."

Gavin shakes his head sadly. "No, love. I didn't survive. And I don't flourish. I just exist. It's all I know how to do."

Leaning in, I kiss him sweetly on his mouth, and he sighs into me. I kiss him a bit harder, and his arms tighten around me. I clutch at his shoulders and kiss him some more, trying to suck out every bit of pain and doubt that I can. I can feel him grow hard beneath me as I straddle his lap, but I pull back from him. "You're wrong, Gavin. When you just exist, you have no emotion. No passion. But when you live… you seize opportunity, you drink of a joyful life, and you're motivated. The man I know… the man I've let into my heart, he's a man that lives."

The sadness in Gavin's eyes melts away and curiosity fill up his gaze. He's listening to me, so I continue. "You suffered unimaginable pain and horror in your young life, and you let it bend you. It bent you over backward, nearly snapping you in half. But it didn't break you. You didn't let it break you."

"Savannah—" Gavin says and his words are husky, filled with emotion.

"The man that held my face and told me that I was the strongest heroine he's ever known, that is a man who is living his life. The man who touches me so sweetly and does the loveliest of dirty things to me... the man that makes me crazy with lust and causes me to scream at the top of my lungs... that's a man that is filled with passion. The man that writes such amazing words and sucks you into his story... he's a man filled with genius and creativity. You're sad, Gavin, and that's okay. Let me share it with you, but don't ever think for a minute that you will ever be a man that is content to just exist."

Gavin stands from the couch in such a swift move that I yelp in surprise. He grabs me by the back of my hair, pulling my face back and kissing me hard. Kisses me with passion and yearning and a zeal to make the most of this very moment we're sharing.

He carries me to the stairs and up to his second-floor bedroom, his lips never leaving mine. I feel something different. In the way he touches me, in the way that he stares at me. He's opened himself up to something that he never did before... something he had held himself back from, and I realize what it is in the moment when he lays me on the bed and looks down at me.

He needs me.

Gavin Cooke, a man who swam through darkness and torture, drowned himself in the ecstasy of the next big high and probably fucked his way through half of London so he could forget his demons, rose from the ashes having survived, but having done so while being utterly alone.

Now he's not. Now he knows that he has one other person in this world who is willing to share the burden of his sadness. And I can see it in his eyes… right this minute, that he is acknowledging that he needs me.

And God help me, I think I need him too, because he's made me feel and experience things I never thought were possible in my narrowed existence.

Gavin crawls onto the bed, up my body, and lies down on top of me. He kisses me again, this time with more care than he has ever taken with my lips. He moves slowly but deliberately, pressing his mouth into mine, sucking on my bottom lip, giving me a soft bite. His tongue moves against mine. He angles his head to go deeper and possess me more thoroughly.

He kisses and kisses and kisses me, making no other move to touch me other than to stroke my face.

I can feel his erection laying thick and long between my legs, yet he doesn't even move his hips to grind into me. This isn't about sex right now, although I know that's coming.

It's about him showing me how much he cares for not only what I just said to him downstairs, but also for the person I am.

He finally... yes, finally, because I am starting to fill up with a crazy burning for more of him, peels my clothes away, letting his lips travel over every bit of exposed skin. He silently caresses me with his hands, his tongue, and the very breath that rushes out of his mouth. I wriggle and moan, and even beg him to give me more, but he takes his sweet, filthy time with me.

When I'm completely naked, he rolls from the bed, standing briefly to disrobe, his eyes never leaving mine. When he crawls back in and lies back down on top of me, my heart hammers a hungry tune for him. I can feel his warm erection between my legs, pulsing and jerking with need. But he does nothing more than start to kiss me all over again, now whispering the sweetest of words that I've ever heard come out of his dirty mouth.

Sweet... your skin is so soft. I could kiss and lick at it for days on end.

Your nipples... so perfect. Your breasts, your stomach, your hips. All so fucking perfect.

Touching you is the best part of my every day.

We could live to the end of time, and even when the sun would finally die out, I'd still never have enough of you.

Oh, Gavin… my poet.

When he finally rises up just a bit, he looks down at me. He is suspended on one hand while, with the other, he takes himself in hand and guides it into me. He slides in easily, because I'm so ready for him, and when he's seated to the hilt within my body, his eyes flutter closed and he sighs.

When he opens them again, he leans down and kisses me gently. After he pulls back from my mouth but before he gives the first move of his hips, he whispers, "Thank you."

And in that moment, I'm pretty sure my heart has been enslaved.

TWENTY-ONE

Gavin

"Geez, love… how long exactly does it take for you to get ready? It's just some drinks with your friends," I say in exasperation as I lean against the doorjamb of my bathroom. Savannah has been diligently working on herself for the past half hour. I've watched as she put cream on her face and eyes, some type of frothy stuff in her hair. She then put on makeup—seemed like a million different things went on her face—yet when she was done, she didn't look made up at all. Except for her eyes... her lashes were so long and thick that her eyes practically glowed at me. Then she dried her hair... then she took some type of wand looking thing and ran it through, causing the slight bit of wave that it naturally bore to straighten out and flip at different angles.

Finally... yes, finally, she slathered gloss on her lips, puckered said lips in the mirror, and all I could think about was getting those slick, wet lips around my cock. I had to turn my back on her and walk out the bathroom before I fucked her right then and there.

Christ, she's so fucking beautiful and sexy that she makes my eyeballs burn sometimes. And the way she looks at me, especially after I told her all about Charlie last night, especially after the way we made love... she makes my heart squeeze, contract, jump, shiver, and moan in delight.

I thought a lot about what Savannah said... about how I didn't just exist, but I lived. She told me I had been bent but never broken. And I suppose she's right, to some extent... I slogged my way through the darkness that I let overtake my life for a while. I managed to pull myself up and write a book, and when additional opportunity came my way, I managed to remove myself from the life that was dragging me under and get a fresh start here in the Outer Banks. Yeah… I did that all on my own. Crawled out of the deepest hole I could have ever been able to dig for myself.

But where Savannah doesn't acknowledge the full story is where she didn't mention her part. I may have dragged myself up to the edge of the hole, but I think I was hanging onto the edge with my fingertips. Barely… just barely.

I didn't get out of that fucking hole until she wandered up, looked over the edge at me, and smiled. I didn't get out of that hole all the way, until just last night when she grabbed ahold of my wrists and with every bit of strength, care, and kindness, pulled me up out of it the rest of the way.

I woke up this morning, after having pondered that all night while I held her in my arms, and realized that I could have a different life than what I thought, starting today.

Starting right this very moment where I want to really start it off right by walking back into that bathroom, stripping her naked, and feasting on her body for hours.

"I'm ready," she says, coming out of the bathroom.

"Finally," I grumble, pulling her into my arms. "You look fantastic. Smell even better. I know for a fact you taste fucking amazing. Want to give me a taste?"

She nods, so I lean down. I kiss her wet lips, tasting vanilla and mint on them. Then I release her, or else we'll never make it out of the bedroom, and I know she's dying for me to meet her friends.

I briefly marvel at how fast all of this seems to be moving between us. Just a little over two weeks ago, I was snarling at her and she was cowering from me. Then I fingered her in my Maserati, and things definitely changed then. After I fucked her for the first time, I knew that sex would never be the same for me again. And last night... after we talked about Amanda, Charlie, and my addictions, she liberated me from the rest of my darkness with just a few small, comforting, but heartfelt, words.

And now, here we are, and she wants me to meet her friends.

I'm up for the challenge, of course. After the things I've been through, nothing scares me. Except the prospect of losing Savannah, when I just found her. So, maybe I am a little nervous they won't like me. Particularly Brody, who I can tell is very protective of her.

Yes, forget her pack of girlfriends… Brody is the one whose approval I'm going to need to get.

"Are you having fun?" Savannah says as she saunters up to me with a flushed grin on her face. She's at that place right now where she borders between slightly buzzed and really buzzed, and she's fucking charming as all get out.

I was watching her play pool with Hunter, my eyes either pinned to her ass or the slight cleavage she shows when she bends over. Every once in a while, my gaze will stray to make sure no other guys have their eyes pinned to her ass or tits, which is something I wouldn't take kindly to.

"Loads of fun," I assure her, but while her friends have all been nice… except Brody, who seems a bit reserved, I'd much rather take her home and spend hours making her scream.

"So, where do you stand on PDA?"

"P-D-what?" I ask, confused.

"PDA… public displays of affection," she says seriously. "Some guys don't like that, and I'm curious where you stand?"

Reaching out, I place my hands on her face and draw her closer to me. "I'm not sure. Let's test it out first... see if I like it or not."

Bending down, I touch my lips to hers, with only the intent of grazing their fullness. But she presses in to me, opening her mouth and slipping her tongue in. I'm powerless not to reciprocate, so I do... giving her a deep, sensual kiss, so that when I pull back she is dazed and weak-kneed.

"I think I like it," I murmur as I release my hold.

Her fingertips come up to rub her lips thoughtfully, and she stares at me intently. "I really like it too."

My hands slip to her waist and wrap around her lower back, pulling her in flush against me. "When can we leave?"

"Already?" she asks in disbelief. "We just got here."

"Three hours ago," I point out, and while I have indeed been enjoying myself, I'm dying to get her alone.

"*Pfft*," she says, waving her hand dismissively. "What's three hours in the grand scheme of things?"

Laughing at her near-drunken silliness, I bend down again and give her a quick kiss on her mouth. I put my lips near her ear. "It's three hours too long without feeling your sweet pussy wrapped around my cock. I'm dying here, Sweet. I want to leave so I can fuck you."

"Oh," she breathes into my neck and then pulls back to look at me. "Why didn't you say so? That sounds like so much more fun than hanging out here."

I give her a huge grin and release her waist, only to take her hand. "Let's say our goodbyes then."

I turn to start walking her over to where the girls are all standing, only to practically run into Brody. He's holding a bottle of water in one hand and glass of Scotch in the other.

Handing the liquor to me, he says, "I bought you a drink."

I take it from him, heaving with frustration on the inside, and say, "Thanks, mate. You didn't have to do that."

You really didn't have to do that.

"Oh, sure I did," Brody says affably, although I sense an underlying tone of censure in his voice. "Besides, I thought we could have a chat."

I cock my eyebrow high, to let him know just what I think of that, but then turn to Savannah. "Why don't you go hang with the rest of the gang for a bit, love? Let Brody and I get to know each other a bit better."

Savannah's eyes flick between Brody and me for a moment, then she sighs rather audibly. "Fine. But hurry up, Filthy. You have promises to fulfill tonight."

I wince internally over her words because Brody seems to stiffen up beside me as we watch her flounce off to join Gabby, Alyssa, Casey, and Hunter.

Taking a sip of Scotch, I watch her thoughtfully. She's fucking perfect. Perfect for me, that is, and I have to wonder what this means for my future. Just a few days ago, I had high plans to jet back to London when I finished my manuscript. Now I have no clue what to do. I definitely see something with Savannah for the future; I just don't know what it is. I'm pretty confident it wouldn't involve marriage, because with marriage comes the expectations of children. Savannah is the type of woman that would want children. Lots and lots of them, but that is something I crossed off my bucket list long ago and will never put back on.

I had my one chance at a child, and I failed miserably. I'm never going through that again, because the pain far outweighed the good. I'm never taking the chance of having to go through that pain again.

"Some deep thoughts brewing in that head of yours," Brody says, and I turn around to blink at him. I had completely forgotten he was standing there.

"Savannah's a deep woman," I say. "She deserves deep thoughts, don't you think?"

"She deserves the best thoughts," Brody says, and I don't miss the ominous tone in his voice.

I take another small sip of Scotch, appraising the man standing before me that Savannah has so much care and respect for. I have to say... the protectiveness in him over my woman both assures me and pisses me off. It's nice to know Savannah has had someone looking over her, but that's not needed anymore, so I decide to lay it on the line. "What's on your mind, mate? Spill it."

"I don't want to see her hurt. Savannah is a special woman; no doubt, you already know that. But she wounds easily."

"I have no intentions of wounding her."

"What are your intentions, then? You're here just temporarily, right?"

I turn my head and watch Savannah as she sips at her beer and laughs at something Gabby says. If she laughed with me like that every day, I'd have to seriously consider staying with her forever. Or convincing her to come with me back to England.

Regardless, the point being, I don't think I can give her up.

Turning back to Brody, I tell him honestly. "My original plans were to leave as soon as I finished my manuscript. But I'm thinking that's easier said than done at this point."

Brody seems to like my answer, and I can feel some of the ice melt away. "So what's the problem? You can write anywhere, right?"

"That I can," I tell him. "Seems like a simple solution, right?"

He claps me on my back and laughs. "Dude, there's nothing simple about relationships. If it were easy, everyone would have them."

"You make it look easy," I point out. "You and Alyssa… you're about as tight as I've ever seen two people."

Brody's eyes go soft as he looks at her. "We share a bond that's hard to explain."

Holding up my glass of Scotch, I give it a little shake. "I've got a glass of liquor to sip at, so I got the time."

With appraising eyes, Brody stares at me. I can see the moment he feels like I'm worthy to hear his story, and it doesn't have a damn thing to do with anything he knows about me. He's trusting Savannah's instinct about me.

Leaning back against the wall, Brody fiddles with the plastic cap on his water bottle. "Did Savannah tell you I was in prison?"

"Yeah… just that it was a drunk driving accident, someone died, and you went away for five years."

"That's part of the story. The other part… the part that only a select few know, and that select few includes Savannah… was that I wasn't the one driving the car. I foolishly took the fall for my girlfriend because she begged me to… and I paid the price by losing everything that was important to me. I lost my freedom, my medical career, and my family for a time. She took everything from me."

My jaw drops as I realize, at this very moment, Brody and I share something in common. We've both had loves who had taken something away from us. Granted, it was two very different ways in which we were hurt, but still hurt by women in a profound way all the same.

"I was pretty broken when I came out of prison," Brody says as he continues his story. "Had given up on life… on people… on my family. I was existing in a world I didn't know."

His words are like a sucker punch to my throat, because I know exactly what he means. I know exactly how that feels. I open my mouth to talk, but my throat catches because of the rawness sitting there. I clear it and say, "How did you survive it?"

Brody turns from me and nods his head toward Alyssa. "I survived it for her. Because of her. All her."

As I sip at my Scotch, Brody tells me how he had kept it a secret from everyone that he had not been the one driving. He told me that Alyssa came into the secret by mistake, by overhearing a conversation between Brody and his ex-girlfriend. How she kept his secret, and all the while shared his hurt and pain. How every time he was with her, talked to her, touched her… it became more and more bearable, until finally… he just couldn't remember the darkness anymore.

He didn't say it in quite those flowery words, and hey… I'm a writer so I tend to expound, but that was the gist of what he was telling me. By the time his story is over, I'm staring hard at Savannah because she's offering me the very same path to salvation that Alyssa offered Brody.

This is not news to me. I figured that much out all on my own last night. But the moral of the story is the same… that not all women are created equal. That as humans, we can have untold suffering and still persevere and, above all else, there can be a full life after heartbreaking misery.

I suspected as much, but at least Brody is living proof that it is so.

Savannah and I end up staying at Last Call for the rest of the night rather than leaving to get our fill of each other. At this point, after listening to Brody, I'm pretty sure I'm not going anywhere after this manuscript is finished. I'll have days and nights and more days and nights with Savannah, so the next few hours aren't going to break me if I have to just watch her having fun with her friends from afar.

When we leave, Savannah is blitzed, and I'm thankful I limited myself to just three drinks the entire night, the last one having been drunk almost an hour and a half before we left. I'm completely fine to drive.

Where I run into trouble is when Savannah—who is a little too inebriated—decides to knock off an item from my sex wish list. She tries her damnedest to get me to pull the car over on the side of the road, so she can fuck me in my car.

I groan at the thought and groan more when Savannah leans over in the seat and palms my raging hard-on. She even leans over and kisses me through my jeans.

"Get back over in your seat, Savannah," I tell her gently. "I don't want you slipping out of your seatbelt like that."

"Then pull the damn car over, Filthy, and prove to me why you earned that nickname."

Chuckling, I grab her hand and bring it to my mouth, giving her a soft kiss on the tips of her fingers. "Oh, Sweet… you are absolutely perfect for me."

She giggles as she turns to look at me. I give her a brief glance. Even though her blood is swimming with alcohol, her gaze is serious and intent. "I'm so fucking perfect for you, Filthy. We were made for each other."

I can't hold her gaze for long because it belongs on the road, but I murmur in agreement. "I think you're right, love."

TWENTY-TWO

Savannah

I'm overwhelmed. Positively overwhelmed by Gavin's fame. I had no clue.

We arrived in Chicago yesterday afternoon, where we promptly checked into the hotel. Then Gavin stripped me bare and made me come three times to his one. We showered, got dressed, and went out for some Chicago-style pizza. I loved it. He hated the doughy mess, proclaiming that New York-style was the only way to go.

I laughed at him then, and I laughed repetitively with him as we walked the streets of The Windy City, finally ducking into a small bar because it was practically Antarctic weather outside. We sat in a small booth in the corner, and I drank wine while he drank Scotch. We held hands, talked, laughed, and laughed some more. When it was midnight, he bundled me back in my winter coat, which I had to buy for this trip because I didn't own one, and we walked back the five blocks to our hotel.

Back in the room, I let the two glasses of wine impassion my desires for this beautiful man. I pushed him down on the bed, unbuttoned his jeans, and stroked him with my soft hands. Then I put my mouth on him, and I licked, kissed, sucked, and licked and sucked, while his hands fisted my hair and his hips kept pushing up from the bed. His moans fueled me on, and I devoured him down without giving him any mercy.

"Christ, Sweet," he panted when I was done. I crawled back up to lay beside him on the bed with a satisfied smile on my face.

"You give amazing fucking head," he murmured while gathering me in close.

I smiled, completely happy with my life in that very moment.

I got even happier when Gavin tore my clothes off and extended the favor back to me.

The next day is when I got slapped in the face with Gavin's success. His agent, Lindie Booth, met us in the hotel restaurant for breakfast. She was a no-nonsense type of woman… tall, regal, with jet-black hair and even blacker eyes. I guessed her age to be about fifty. When Gavin introduced me with an arm around my shoulder, she briskly shook my hand and said, "Pleasure."

Then I was forgotten, and it was down to business.

As I ate my egg-white omelet, Lindie went over Gavin's afternoon schedule, which included an appearance on a popular, national TV talk show, his signing at a major book retailer, and a party being thrown by his publisher for several of its more successful authors.

"Savannah… you should go out and see the city today," Lindie had said as she looked across the table at me. "Gavin will be extremely busy, and we can send a limo to pick you up at the hotel for the party."

"Savannah's staying with me," Gavin said before I could even open my mouth to respond. "She's my assistant."

"But... I have an assistant for you for the book signing, and I'll be with you at the talk show," Lindie said in disbelief.

"And yet, Savannah will still be there with me for both," Gavin said smoothly, and took a sip of tea that he had ordered rather than his customary black coffee.

Lindie huffed and said, "Fine," in a voice that didn't sound all that fine, but then she moved on and prattled about various other engagements he had to attend in the next several months.

When Gavin walked on stage at the talk show and the audience went nuts over him, that's when I started to get overwhelmed by his fame. The women were standing and screaming for him, many holding up a copy of *Killing the Tides* in their hands. I stood just off stage behind a partial wall so I could see Gavin, the talk show host, and about half the audience.

I was so proud with how he handled himself, addressing questions from the host and the audience. He cheekily talked about the erotic scenes, giving away no clear details of what drove his passion for writing them, but hinting thoroughly that they were extremely hot, and this I can attest to. Reading Gavin's book made me squirm more than once.

I almost couldn't breathe when one of the audience members asked Gavin if he was in a relationship with anyone.

He never missed a beat. "Absolutely."

I about died when the talk show host asked, "And is that where you get all of those hot sex scenes you write about?"

I was mortified, but strangely pleased, when he gave a cocky grin and said, "There are no words I could write that would ever do justice to what we do behind closed doors."

Mortified… pleased, and yes… I preened.

Lindie, who was standing beside me, just snickered.

The book signing was an entirely different matter. Whereas at the talk show, he was separated from the fans by a huge production stage, at the book signing, they were right up in his face. Now, granted, most of the people that came to have him sign their books were quite lovely. They were starstruck for sure, often clutching their hands to their chests with breathless excitement, or squealing over his inscription in their books. But a few… not-so-lovely ladies wanted pictures, and they pressed in unconscionably close to him. As his "assistant," I had to take picture after picture of young, hot women putting their hands on my man and making outright lewd suggestions to him.

One woman, who was dressed in a slinky, black dress that hit mid-thigh with high-heeled, black leather boots and a cloud of curled hair around her painted face, actually handed Gavin her phone number.

"Call me when you get through with this signing, Gavin," she said as she looked him direct in the eye. "I'll show you Chicago like you've never seen it."

To give Gavin credit, he handed the phone number to me and told the woman with a charming smile, "Now that's an exciting offer, love, but unfortunately, I have plans tonight."

My head snapped toward him even as I crumpled the paper in my hand. The woman never gave me a glance.

Unfortunately? Did he just say unfortunately?

I glared at him even as the woman was not about to give up. "Next trip then?"

"Sorry, love. I'll have plans then as well."

I waited for the woman to move out of line so the next hundred people standing there could get their turn, but apparently, there wasn't much going on upstairs underneath all of that curly, dark hair. She leaned over the table, which effectively spilled half her boobs out of her dress. "You do understand what I mean when I say I'd show you Chicago like you've never seen it before?"

Gavin... that scoundrel, tilted his head back and laughed. He looked the woman in the eye and said, "I do, indeed, understand you. But this lovely lady sitting next to me," and here he paused to put his arm around my shoulder, "would have something to say about it. You see, she's the one that all my plans revolve around, and I'm quite positive she would not want me seeing Chicago with you."

My face had flamed beet red over his proclamation, and I couldn't even take joy in the way the woman huffed and then slunk away from the public humiliation Gavin just handed down to her.

He leaned over to me and whispered, "You're beyond cute when you're jealous."

I nudged him in the arm and hissed, "I wasn't jealous."

"Sweet... it was rolling off you in vibes. So fucking cute."

I held my tongue because the next fan in line walked up and had a semi-legitimate conversation with Gavin about his book, and my blood pressure started to ease.

"You are stunning tonight," Gavin says as he holds me close and we sway to Norah Jones' *Come Away with Me*.

His publisher's party is a sight to behold, taking up the entire grand ballroom of Chicago's Waldorf Astoria. Ice sculptures, a ten-piece band, caviar, champagne, tuxedos, and ball gowns. It's an entire world away from where I live, yet dancing here in Gavin's arms, I feel completely comfortable for the moment.

"Although I would have preferred buying you a dress," Gavin says as his thumb strokes my lower back, "I'm going to have to admit this one you borrowed from Alyssa is beyond amazing."

When Gavin told me there would be a black-tie event we'd have to attend, I went into a panic. I didn't own a ball gown, and I certainly didn't have the money with which to buy one. He had offered, gallant and sexy man that he is, to buy me one, citing that it would just be a write off for him to be able to dress his "assistant," but I declined. Despite all the intimate touches and shared orgasms, I didn't feel comfortable with Gavin buying me expensive clothing.

Alyssa, heiress to a fortune and luckily my exact size, came to my rescue and pulled me into her closet the day before yesterday, telling me to take my pick of dresses to borrow. My eyes bugged out of my head as I rifled through the rainbow of silks, chiffons, and velvets.

I chose a simple, champagne-colored, strapless sheath gown that was ruched at my breasts and fell in a straight line to the floor. It had a long slit up the back, and Alyssa gave me a pair of matching strappy sandals that I'm betting cost more than three months' rent to go with it.

"I'm glad you like the dress," I tell him, and then mischievously add, "I'm going to enjoy you taking me out of it more."

Gavin chuckles and squeezes me tighter to him. "Where did my shy Sweet go? You're so bold now."

"You like it," I tease.

"I love it," he says solemnly and bends to kiss me under my jaw. "How much longer do you think we need to stay?"

"Well, since you're one of the guests of honor, I'm thinking it would be poor form to leave before dinner," I say sadly, because honestly, there's nothing I'd love more than for Gavin to whisk me back to our hotel room and practice dirty things upon my body.

"I can't wait to have you all to myself," Gavin murmurs. "The things I'm going to do to you tonight."

I can't help the shiver that wracks my body, his words slicing right through my skin and taking my nerves hostage.

"You have the most powerful words," I tell him while stroking the silk piping on his lapels. "They threaten to drop me to my knees sometimes."

"Then we're even," he says as he spins me around and dips me low. His face hovering over mine, he whispers for my ears only, "Just looking at you makes my knees weak."

He lifts me up again and, as the last notes of the song fade away, gives me a lovely PDA kiss. I sigh. When he pulls back, I touch his face and ask with wonder, "How did I get so lucky to find you?"

Gavin smiles... with understanding, with sadness, and even a little touch of humility. "I'm the lucky one, Sweet. Nothing is ever going to be the same again."

No, nothing will be the same. My body, for one, will never respond to another man the way it responds to Gavin. That's not because of any special talent on his part, although he has talent in spades. His tongue for instance.

I won't respond to another because my heart is tied up with Gavin now in a way that has never belonged to another man before. It's been completely enslaved by him, and he alone has the power to cultivate or destroy it, but whatever he chooses, my life is on a different path now.

Gavin leads me off the dance floor by my hand. Halfway back to our table, I'm struck with sudden inspiration. Tugging on his hand, I get him to stop, and he looks at me with a smile.

Stepping in close, I rise up on my tiptoes and whisper to him, "I think I want to get filthy with you."

His eyebrow cocks at me in amusement, and he leans in and kisses my nose. "You think or you know? Because I assured you I'd do you right tonight."

"Not tonight… not later. Right now."

Molten heat flares in Gavin's eyes, and his hand squeezes mine reflexively… almost painfully. His voice is rough when he asks, "Right now?"

"Right this very minute," I confirm.

Gavin spins on his foot and starts walking with large strides to the doors of the ballroom. I have to run to keep up with him, my one hand firmly grasped in his, the other holding up the long length of my dress so I don't trip on it. He leads me out of the party, down a hall, and straight to the ladies' bathroom. Pushing the door open, he strides right in, pulling me along, only have to have several women all wearing gowns and applying lipstick turn to look at him and gasp.

"Fuck," he mutters and backs out, pushing me along.

He starts walking again, down another hall, randomly checking doors. One says, "Accounting," another says "Food Services." All locked.

I can feel the frustration rolling off him in waves, and I have to struggle not to giggle. Finally, he finds a door that says, "Service Staff Only" and pushes through. It leads to another corridor, this time paved with white tile rather than the sumptuously, deep carpeting in the public part of the hotel. On the third door he tries, which says "Janitorial Supplies," he hits pay dirt, and the door swings open. He pushes me through and follows me inside.

The light comes on automatically, apparently by sensor, and I glance around in interest at row after row of metal shelving stocked with a variety of cleaning agents, paper products, and linens.

Thankfully, there's a lock on the door, which Gavin gives a quick turn, and the click causes me to turn and face him.

He smiles at me sinfully.

Then he's on me.

In one large stride, he's pushing me backward until my back hits against the far wall. He grabs fistfuls of my dress and drags it up, leaning sideways and back a bit to get a look at what I have on underneath. I know he's pleased when his nostrils flare at the champagne-colored lace thong I bought to match the dress.

"Oh, Sweet," he breathes out in a rush. "So fucking sweet."

His hand comes down between my legs and fingers the edge of my panties. He strokes me softly, almost as if he's considering his next move. My blood is on fire and the prospect that we've just left a party where Gavin is surely to be missed, and are in a supply closet in a major luxury hotel that is no doubt frequented by the staff, has me buzzing with nervous energy and lustful need.

"Um… baby. We're kind of on short time… don't you think we need to get at it?" I ask sweetly.

Gavin groans and slips his finger into my underwear. "Need to make sure you're ready… that you can take me."

When his finger slides into me, he finds that I am indeed ready, because just the prospect of what we are about to do was all the foreplay I needed. My hips flex hard against his hand, driving his finger in deeper.

"More," I demand. "Now."

Gavin groans again and his hand gives a hard pull against my underwear, shredding the flimsy lace down one side. The remaining remnants flutter down my leg, catching at my ankle. I'm pinned by Gavin's eyes as he stares at me hotly, all the while working at his fly. His cock springs free and my hands immediately go around it, stroking the velvety hardness.

"No time for that, love," he pants and reaches down to pick me up. My legs go around him, he pushes me back into the wall again, and his cock nudges at my entrance. "This has to be hard and fast."

He slams into me, and I burn in pleasure. My hands grip onto his shoulders, and I bring my mouth down onto his hard. We both groan with mutual satisfaction, and his hips start pumping against me quickly. He thrusts in, pulls out to the tip, perfectly timing it and tunneling back into me again.

Every nerve I have is on fire, my blood singing in joy over the way he feels inside of me, and I urge him on. "Harder, baby. Faster."

"You're killing me, Sweet," he groans into my mouth and fucks me harder and faster.

"I'm getting close," I tell him because I can feel the quickening of my pulse and my muscles starting to tense up all over.

"Me too," he pants as he pushes his face against my neck. His lips latch onto my delicate skin, and he sucks at me hard.

Moving his hand between my legs, his thumb finds my clit and he starts circling it with swift pressure, matching the strokes of his cock as it works me over.

He's brutal, he's brilliant, and he's completely mine.

Suddenly, I'm shattering, my hands coming to his head and my nails digging in his scalp. He slams into me one more time, so hard, I think I might have a bruise on my lower back, and then he is murmuring into my neck. "I'm coming. Fuck, I'm coming so hard."

Start to finish, even including the time that Gavin knelt down and used my torn panties to clean his semen from between my legs, we couldn't have been gone for more than ten minutes top. But damn... that was probably the best ten minutes of my life, and I was hungry to do something like that again real soon.

TWENTY-THREE

Gavin

    I'm exhausted. Only a week back from Chicago, and then I was jetting back out to The Big Apple. I've been in New York for two days, which were two days too many in my opinion. I had two book signings, a meeting with my editor, a meeting with the marketing team for my publisher, and finally, a meeting with Lindie. I was on the go constantly, meeting people, talking about my work, and promoting myself.

I hated every fucking bit of it, mainly because I had to leave Savannah back home. She was supposed to come with me but the night before we were to leave, she wasn't feeling well. By the next morning, her nose was running, her voice was hoarse, and she was coughing so hard that I was afraid she'd expel a lung.

I immediately jumped out of bed when I heard her, got her some Tylenol and orange juice, then pulled my phone out of my pocket.

"What are you doing?" she had croaked while she looked up at me weakly from the bed.

"Canceling my trip," I told her as I flipped through my contacts for Lindie's number.

"No you're not," she said, and her voice sounded like it was coated in razor blades.

"Babe… you're sick. I'm not leaving you."

"It's a cold, Gavin. Just a cold, I'm sure."

"I've never heard a cold sound like that," I retorted, and she gave a deep, lusty cough as if to prove my point.

"You're not canceling," she said firmly. "I just need some cold medicine and rest. I'll be fine in a few days' time."

"And who will take care of you while I'm gone?" I growled at her.

She grinned at me then... her nose red and runny, and she fucking grinned at me. "You are so cute when you play mother hen," she said with a laugh, and then another cough. "But I can take care of myself."

"Let me at least take you to the doctor," I told her, stuffing my phone back in my pocket.

"You can't. You have to pack and get to the airport, but I promise I'll go to the doctor if I'm not feeling better by tomorrow. Okay?"

I grumbled then, muttered a curse word under my breath, and watched as she grinned at me again and started clucking like a chicken. "Mother hen," she teased.

I reluctantly packed, tried to give her a kiss before I left, to which she refused because she didn't want me to get sick. I then had to point out that I had fucked her silly the previous night and had my mouth all over her, including my tongue down her throat, and that I wasn't that worried about getting sick. She still refused me and offered me a handshake.

I refused the handshake, crawled on the bed, and nuzzled my face in her neck. "Take care of yourself, Sweet."

She sighed, stroked my hair, and murmured, "You too, Filthy."

I called her yesterday. She had indeed not gotten any better and, as promised, went to the doctor. She sounded horrible but managed to tell me that he put her on some antibiotics and gave her a kick-ass cough syrup that she thought might have caused her to hallucinate that pink elephants were trampling through her room. I, of course, didn't think that was funny and almost got on a plane right then and there to rush home to her, but she laughed softly into the phone, then hacked up another lung, and assured me she was fine.

As I was getting on the plane to come back this morning, she had texted me to tell me that she had to go work at The Haven because Jimmy, the guy that normally covered the Saturdays, was sick.

I texted her back with a pointed reminder, *You're sick too. Stay in bed.*

I'm not as sick as Jimmy. Plus, I feel better today, she replied.

I wasn't happy with her flippant attitude over her own health, and I made my displeasure known. *I'm going to redden your ass with my hand when I get home.*

She was not intimidated. *Promises, promises.*

Pulling into The Haven, I don't see any other vehicles. This is the second time I've been here, the first just last week when we got back from Chicago.

Savannah wanted to get a few volunteer hours in and had asked if I wanted to come. I didn't particularly, but I was making amazing progress on the manuscript now with Savannah's help on all the other crap I had to handle, and frankly, I didn't want to be away from her.

So I said yes.

And I had fun.

It was hard work, but seriously... how can playing with cute puppies not be fun? And yes, maybe I played with the dogs more than I helped Savannah, but she just smiled at me while shaking her head, and I let her do the dirty work while I rubbed every dog's tummy at least a dozen times.

Pulling around back, I see Brody's truck but not Savannah's car. He comes walking out of the kennel just as I exit the Maserati.

Brody gives a low whistle. "Damn, dude... that is a sweet ride."

"You can take it out for a spin any time you want, mate," I tell him as he walks around it, eyeing the sleek lines and shiny paint.

"I'll take you up on that sometime," he says, and then adds on, "Looking for Savannah?"

"Yeah... just got in from the airport, and she said she'd be here."

"She was until about an hour ago, when I found her practically keeled over on the floor. She's way too sick to be working today."

Cursing, I walk back toward my car. "Thanks. I'm off to go spank her for getting out of bed when I specifically told her not to."

"Give her a whack from me," Brody calls out, and I shoot him a wave as I get in my car to go take care of my girl.

I find Savannah in my bed—our bed really— curled up in a fetal position with the blankets pulled up under her chin. Her forehead is sweaty and her skin clammy. Sitting on the edge of the bed beside her, I stroke her head lightly and say, "Savannah... baby... I'm home."

Her eyes immediately open and focus on me, and a sleepy smile comes to her face. "Hey," she says, and her voice still sounds like a frog is stuck in her throat.

"Not feeling any better, I see."

She shakes her head and coughs into the crook of her elbow.

"And didn't I tell you to stay in bed? Brody said you were practically passed out on the floor today," I chastise her.

Savannah's eyebrows draw inward, and she whines to me, "I wanted to be better. I wanted to be better because I knew you were coming home today and look... I even put on sexy underwear because I wanted to seduce you."

She pulls the covers down, and she is indeed in some sexy-as-fuck lingerie... black, see-through lace, and no matter that my girl has a red nose and snot running out of said nose, my cock twitches at her beautiful, lace-clad body.

I pull the covers back up around her and tuck them back under her chin. "Bad girl. You had no business being out of bed, and you certainly are in no condition to prance around in that get up, trying to get me all hard, knowing I can't take advantage of you. I'm so going to tear your ass up when you're better."

She's feeling well enough to give a soft laugh over my non-existent threat, and then she gives me a tender smile. "I missed you."

"I missed you, too," I tell her as I lean over to kiss her forehead. "Now, when was the last time you ate?"

She shrugs her shoulders, and I give her a disapproving glare. She grins back at me.

"Chicken soup, medicine, and then I'm ordering you to sleep while I get some work done, okay?"

"Okay," she says sleepily, rolling back over to close her eyes while I go fix her some lunch.

"You're going to get sick," Savannah grumbles.

"I'm not going to get sick," I tell her and squeeze her closer.

My well-laid plans to feed her, medicate her, and then go to work have been waylaid. I took one look at her lying in bed, realized how much I had missed her the last two days, and said, *Fuck the manuscript.*

I stripped down to my underwear and crawled in bed with her. I pulled her into my arms over her protests that she'd make me sick and tucked her in tight.

We watched TV for a while and Savannah dozed on and off, occasionally coughing… a wheeze here and there. She wasn't running a fever though, so I just let her sleep while I held her. At six o'clock, I got up and heated us up some more soup, made her take her antibiotics and cough syrup, and then ran a bath for her.

She was a bit shaky while I peeled the black lace off her body and helped her step into the tub. I sat on the ledge while she washed herself, leaning over and helping her every once in a while, just so I could touch her.

"Bad boy," she whispered hoarsely, and I couldn't agree with her more.

After I got her out of the tub, I dried her body and her hair. Slipping one of my T-shirts over her head, I packed her back off to bed. I knew I should go and work on the book some more, but I couldn't help myself and crawled back in bed with her.

Savannah laces her fingers through mine and snuggles in closer to me. "Are you close to your parents?"

I squeeze against our threaded fingers and stroke her hip with my other hand. "Sure. I mean... we're pretty close. After Charlie died and I sort of went off the deep end, things were strained for a while, but my parents were like fucking rocks for me."

"I'm sure they were devastated," she says softly.

"Yes... completely. Not only for their grandchild but for their son as well. What about your parents?"

"They're pretty awesome. Of course, I told you they gave me tremendous support during the whole Kevin thing."

My body involuntarily tightens when I think about "the whole Kevin thing." I'd like to look his sorry as up and beat the ever-loving shit out of him.

"I'd love for you to meet them sometime," Savannah says timidly.

Meet her parents?

Hmmmm... now why isn't that causing a pit of fear in my stomach? Why does that idea sound appealing to me?

Oh, I know why... because that's Savannah admitting to me that we have something pretty fucking deep here, just as I was suspecting.

"Too fast for you?" she asks quietly.

"What?" I ask, blinking. "Is what too fast?"

"Meeting my parents. You got awful quiet when I suggested it."

Turning on my side, I lay my head on her pillow so we're practically nose to nose. "I'd love to meet your parents, Sweet. Tell me more about them."

She smiles and takes in a deep breath that, to my ears, sounds like it may be a little clearer. "Here's their short bio. June and Brian Shepherd, married for thirty years this coming summer. They doted on their only, and quite angelic, child, Savannah. Mom is a secretary for an accountant, and Dad is an electrician. They're kind of shy, so you know I come by it honestly, but they have the best hearts in the world. You'll adore them."

"I'm sure I will." *Just like I adore you, sweet girl.*

"Did you always want to be a fiction writer?"

"Always," I tell her as my hand winds around her waist, and I pull her in tight.

"Have you written any other books?"

"A few," I tell her. "Although they're rubbish."

"No way," she denies me. "I've read your work. It's amazing."

"Yeah, but you read my work post-Charlie. I wrote from a very dark place and it showed through in my writing. People like that shit for some reason."

"What are your other books like?"

"High fantasy... knights, castles, and dragons sort of stuff. No romance. No sex."

"Can I read some of it?"

"Sure, babe. Anything you want," I tell her as my hand slides down from her back to her hip. She didn't put any underwear on after her bath, and my hand snakes down further to caress her bare bottom.

She sighs and pushes in closer to me, until she's pressed right up against the erection that had started growing the minute my hand touched her sweet ass. Savannah swivels her hips against me, giving me a slow grind, and I groan and push away from her.

"Uh-uh," I admonish her. "You're sick."

"Sorry," she mumbles, casting her eyes down toward my chest. "I know I look awful."

Sliding my hand up her body, I bring my fingers under her chin and tilt her head up to me. Leaning in,

I give her a kiss and then rub my nose against hers. "You don't look awful. You look as beautiful as ever and you can feel I got a fucking hard-on, so you know I'm turned on by you. But you need rest. The sooner you get better, the sooner we can get back to the fucking."

Her cheeks flame hot, but she's bold as brass when she says, "I'm not tired though."

"Rest," I affirm.

Giving me a coy smile, laced with a bit of evil, she says, "I could... you know, relieve *you* if you wanted. I hate thinking about you laying there, all hard, pulsing, and aching..."

"God, you're so bad," I groan, and I turn my face into the pillow. She laughs softly at me and tries to push her hand down in between our bodies to touch me. My hand immediately stops her. "Savannah... so help me God, if you don't stop, I'm going to tie you up."

"Now, that's what I'm talking about," she exclaims as she tries to grab my cock.

Releasing my hold on her, I roll out of the bed and glare down at her in disapproval. She fucking grins back at me. "Where are you going?"

"I'm going to either take a cold shower or jack off, you heathen woman," I snarl at her.

She grins even bigger. "Can I watch?"

"Fucking death of me," I mutter as I turn away from her and head into the bathroom. For good measure, I shut the door behind me and lock it so she won't be encouraged to get out of bed when she should be resting.

I walk up to the vanity and rest my hands on the edge, lifting my face up to look at myself in the mirror. I'm met with my reflection wearing a big ass fucking smile on my face. I positively beam.

A smile that Savannah put there, and I don't ever want to lose again.

Reaching down, I tug on my cock through the material of my boxer briefs and consider jacking off. Then I decide against it, because if Savannah has to wait, I will too. Starting the shower, I wait for the water to heat and step out of my underwear. Just as I open the door to step in, I hear Savannah rattling the doorknob.

"Filthy boy," she calls out, her voice still raw so I know she should be resting. "Can I please come in and watch?"

"Go away, Sweet," I growl. "I'm not letting you and your wicked ways in."

I hear her laughing at me and then it's silent, so I assume she finally heeded me and went back in bed.

TWENTY-FOUR

Savannah

God, I'm so freaking horny I can't stand it.

Me... Savannah Shepherd, the woman who can count the number of men she has been with on half of her right hand. The woman who didn't know multiple orgasms were possible. The woman who had never had a man in her mouth.

So freakin' horny.

After two more days of bed rest, where Gavin catered to my every need, he finally let me up and about. He wouldn't let me do anything but sit on the couch, forcing soup and the antibiotics down my throat. Two more days after that, when he hadn't heard my cough for at least eighteen hours, he proclaimed that I was "on the mend."

On the mend, my ass. I am fully mended. Sure, I have a few more days of antibiotics left, which I will dutifully take, but I'm feeling fine and like I said... horny as hell.

I can hear Gavin up in his office, that damn chair he sits in squeaking and groaning periodically. I don't dare disturb him up there, because that's his private space and I know his mind is elsewhere.

Deciding to occupy my time, I mop the kitchen floor, dust the furniture, and do our laundry. When I finish, I'm not the slightest bit tired and slightly perturbed that Gavin hasn't come down once to check on me. According to him, I was practically dying just two days ago.

Did I also mention I'm sexually frustrated?

With a determined straightening of my shoulders, I grab the vacuum and haul it up to the second floor. I walk into Gavin's bedroom, unwind the cord from the back, and plug it in. I start on the far side of the room, closest to the bed, and start cleaning the rug. I start counting... slowly to myself, *One, two, three...*

I push and pull on the vacuum, bending to get it under the bed. *Four, five, six, seven…*

A few more strokes near the nightstand. *Eight, nine, ten…*

"What the fuck, Sweet?" I hear Gavin before I see him. Turning, I watch as he stalks over to the wall plug and pulls the cord out. The vacuum winds down to utter silence.

Ten seconds. Impressive.

"What?" I ask, my eyes wide and innocent.

"You're vacuuming. You should be resting."

"I'm not sick."

"You're still taking antibiotics. You're sick."

"Am not," I tell him as I drop the vacuum handle, and it falls to the floor. Reaching down to the hem of the long sleeved T-shirt I'm wearing, I lift it up and pull it over my head, dropping it carelessly on the floor.

Gavin watches me intently, swallows hard, and asks, "What are you doing?"

"Seducing you," I say matter-of-factly.

His eyes roam over the peach, satin bra I had carefully chosen after my shower a few hours ago. I personally know it happens to go well with the olive tone of my skin, plus it plumps my breasts up nicely.

My hands go to the buttons on my jeans, and I shimmy out of them, kicking them over my bare feet.

Gavin's eyes feast on the matching peach panties I have on. Just to keep his attention there, I bring my hand up to my stomach, idly stroking the skin there with my fingertips. Then I drop my hand, skirting one finger under the top elastic band.

"You should be in bed," Gavin says thickly, his eyes pinned to my hand as it sinks lower into my underwear.

"I plan to be," I tell him throatily, begging him to move toward me.

The most I get is he drops the vacuum cord from his hand and balls his fists up tight. With a sigh, he says, "Savannah… baby… you need to rest. You have bronchitis. You don't need to be cleaning, and you sure as hell don't need to be wasting your precious strength fucking me."

I'm losing him. I thought the minute I stripped, he would be mine, helpless to fight the lust that I know I can induce. What I didn't count on was for him to be a caring, upstanding man that doesn't want to take advantage of what I'm offering at the risk of possibly hurting me.

Stupid man.

Taking two steps, I reach the edge of the bed and crawl onto it. I position myself in the center and rise up with my elbows supporting my weight, which I happen to know thrusts my breasts outward in a provocative fashion. "Baby... filthy boy... I feel fine. I feel great, as a matter of fact, except for this aching I have right between my legs. I need you."

"Christ," Gavin mutters, taking half a step toward me.

"If you don't come over here right now and give me a massive orgasm, I'm going to have to take care of myself."

"You wouldn't," he declares officiously.

"Watch me," I tell him boldly, and my hand snakes back down into my panties again... way, way down.

I touch myself with my index finger, stunned to find myself unbelievably wet. Pushing further, I lightly touch my clit. My hips fly off the bed, and a strangled moan comes out of mouth.

Gavin is on me in a second, ripping my hand from between my legs and crushing me with his body. His lips are on mine, his tongue deep in my mouth. He kisses me with a wild, pent-up energy, like a tiger being released from a cage, that hasn't eaten for a month, and there's a nice, juicy steak waiting for him on the outside.

"Fuck, Savannah." He practically shoves a growl down my throat. "You drive me crazy."

"That was the plan," I moan, pumping my hips upward to rub against his hardness.

Gavin lifts his mouth from mine and looks at me carefully. "Are you sure you're okay?"

"I'm fine," I tell him with a smile, kissing his chin, his jaw, and flexing my hips again.

"I'll be gentle," he promises me.

"Don't you dare," I growl back at him.

He gives me a feral smile and plunges his tongue back in my mouth.

The bedroom is semi-dark, the light from the TV casts flickering blue shades over our bodies as I lay in Gavin's arms. One hand is stroking my back, the other my hair.

We stayed in bed all afternoon, testing our spirits and our stamina, stopping to nap, once to eat, and then going at it again. Ten minutes ago, Gavin came inside of me supremely hard, nearly dislocating my hips with his last violent thrust, and then kissed me softly for another two minutes. When he finally lifted off my body and rolled to the side, he said, "I'm done. You've depleted me. I've got nothing left for you, love."

I giggled and rolled into him, placing my head in the crook of his shoulder and my arm across his waist. His own arms gathered me in close, smoothing over my back and my hair, and I felt more cherished than I ever had in my whole life.

"I'm almost done with the manuscript," Gavin says absently.

"That's wonderful," I tell him, threading my leg in between his, enjoying the way his coarse hair rubs up against my smooth skin.

"Will you read it?"

Lifting my head up, I look at him with excited eyes. "Are you serious?"

"Of course, I'm serious," Gavin says with surprise that I'd even ask. "Your opinion matters to me."

My fingers idly move over Gavin's stomach, stroking the rolls and peaks of his pecs, letting them bump along the ridges etched in his stomach which involuntarily contracted when I touch him. I let my fingers twirl in the dark hair that starts just below his belly button, and I want to inch my hand down further, but Gavin seems to think I've broken him this night.

"What are you going to do? Now that you're finished?" I ask him hesitantly, because we haven't spoken of a future past his manuscript.

Gavin came to the Outer Banks to escape the spiraling pit of destruction he had let himself sink in to. He came specifically to write a book, and now that was almost done. Now... he has no reason to stay.

"I'm not sure," he says carefully. "I have to go back to England at some point to take care of the house. Get Charlie's things."

Gavin had told me that his house in Turnbridge Wells... the one he lived in with Amanda and Charlie, had just recently sold. While his dad had a lasting power of attorney and was able to handle the details of the sale, all of Gavin's and Charlie's belongings had been packed up and moved to his father's house for temporary storage.

"But, there's no rush to do that," he continues. "My dad said I can keep the stuff there for as long as I want. Until I decide where I want to live permanently."

I'm silent, not knowing what to say. What I really want to say is, "Don't leave. Stay here with me forever and let's build something together."

But my anti-heroine tendencies creep up at the most inopportune times, and I remain silent. Gavin remains silent too, and I take that as utter proof that he really doesn't have any inkling as to what he wants to do. Time ticks by, and my eyes travel to the TV, which has been muted. An old re-run of *Buffy the Vampire Slayer* is on, and I amuse myself for a bit, trying to guess what crazy and snarky things Buffy might be saying at this very moment.

"Sweet?" Gavin calls to me quietly.

"Yes, Filthy," I answer demurely and although I can't see it, I can feel him smile.

"What if I told you I wanted to stay here... with you?"

My head pops up, and I angle my shoulders so I can face him. "Are you serious?"

"Maybe," he says with a sly smile. "Depends on what your answer is."

Rolling over, I flip my leg over Gavin's and sit up straight while I straddle his lap. His hands come up to rest on my thighs, and I don't have one bit of embarrassed shyness over my complete nudity on display before him. He's licked every bit of modesty away.

"Gavin... I don't have any explanation for the connection we've made these last several weeks, but I do know this... I don't care if this seems fast, or furious, or crazy. I know I've never felt this way about anyone in my life, and it would make me so happy if you stayed. Deliriously happy, in fact."

His hands rise up from my thighs and he cups my breasts in them, using his thumbs to gently circle over my nipples. His eyes watch the movement of his hands, and he seems lost in thought… pensive and a bit unsure.

Maybe I overstepped my bounds. Maybe I said too much… seemed too excited. Maybe I've turned him off to the idea of staying with me, and he's trying to figure a way out of this mess he just created.

"Charlie's in England," he says as his hands still against me.

"Yes," I acknowledge. "He is."

"I'd want to go back… to visit his grave."

My hands come up and clasp Gavin's, holding him tight against me. I squeeze his fingers gently. "Of course, baby. You can go back whenever you want."

"I want you to come with me," he says, still with his eyes focused on where our hands are now mutually joined across my chest.

"Yes, I'll go with you. Whenever you want."

"And you'll live here with me?" he says as his thumbs starts to move again across my nipples, and I can feel him start to grow hard underneath me again.

"Yes, I'll live here with you, Filthy."

"Will you continue to be my assistant… help me… travel with me?" His eyes never lift to mine, instead they still gaze vaguely at where his hands work my breasts.

"Yes, all of that," I tell him firmly.

Finally... his eyes lift, and they seem to sparkle in the reflective light of the TV. They are wide, open, and vulnerable when he asks, "Will you also start falling in love with me?"

My breath catches in my throat, and my heart expands to about ten times its normal size. I reach one hand out and lay it along Gavin's cheek. His eyes close briefly from the touch, but he opens them up just as quickly to await my answer.

"Yes," I whisper to him. "I'll start falling in love with you. I promise."

"Good," he whispers back. "Because I've already started that process with you."

Pressing my palms to the pillows beside his head, I lean down and kiss him gently. When I pull back, I give him the tenderest of smiles. "Falling in love with me, huh?"

"Falling deep," he confirms.

"Me too."

"That's fortuitous for me," he says with a grin.

"Is this too fast?" I ask, worried that maybe we're seeing something that we want to see but that shouldn't be quite visible yet.

"Not fast enough, in my opinion," he says, and then moves his hands down to play between my legs.

My head falls back at his first touch, and I reach behind me with one hand to stroke him. He's already rock hard, still slightly moist from our last round of lovemaking.

"I thought you said you were done?" I ask on a gasp when he slips a finger in to me.

"I'll never be done with you, Sweet. Never."

TWENTY-FIVE

Gavin

"Savannah!" I yell from my office chair as I stare at the manuscript on my laptop.

"What?" she yells back from somewhere on the first floor.

"Come here," I call out, leaning back in my chair and gazing at the computer with a smile.

"No," she yells back with a whiny voice. "That's three flights of stairs, and I'm still sick."

"Bollocks. You've had no problem letting me fuck you the last three days, silly wench, so three flights of stairs shouldn't be a problem. Now get your sweet ass up here."

I can actually imagine the grin on her face, and I listen as her feet race up the stairs toward me. When I hear her at the top, I swivel the chair around and face the door. She comes barreling through and launches herself onto my lap, her arms wrapping around my neck. The chair moans and groans under the added weight and movement.

"What's up, pup? Want a little afternoon quickie?"

Why yes, yes I do, but I don't voice that out loud.

Instead, I turn the chair back around toward my desk, swiveling both our bodies, and point at the laptop. She leans forward, peers at the screen, and reads the two words at the bottom.

The End.

"Filthy," she squeals as she squeezes me in a bone-crushing hug, nearly strangling me. "You finished."

"I finished," I tell her, both happy and sad all at once. It's a definite cause for celebration when an author finishes a story, having poured blood, sweat, and tears into the words. But you're also sad and empty at the same time, because you're leaving behind the same blood, sweat, and tears. There's also a nervousness… a fear that maybe what you wrote wasn't worth the blood, sweat, and tears that leached out of you onto paper. Particularly following up a huge hit. Is this book just as good? Will the fans love it or will I have let them down?

Savannah scrambles off my lap and tugs at my hand, so I stand up. I bend down to hug her again, perhaps catch that sweet mouth in a kiss so we can begin the celebration, but she pushes me to the side, steps past me, and sits in the chair. It squeaks loudly as she pulls it up to the desk. Her hand reaches out to my laptop as she says, "I can't wait to read this bad boy."

Quick as lightning, I slap lightly at her hand in admonishment, and she gives a yelp as she draws it back, narrowing her eyes at me. "What did you do that for?"

"No reading just yet. We're taking a trip."

"A trip?" she asks dubiously.

"Yes, a trip. We need a vacation."

"A vacation?"

"To a beach."

"A beach?"

"Are your brains addled, love?" I ask her as I pull her up out of the chair, wrapping my arms around her waist and leaning down to kiss her neck.

"But we live on a beach," she says breathlessly as I kiss behind her ear.

"A bloody cold beach in the winter," I point out, moving my lips to her jaw. "I want to go somewhere tropical with you."

"Mmmm. Tropical," she moans as my hand comes up to cup her breast.

Releasing her, I grab her hand and start out of my office. "So let's get packing."

She follows me down the stairs and into the bedroom. I go in the closet, pull out a suitcase, and toss it on the bed. Heading to my dresser, I open the top drawer, pulling stuff out and throwing it in the suitcase. "We'll get me packed up, then go to your house and get whatever else you need."

Savannah's hands on my lower back cause me to falter, and the kiss she presses into the middle of my back stops me. Turning to her, I look down at her beautiful face as she stares up at me with warm eyes. "Before we go, I think you need to be congratulated for a job well done."

"I do?" I ask, my lips curving into an anticipatory leer.

Her tiny hands work at the button of my jeans, and then slowly unzip the fly. My breath catches as she pushes her hands inside right at my hipbones and pushes the denim down. She pulls the front of my briefs down, and her hand gently takes my cock. It immediately starts to swell as she moves her soft hand up and down.

"Yes, you need something special," she murmurs as she drops to her knees before me.

"Something special?" I breathe out in a long rush.

"A congratulatory prize," she whispers as her tongue flicks out over the head of my dick.

"A prize," I repeat in a daze.

"Are your brains addled, love?" she teases me, and then takes me fully into her mouth.

Yes, my fucking brains are completely addled when it comes to Savannah. I stroke the top of her head while it bobs up and down on my cock. I watch her with hot eyes and a warm heart, balls tightening and my chest thumping like a drum.

God, I'm falling in deep…

"You wanted to go somewhere tropical, here we are, and yet, we haven't left the room yet," Savannah complains as her head rests on my thigh and my hand strokes her backside. We just got done having a math lesson… one that involves adding two people, two mouths, and equaling the sweet number of sixty-nine.

"This room is awesome," I tell her with a light slap on her ass. "Why would we ever want to leave?"

Savannah lifts her head and looks around the room. She looks back at me, her lips swollen from the unbelievable blow job she just gave me and her neck flushed from the stupendous orgasm I just gave her.

"It's a pretty awesome room," she agrees.

Best I've ever been in as a matter of fact.

After we'd ran around like two kids in a candy store packing our bags four days ago, we actually stopped and looked at each other stupidly, having realized we had no clue where we wanted to go. So we jumped on my laptop and did some searching. Two hours later, we decided on Jade Mountain in St. Lucia.

The resort was small and catered heavily to its clientele. Each room came with its own personal butler, who was available via a cellular phone 24-7. But that wasn't the best part. No, the room was the best part of this entire trip.

It was huge and square with no internal walls. A large, king-sized canopy bed with mosquito netting draped over it took up one wall. Along another wall was a bathroom that sat up on a raised dais. The toilet was sheltered by a small, three-foot tile blocked wall to afford some privacy, but the shower stood out in the open. The middle of the room bore a couch, two chairs, and a coffee table, and just to the right of that was a small, indoor pool. But the coolest feature, by far, was the fact that the room only had three walls. The fourth wall was gone… non-existent, and the room completely opened up to the outside with a fabulous view of the Piton mountains and the clear waters of the Caribbean. The indoor pool actually started inside of the room, at the base of the raised bathroom, and ran lengthwise outside to the large outdoor deck stacked with teak furniture, potted tropical plants, and hummingbirds that zoomed around the blooming flowers. Each room was constructed to have utter privacy. Even standing on our deck and leaning over it, the way the resort sloped down the face of one of the mountains, you couldn't see another room above, below, or to the left and right of us.

Didn't mean you couldn't hear the other people all around us. We found that out our first night when I made love to Savannah on one of the deck chairs. After she cried out loudly as she came, we heard someone above us snickering. She tucked her red face into my shoulder and hissed at me to take her back in the room.

Instead, I dumped her in the warm pool and jumped in behind her. We played, splashed, then kissed some more, and my dick just never seems to quit with Savannah because before you knew it, I was hard again.

Then I was inside of her again.

Then she was screaming again.

Then snickering could be heard from above us again.

By the second day, we didn't give a shit who heard us and had completely eschewed all clothing except when the butler came to our room to deliver food.

"I suppose we could get out... go do something," I muse as my hand slides up her leg.

"Hmmm," she moans, as I get closer to her sweet spot. "Like what?"

"We could go lie on the beach, go snorkeling, mountain biking, sailing... you name it, Sweet. We can do it. As long as it involves you wearing that white bikini you brought."

"Why would you want me in a bikini when I do nothing but walk around naked all day and night here?"

I shrug my shoulders. "Good question. We're definitely not leaving this room since we have to put clothes on."

"How, in the order of the universe, does a derelict drunk of an author meet an incredibly sweet photographer and end up with her on a hot, white, sandy beach in the Caribbean, where she makes sweet love to him day in and day out, and his heart gets hopelessly lost to her?"

Yes, we finally put on clothes and made it down to the beach.

And yes, Savannah's white bikini is getting me quite hot and bothered.

We're lying side by side on wooden lounge chairs. The sand is warm and soft... super fine, white crystals that sparkle in the sunlight. The water is an unbelievable clear blue, transparent as glass, and also sparkles in the sunlight. Savannah is holding my hand, our fingers lightly laced together as we bake under the sun, sip Mojitos, and watch the day drift by.

I don't ever want to fucking go back. In fact, I wonder if I could rent a room here at Jade Mountain, keep Savannah naked, and write my next book from here.

"I find it odd that the universe gives you the talent to write dark, erotic, thriller-type books and yet, you sit there now and spout the most beautiful words to me. Put those in a book, sell them, and you'll have women falling at your feet," she says while gazing out over the water.

I turn my face to look at her. She has her hair piled on top of her head in a messy knot. Large, oval sunglasses sit on her delicate face, and her lips glisten from the rum drink she just took a sip of. Her bikini stands out stark against her tanning skin, being nothing more than a four triangles of material held precariously closed by a few strings.

"Is your heart getting hopelessly lost to me as well, love?"

She turns her head slowly to me, and although I can't see her eyes behind the dark frames, by the set of her chin and the way she squeezes my fingers, I know she's serious when she says, "So lost that I don't know if I'd even be able to find where it went."

"I'll tell you where it is. It will be residing right next to mine. I'll give you access to it any time you want, but I think I'll keep it buried with my own, just for safekeeping."

We stare at each other a moment more, letting our sappy words hover in the humid air, and then

Savannah snorts. Her free hand comes up and she covers her mouth trying to stifle herself, then her head is thrown back and she's laughing with gusto. I laugh with her, and it feels fucking awesome.

"God, we're so corny," she sighs as her giggles die down.

"Okay, so let's talk seriously," I tell her with a final grin and turn my face back to the water. "You said you'd continue on as my assistant, which I'm not letting you back out of by the way, but I think you should also do something with your photography."

"Like what?" she asks lazily, taking another sip of Mojito.

"Whatever you want. What was your primary goal when you graduated college?"

"I wanted to do wildlife photography. Then I wanted my own place where I could lock myself away in a dark room and develop my pictures. Then I could frame them and sell them, and get rich, rich, rich. But mainly... I just want to take the photos of the animals. All that other stuff is just so I have a way to support my habit."

"So, when you say photos of wildlife... you mean like on the plains of Africa type wildlife?" I ask, not really liking that idea. First, it would put her too far away from me, and second, I didn't relish Savannah getting eaten by a lion.

"Any type," she clarifies. "Doesn't matter the type of animal. As long as it's wild and in its natural habitat."

"So, you should do that. You should take certain days to make sure you get out and shoot that type of stuff."

"And do what with it?" she scoffs. "There's not a huge market for that type of photography."

"You can do whatever you want with it, Sweet. Sell it to magazines, give it as gifts, or display it in an art gallery. Hell, publish a fucking book of your photos. I can help you get that done."

Savannah turns to look at me again and even without seeing the feeling in her eyes, I can tell she has skepticism on her face.

"The point is," I tell her solemnly, "is that you can do whatever you want, even if it's only to take the photos for your own pleasure, and we can look at them together while we cuddle on the couch and drink wine."

"You make everything seem so easy sometimes," she murmurs.

"It's never easy, baby. But you have a passion for it... and it's oh so much fun. So I hereby proclaim that when we get back to civilization, provided I agree to go back, then you are immediately setting up some time for you to get out each week so you can get back to following your dreams."

I get a soft smile from Savannah and she turns her face away from me, lifting it up to the hot sun. I stroke her fingers and close my eyes.

"Gavin?"

"Yeah?"

"Are you for real?"

Her words are so soft... so unsure, I immediately sit up on my chair and swing my legs over to her side. Tugging on her hand, I urge her to sit up and face me. When she does, I pull her sunglasses off her face so I can see her eyes, and I take mine off so she can judge my truth as well.

"Why the doubt, Sweet?"

"It's just... stuff like this doesn't happen in real life, and it certainly doesn't happen to me. You're larger than life, and I feel dwarfed. You're dark and mysterious. Sexy and charismatic. Your touch leaves me breathless, and your words hypnotize me. I feel both lost and found with you, yet many times, I feel in between those two places, which is way worse that just being lost."

I tilt my head to her and give her an understanding smile. Pulling on her hand, I say, "Come here, baby. Sit with me and let me tell you all about it."

She stands up and lets me pull her on top of my lap, arranging her legs in a good straddle. I love being this close to her, face to face, pussy to cock.

"You'll get a boner in this position," she says confidently, slyly. "You always do."

"I don't give a fuck." I smirk at her. "I like you this way."

"But everyone will see," she says as her eyes glance around the crowded beach.

"Again, don't give a fuck. They might see but you are the only one feeling it."

She sucks her lower lip in between her teeth for a moment, considering my words. She lowers her hips down and makes contact with the hard-on that is indeed starting to tent my swim trunks.

"Mmmm, feels good," I tell her but then still her progress with my hands on her hips. "Now, what were we talking about?"

"We were talking about the fact that I'm not good enough for someone like you... not really."

Leaning forward, I place a soft kiss on Savannah's breastbone. Her skin is hot and there's a tang of salt on my lips when I pull back. Looking up at her, I talk to her with utter transparency. "Savannah... Sweet... you have it all backward. I'm the one that's not good enough for you. Your light shines so brightly that I'm merely thankful to be standing near enough to let one of the rays touch me. You say you feel dwarfed by me? Well, I feel utterly overwhelmed by you. My skin hums whenever you're near, and my heart threatens to leap out of my chest like an excited puppy. I've never felt that something was so right... so meant to be. It doesn't have any reason to it, but then again, feelings and emotions aren't meant to. All I know is that my gut, my heart, my brain... the cock that's pushing up against you, they're all telling me that you're the one. So, no more doubts. Okay, baby? We're good for each other, and that's all we need to worry about right now."

TWENTY-SIX

Savannah

"Are you sure you want to do this?" I ask Gavin, which yes... I know it's for the third time.

"I'm sure," he says as he pulls several bottles of wine out of the rack and sets them on the kitchen counter.

"I'd understand if you weren't sure," I prod at him.

"I'm sure you would understand."

"I mean… we can cancel, if you want."

"We can't cancel," he says and yes, that's a smirk on his gorgeous face.

"But if you want—"

Gavin turns on me fast and pulls me to him. He kisses me hard, swiftly, with power and control. "Shut up, Sweet. They'll be here in ten minutes, and you're wound up tighter than your own pussy. What's up?"

I hardly even blush anymore because his dirty talk is getting easier to digest. "It's just… I'm nervous about everyone coming over."

"Why?" he asks as he kisses my forehead. "I've been around all your friends before. I think they like me, right?"

"Seemed to," I grudgingly admit.

"Then what's the problem? You wanted to invite them over for a get-together, and I told you I thought it was a fantastic idea. This will be fun."

Sighing, I give him a squeeze and then pull out of his embrace. Turning to the refrigerator, I start pulling out all the finger foods I made. A veggie tray, sliced cheeses, grapes, and deli meats. A pot of spicy meatballs simmers in a crock-pot on the counter, and another holds a warm, buffalo chicken dip. "You're right. It's just… things have moved kind of fast for us, and I don't want them to judge me."

I expect further words of comfort and encouragement from Gavin, but he merely says, "Fuck 'em if they judge us. You don't need them."

Lifting my gaze to his, I see anger and protectiveness. "That's kind of harsh," I murmur. "And I do need them... they're my friends."

Gavin grabs the Macallan from the various bottles of liquors and mixers he brought up from the bar downstairs. Pouring himself a glass, he takes a sip and says, "The way I see it... maybe you're nervous because you doubt what we have is real. You said it's too fast—I said it's not fast enough. Maybe we're not on the same page like I thought."

I blink at him in surprise, taken aback by the resentment in his words. "What? No, I don't feel that."

"If your heart is true, and all the things you told me in St. Lucia were true, you wouldn't worry about what others think. You'd accept what it is and revel in it."

Pushing away from the counter, I walk to Gavin and step in to him. Wrapping my arms around his waist, I place my cheek to his heart and hear it galloping away. He doesn't respond for a moment, then finally sits his glass down and places his arms around me, leaning his cheek to the top of my head.

"Filthy boy," I say gently. "My heart is sure. My body is sure. Don't be mad that I'm nervous. It's not that I doubt you, but I doubt my friends and that they won't see clearly. I just desperately want them to see the same thing that we see. I want the validation that what I'm thinking is the best thing to have ever happened to me isn't a figment of my imagination."

Letting out a deep breath, Gavin murmurs to me, "I'm sorry. You're the best thing to have happened to me too, and I don't want you to ever doubt my feelings on that."

"I don't. I couldn't. You've shown me otherwise, too many times and in too many ways."

We've been back from St. Lucia for just over a week, and I'm still riding on the high of the time I spent alone with Gavin. We had no worries, no obligations, only each other. The things he did to me… the words he spoke. It piled up, all on top of the other, until I was smothered in a blanket of care and devotion. I left St. Lucia knowing that I had found my other half, and I want to shout it out to the world.

I'm just terrified the world is going to shout back at me, *Sucker!*

The front doorbell rings, and I pull back to look up at Gavin. He takes my face in his hands, and peers down at me with searing intensity. "Just remember this, and this is the only thing you need to take away from this conversation. After tonight is over, and all your friends unanimously give their blessing on our relationship, I'm going to fuck you so hard that you're going to pass out from the pleasure. In fact, I'm thinking there might be some rope involved. You tied to the bed... legs raised high... my mouth on your pussy, until you come over and over and over again. I can't fucking wait."

My eyes practically roll into the back my head, and my panties go damp at the thought. Gavin did that on purpose... gave me a dose of my Filthy so my worries would go out the window. So I'd have something to look forward to, and so I wouldn't forget that while the words between us seem to abound, we also have amazing combustion in the sack, which is further testament to the "rightness" of what we have.

"Oh, Filthy." I sigh heavily. "You always know what to say to get my knickers wet."

"Knickers?"

"Yeah... I've heard you say that a time or two."

"I know... but it sounds weird coming from a Yank."

I grin at him, he beams at me, and all of our doubts and misgivings are forgotten. He gives me a quick kiss and then pushes me toward the door to greet out guests.

"Girl... you don't waste any time, do you?" Casey says to me with a wink as she leans her elbows on the kitchen counter and smirks at me. "From employee to live-in lover in a month's time. Nice."

"Leave her alone," Gabby snaps as she dips a piece of celery into the buffalo chicken dip. She takes a bite, groans, and looks at me with praise in her eyes. "Oh my God, Savannah. This is so good. I have to have this recipe."

"Yeah, leave our sweet Savannah alone, Case," Alyssa says in agreement.

"What?" Casey says with her arms outstretched in mock surprise. "I'm just saying... our girl hasn't looked at a man twice since we've known her and now she's shacked up with a wealthy, famous author, who is smokin' hot by the way. Well done. My point is... I'm totally fucking jealous of her."

We all laugh, lift our glasses, and clink them together. Sliding my eyes over to the living room, I see all the guys standing around talking with plates of foot in their hands and one eye on the hockey game that Gavin put on when Hunter requested it. As if he can sense me staring, Gavin turns his head to me and his eyes are tender. He gives me a private smile and turns back to something Brody is saying.

"Well... I think it's wonderful," Alyssa says. "From the time of my first kiss with Brody to the time we started shacking up with each other was only a few weeks."

Gabby nods her head. "The heart knows what the heart wants."

"Wait? We're talking hearts here?" Casey asks in bewilderment. "I just thought this was sex. If hearts are involved, I am so not jealous."

Laughing at Casey, I throw a grape at her head and miss. "You're so jaded, Casey. One day, love is going to hit you so hard that I'm going to just snicker at you while you stumble around all drunk from it."

Leaning in closer, Gabby whispers, "So... is it love then?"

The other girls all lean in to hear my answer. A quick glance at Gavin and my heart starts to pound... as if it's calling out to his. Turning to face the girls, I whisper back. "It is for me. I just haven't said it out loud yet."

"What about him?" Alyssa asks, voice hushed.

"I don't know... I think so. I mean, we've opened up a lot with each other about our feelings, but we just haven't come out and formally said we love each other."

Alyssa snickers. "There's nothing formal about love, Savannah. It's hot, messy, and totally disjointed. My guess is you'll say it at exactly the right moment, without any planning."

"And if he doesn't say it back?" I ask fearfully, because all along, I've thought that Amanda must have surely killed Gavin's ability to love another woman again.

"You determine how important those words are and decide what to do from there. Love is about so much more than just words."

"Okay," Casey exclaims as she refills her wineglass. "This conversation is turning far too morose. I say we discuss something else... like... how is the sex, Savannah? I mean... look at Gavin. You just know that man knows his way around a woman's body."

All four of our heads swivel to Gavin and thankfully, he doesn't notice.

"Am I right?" Casey asks and three heads turn to look back at her while she levels her gaze at me.

Leaning inward to whisper again, I say, "You don't even know the half of it."

"Tell me at least a quarter of it then," Gabby says excitedly.

Grinning, I say, "Oh girls… the things he does with his hands and mouth alone are worth dying for."

Alyssa rests her cheek in her hand and sighs. "Brody's good with his mouth too. I love that. Don't you love that?"

"Hunter too," Gabby says. "It must be a Markham twin thing."

We all giggle and sip at our wine.

"No fair," Casey grumbles. "I haven't gotten any good oral in ages."

"That's because you haven't found the right guy, Casey. A guy that is really in to you is going to worship you with his mouth," Alyssa points out.

"Yeah, but that implies a relationship," Casey states firmly. "And as you old, monogamous women know, Casey Markham doesn't do relationships."

"Then you can forget the mind-blowing oral sex," I tell her before popping a few grapes in my mouth.

"Well, let me live vicariously through you at least," Casey says. "Tell me what he does with his mouth."

It's been all fun and games talking with innuendo, but I'm not about to share the intimate details of what Gavin does to me. That's for me alone. But I do give her this. "Let's just say my nickname for him is 'Filthy'."

Casey gasps. Alyssa sighs. Gabby says, "No way."

"Yes, way," I say with a grin, proud of myself that I shared something shocking with my home girls.

"Hey Filthy," Casey calls out into the living room, and all four men turn around to look at her.

I slump down to the counter, my face flashing neon scarlet. Gabby and Alyssa giggle. A slow, sexy smile comes to Gavin's face, and he starts to walk into the kitchen.

"What is it, love?" he asks as he looks at Casey with curiosity. His eyes flick to mine, and he takes in the droop to my shoulders and the pain of embarrassment on my face.

"I'm just wondering," Casey says without preamble. "What exactly did you do to our sweet Savannah to make her give you your nickname?"

Gavin gives Casey a knowing smile and steps around the counter behind me. His arms slip around my waist, and he pulls me up straight from my hunched position. His face goes down and nuzzles at my neck for a moment, before looking back up to Casey.

"Now, Casey-love, I wouldn't invite you into our bedroom, just as sure as you wouldn't invite me into yours. But let me just say... my brand of filth compliments Savannah's sweet very well. It's a match made in heaven, I'm thinking."

"Good one," Casey says as she nods her head up and down.

Gabby and Alyssa sigh again.

Turning me in his arms, Gavin leans down, gives me a soft kiss, and then says, "Now, Sweet... stop telling the girls all of our sexy secrets or there will be no ropes for you tonight."

He turns around to leave, and I'm left with three women staring at me with mouths agape.

"Did he say ropes?" Alyssa asks, astonished.

"That's so hot," Casey mutters.

"We're so stopping at the store on the way home for some rope," Alyssa says.

And we all bust out laughing.

Speaking of ropes, my legs are half asleep because of the soft, nylon rope stretched under the back of my knees and tied to the posts of the headboard behind me. Gavin had pulled them firmly before knotting them, causing my legs to spread wide and raise half my ass off the bed.

His face has been in between my legs for the last thirty minutes, and I've lost count of the major and minor orgasms I've had. He gently licks at me now, murmuring words against my wet flesh that I can't understand, but I am beyond all reasoning or care of understanding.

"Enough," I rasp out. I would push Gavin's head away if my hands weren't also tied to the headboard.

Lifting his head, Gavin's eyes are dark and fevered as he looks at me. "You are so fucking sexy like this. I don't think I'm ever letting you out of this contraption."

"My legs have fallen asleep," I complain without much vigor.

"Then I guess I'll just have to concentrate your feelings elsewhere, right?" he asks, before lowering his mouth back on me again.

I'm bound so thoroughly, my hips can't even reflexively jerk against the insane pleasure he's giving me right now. My body is completely helpless... I can't move an inch, which only makes me focus on the sensations he's creating all the more. My awareness of what he is doing is so heightened that it makes the pleasure sharply exquisite.

He's merciless. Absolutely focused and

determined to make me come again, and I have to wonder what his ultimate agenda is. He's showed me pleasure over and over again since we first came together, but he is relentless in his pursuit to drive me mad with need for him.

I sob, I strain against the ropes, I tell him to stop, and I beg him. He keeps on and on, murmuring words against me in between licking and sucking, and my brain becomes overloaded with sensation.

When I finally come again… what was that—four or five times—I momentarily black out by the conquering force of convulsions ripping through me.

When I come to, Gavin is kneeling by my knees, holding a pocketknife in his hands. He cuts one leg and then another free, and I groan as the blood rushes back through my sore limbs.

Lying down beside me, fully dressed still, Gavin starts rubbing my legs to help increase the circulation. I grit my teeth through the pins and needle-like pain but silently think to myself… that little bit of discomfort was so worth it.

"That was all kinds of hot," Gavin says as he massages my calf.

"*That* was amazing," I murmur.

"Told you I was going to make you pass out," he says with a confident smirk.

"*You* are amazing," I tell him.

TWENTY-SEVEN

Gavin

I've always known February in London is gray and cold, but it seems more so right now. I'm sure that has nothing to do with meteorology and everything to do with the fact that I don't want to be here, and that I'm here without Savannah.

The last few weeks have been unbelievably good to me. Savannah read my manuscript and declared it a masterpiece. I read back through it two more times, making some revisions and tweaking a few plot points. During the day, I would work up in my office, and Savannah would work down in the kitchen, managing all of my author affairs. Sometimes she would take the day and drive throughout eastern North Carolina. She'd pack her camera bag, a sandwich, and her phone so I could text her occasionally. She would come home at night, upload her photos to the computer, and we'd go through them together while eating dinner.

At night… and I mean every fucking night, and more often than not during the day too… I would be inside of her, stroking and pumping my way to an even deeper connection with her, poured forth in orgasms and sweet, whispered words. I couldn't get enough of her… can't get enough of her. I keep asking myself, when will it ever be enough? Something always screams back at me… never!

With my manuscript finally turned into my editor and a few weeks' time before I needed to start on my next one, I decided to go ahead and knock out a quick trip back to the homeland. My main goal was to see my parents and go through all the stuff my dad had packed up from the Turnbridge house. I planned to donate most of it, but I knew there would be a few things I wanted to keep. That goofy, blue octopus of

Charlie's and, of course, all the photos I had ever taken of him. If I'm going to make my home back in Duck, North Carolina, said home should be filled with pictures of my son. I realize that thinking about photos of Charlie doesn't pain me as much as it used to.

Savannah isn't here with me only because my timid, little wallflower apparently has never traveled out of the States before and never had a passport. So I left her with a sweet kiss and an order to get to work on her passport, because she sure as fuck was going to come with me on the next visit. With a direct flight from Raleigh to London, I figured we could make several trips a year to see my family and visit Charlie's grave.

My flight leaves tomorrow at eleven in the morning and there's nothing left to do but get a good night's sleep. I declined my parents request to stay at their house in Turnbridge, preferring to get a hotel closer to the airport to save me some time in the morning.

I pull all the pillows from the bed and arrange them on one side propped against the headboard. Grabbing my laptop, I sit down with my back against the pillows and fire it up so I can start outlining my next novel.

All I can seem to think about is getting back to Savannah.

Savannah, Savannah, Savannah. So very sweet, Savannah.

God, I can't believe how bad I fucking miss her. I feel almost weak and powerless to admit it, yet there's no denying that my life is beginning again because of her. It worries me to no end how much I seem to need her... how desperate I am to be in her presence.

I grab my phone and turn it on. Tapping on the favorites button, I hit Savannah's name. She's the only number listed in my favorites.

After three rings, her voice mail picks up and even though I'm not going to leave her a message, I listen to it all the same just so I can hear her voice. It makes a pang of hurt stab in my chest with longing.

Hanging up, I open up a new document on my laptop and flex my fingers. I'm ready to write. Except... my mind drifts.

I wonder what Savannah is doing right now. It's close to noon in the States but time has no bearing. Her schedule doesn't necessarily follow the tick of the clock. She may be out shooting some photos or picking up my mail. Hell, maybe that fucking vacuum cleaner is running and that's why she's not answering the phone. There's a good chance she may be over at The Haven right now, elbow deep in puppies and kittens.

I smile, because although I miss her terribly, I also love her devotion to the things that are important to her. She even has me going to The Haven with her to volunteer, and it's not necessarily because of the altruistic blood running through my veins. It probably has everything to do with the fact that I want to be near her as much as possible.

I'm whipped. Fucking whipped, I tell you.

But how could I not be? I remember telling Savannah that I was fortunate to have just a ray of her light touch me, and truer words were never spoken now that her light isn't here with me in dreary England. The shadows seem darker and my blood icier when she's not around. I long for just a sliver of her brightness right now.

Great... now I'm fucking waxing poetic. I better purge this shit out of my system. I have a fucking erotic thriller I need to write, and there's no room for romantic sentiments. I need to buckle down and write some scenes that involve some hardcore, dirty, fucking. Animalistic fucking.

Groaning, I realize that makes me think of Savannah too, and I can't help the smile that comes to my face when I realize that there isn't much that keeps her far from my thoughts.

I open the door to my house, about to jump out of my skin over the prospect of seeing Sweet in the next few seconds. I had texted her as soon as my plane landed, *On NC soil. Be home in three hours. Be naked.*

She texted back. *K. See you soon.*

I had expected a flirtier response but then I didn't give it much thought because the mere thought of her waiting for me naked had me pushing the Maserati a little too fast during the three-hour drive from Raleigh to the Outer Banks. By the time I got home, I was convinced she'd meet me at the door without a stitch of clothing on.

The house is quiet when I walk in, but I know she's here because her car is out front. The fact she isn't jumping naked in my arms right now is bothersome.

"Savannah?" I call out.

There's no answer, and I think perhaps she's in the shower. I start for the stairwell, but then from the corner of my eye, I see her sitting on the back deck, huddled up under a blanket while she sits on one of the deck chairs, staring at the ocean.

When I open the back deck door, her head swivels to me, and I see something odd in her eyes. Anxiety maybe? Just as quickly, it's gone and a sweet smile shines at me.

She stands from the chair and throws the blanket to the ground. In just a moment of time, she's in my arms and hugging me tight, her face pressed into my chest. I lean down and put my nose to her hair, inhaling the flowery fragrance of my Sweet.

"Hey," I say as I squeeze her and note that she clutches me almost desperately. "What are you doing out here?"

She doesn't answer me at first, but then shrugs as she pulls back a bit. "Just enjoying the view."

Her eyes meet mine for a second, and then drop away, and I know without a doubt that something isn't right. Releasing my hold on her, I grasp her chin with my fingers and raise her face to mine. "What's wrong?"

"We need to talk," she says nervously, and a hard knot forms in the middle of my stomach.

The cold, ocean wind gusts and catches Savannah's hair for a moment, lifting it up so it billows around her head like it's got a life of its own. But then the wind is but a moment of time, and her hair falls back down softly on her shoulders… almost as if it has died. It seems like an ominous premonition to me.

"What is it, Sweet?" I ask gently, although my own blood seems to be racing.

Stepping back from me and crossing her arms over her stomach, as if to give herself a hug, she says quietly, "I'm late."

"Late?"

"My period."

Apprehension and dread boil up hot, and my knees go weak. "Your period is late?"

"Yes," she says quietly but still holds my gaze.

"Fuck," I mutter and turn away from her. Running my hand through my hair, I look out at the ocean and try to think what to do. "We need to go buy a pregnancy test. No sense in getting worried—"

"I already took one. It's positive."

My head snaps back to her. "Are you sure?"

She nods her head and finally averts her eyes from me.

I let my eyes slide from her and back out to the Atlantic. "Fuck," I say again, softly. Then again not so softly, "FUCK!"

White-hot rage lances through me and I don't know where it's coming from, but I'm powerless to stop it. All I see is Charlie's little body facedown in a creek bed, and I know that is something I can never go through again. Spinning back on her, I snarl, "How the fuck did that happen? You said you were on the pill. Was that a lie?"

Savannah's eyes go wide and fearful, and she takes a step backward. "I was... I am," she stutters.

"Well, did you forget to take them?" I ask wildly. "Because please explain how you could be pregnant and on the pill."

With her hands wringing one another, she whispers, "Um... the antibiotics I took... I read they can reduce the effectiveness of the pill."

"Mother fucking Christ," I yell at her, and to anyone else that might be willing to engage in my anger. "Did you know that when you were taking them?"

She nods hesitantly and says, "I think I remember reading that somewhere... but I guess I had forgotten."

"You forgot?" I ask incredulously. "How could you fucking forget something so fucking important?"

Anger fills Savannah's eyes, and she throws her hands outward. "I don't know," she yells back at me. "I just forgot. I wasn't thinking. I'm sorry, but I just forgot."

Throwing my own arms out in frustration, I turn and walk a few paces from her. "Oh, that's just fucking great, Savannah. Just fucking great." I spin around and stride right up to her, grabbing her by her shoulders. "Do you remember when we had our little talk about unprotected sex? Do you remember how I wasn't all that worried about catching something from you, but I sure as shit was interested to make sure you couldn't get pregnant?"

She nods at me, the anger now sapped out of her, and sadness prevalent in her eyes once again.

"Well, did it ever fucking occur to you that was maybe because I didn't want any fucking kids?" I scream.

I'm absolutely out of control at this point, and the urge to destroy something is so strong that I immediately drop my hands away from her, afraid of what I might do. Every bit of tender feelings I ever held for Savannah seem to melt away, and nothing is left but rage at this moment... at her... at the unfairness of the situation.

"I'm sorry," is all she says, and she sounds broken... utterly broken.

A tiny bit of sympathy stabs at my heart for her. I know she didn't intend this, I know this was an accident, but I cannot put myself in that situation again. I take a deep breath and try to expel the anger out.

"This wasn't supposed to happen," I say softly. "I'm not ready for this to happen. I'll never be ready for this to happen."

"I'm not ready for it either," she says. "But it's happening."

The finality of her words are like the clang of a prison door slamming shut on me, and panic starts to rise. I'm not worried about being shackled to Savannah forever, because just before I walked in that door, I had been thinking how lovely that would be. What I'm not ready for... what I don't have the courage to face, is bringing another innocent life into this world, and then suffering the constant fear that it could be ripped away from me again. When I think of how scared Charlie must have been... when I think of how he suffered... No! I just can't do it.

How can in one moment my life be so perfect, and the next it's collapsing all around me? As I look at Savannah's sweet face, a face I've memorized so I can see her in all my dreams, I realize that all of this was probably a sham anyway. Savannah is made for someone to cherish her completely. Someone that wants to share every bit of life with her. A life that includes children.

I, on the other hand, am apparently still rooted in dark desperation to cling to only those things that can bring me comfortable certainty. I don't have it in me to risk my heart again… not with another child. Fear courses through me as I remember that exact moment when I saw Charlie… laying there lifeless. The pain that flowed through my body dropped me to my knees. It was such pain as I have never felt, nor, I vow to myself, will I ever feel it again.

My breathing becomes a bit ragged as the terror of that moment seeps through me. I need space. I need to be away from Savannah and the unprotected life that is growing within her. I shudder in despair and walk back into the house.

Savannah follows me in, watches as I walk across the living room, back through the kitchen, and to the front door.

"Where are you going?" she asks me.

"Out for a drive. I need to think," is all I say, and then I'm out the door.

When I close it behind me, I pat at my pockets with my hands. Wallet. Keys. I'm set.

I get in the Maserati and back it out of the driveway. Glancing up at the house, I see Savannah standing at the kitchen window, looking down at me. I hesitate for a moment before going any further, wondering if she'll stand there and watch until she can no longer see me.

We stare at each other... moments tick by, then Savannah turns from the window and she's gone.

I back out of the drive and onto Highway 12. I have no clue where I'm going. I just know I need to get some distance between myself and the unholy mess I just left behind.

Savannah's sad eyes haunt me, but not enough to make me turn around and go back to her. I drive south through Kill Devil Hills and Nags Head. I think... what to do? Could I possibly raise a child with Savannah?

No, my thoughts scream at me. *No, you don't have it in you. Protect yourself.*

I keep driving, turning off onto Highway 64 and westward.

I drive, and I drive, and I drive. The further I leave Savannah behind, the more the pressure in my chest eases.

I drive west, further and further away.

I turn on the radio, but the sound has no impact on me.

Charlie, Charlie, Charlie. My poor, dead Charlie.

My thoughts wander. I try to remember what he was like when he was alive, but I keep seeing his swollen, lifeless body. I think about the booze, and the drugs… and I want to get high right now so bad I almost itch. The women… countless, nameless women who I turned to, trying to drown out my sorrows. I can see them clear as day… sucking me off, taking it up the ass for me because I said so, asking me to hurt them just a little bit sweeter.

I try to think of Savannah, but her face is blurry. I can still see all those women though, clear as day.

Just as I can see Charlie… dead Charlie.

Blinking my eyes, I see the sign that says Raleigh, I-540 to Raleigh-Durham Airport.

I never hesitate a second before putting my blinker on and taking the exit.

TWENTY-EIGHT

Savannah

"How many times have I told you to stop stocking the heavy items, Savannah?" I hear from behind me. Lifting my head over my shoulder, I see Brody standing in the supply room doorway, glaring at me. He strides over, grabs the case of canned dog food I was lifting onto a shelf from my hands, and easily hefts it up.

"I'm not an invalid," I grumble. "So stop treating me like one."

"No… you're pregnant and you were spotting, so quit being so obstinate."

Turning to the cart laden with supplies, I start pulling off jars of vitamin supplements, stacking them methodically on the shelves. "I was spotting a month ago. The doctor said the baby was fine."

"If you want to keep your job, then do as you're told," Brody says, and his tone of voice doesn't leave room for argument.

Sighing, I keep stacking the smaller supplies while Brody handles the heavier items. We work silently side by side, and I try not to be resentful of his overprotectiveness.

Can't help it though. I am resentful. Resentful that Brody is doing the job that Gavin should be doing. Don't get me wrong; I'm very grateful for Brody and Alyssa. They talked me into accepting a full-time job at The Haven, a proposition I had turned down from them over and over again in the past. But even I know beggars can't be choosers. With a baby on the way, I had no better prospects. Eric certainly wasn't going to hire me back, and the two ladies I cleaned houses for had already hired replacements they were happy with. Unless I wanted to go home with my tail between my legs and a bun in the oven, I really had no choice but to accept their kindness.

Their charity.

Fuck, that burns me up. That I'm stuck in this position, having to prey upon the benevolence of my friends.

Fuck Gavin for leaving me, without a word... without a backward glance.

Like an idiot, I waited. I waited in his kitchen for an hour for him to come back. Then an hour turned into two, which turned into three. At the four-hour mark, I started calling him, but I got his voice mail every single time. I went to bed that night, slept fitfully, and was back up at dawn to wait for him in his kitchen.

I waited at his house for three fucking days. Like an idiot. Then I moved my stuff back home and cried for two more days. The day after that, I went to the doctor's and had a blood test, which confirmed I was pregnant, and I cried again. Both a mixture of happy and sad tears.

I hadn't wanted to get pregnant. One day... sure. But not until I was older. Not until I had accomplished some of my other dreams. But the fact was... I was pregnant and all of a sudden, I had a little life growing inside of me that I couldn't wait to meet one day. I let the tears come again, pretending to segregate a portion of them for the joy that I would have a baby one day soon, and sadness that the man I thought I loved had abandoned me.

After that day, I refused to cry again.

I refused to call Gavin again.

However, I did go to the post office to pick up Gavin's mail the following week, only to find the box empty. I expected it to be packed full, and when I asked the nice lady behind the counter where it all was, she informed me that a change of address form had been submitted and the mail was being forwarded to an address in England.

Tears pricked at my eyes when she told me that, but I refused to let them fall. I swallowed hard... swallowing my heart, my tears, and my pride. I pushed it all down and refused to let it back up again.

In the parking lot, I sat in my car and deleted Gavin's contact information from my iPhone. Within a week, I had forgotten his phone number and now, officially, had no way to get in contact with him even if I wanted.

Weeks.

My life is now measured in weeks.

When I was five weeks pregnant, Gavin left me, and I entered the denial phase. There was no way he could have left me for good. He would be back.

At six weeks, I turned in his post office key and entered the anger phase.

At seven weeks, I succumbed to morning sickness, except it happened every afternoon, not just in the morning. I accepted Brody and Alyssa's offer to work at The Haven, and the smell of dog poop increased my nausea. I was usually able to make it into the bathroom before I puked. I entered the bargaining phase, and pleaded with God every night to let Gavin see reason and come back to me... preferably on groveling knees.

At eight weeks pregnant, I started spotting and had a mild panic attack. The doctor checked me out and a vaginal ultrasound sent me into a fit of maniacal laughter filled with relief when I was able to hear the baby's heartbeat. All was fine I was assured, but I was thoroughly immersed in the depression phase, swallowing my tears and hiding my melancholy from my friends. No one could convince me that all was fine.

At twelve weeks, in a fit of morbid and morose thoughts, and in a need to apparently torture myself, I drove by Gavin's house to check on it. I was slapped in the face by a large For Sale sign planted in the front yard. It wasn't Casey's realty firm, so I had no guilt whatsoever when I put my car in drive and gently drove it into the sign, stepping on the gas with more and more pressure until the thick, wooden post cracked and the sign fell over. Some might call that another round of the anger phase, but I called it acceptance.

I was done.

And now… at seventeen weeks today, I spent the morning in the doctor's office having an ultrasound and was shocked to learn that they could tell the baby's gender. I learned that I'm going to have a baby girl. I smiled so big, so wide… yes, that was called the joyful phase.

"So, are you going to tell me or am I going to have to beat it out of you?" Brody asks amiably.

"Tell you what?" I ask innocently as I look over at him.

He glares at me and waits.

I just stare at him.

He glares at me some more.

"Fine. It's a girl," I say with a tiny squeal of excitement.

Brody grabs me, picks me up, and swings me around until I'm dizzy. He hugs me close, kisses me on top of my head, and shouts in my ear, "That's awesome. I'm so happy for you. I need to call Alyssa and tell her."

When he releases me... sets my feet back on the ground, I do a little happy dance-jig sort of maneuver and Brody laughs at me. We go back to stocking shelves and all is quiet. I start daydreaming of a nursery I'll never have because there's no room in the small, two-bedroom house that I share with Casey. However, I still imagine it filled with frilly, pink curtains, pink and gray elephants on the comforter and walls, and plush, white carpeting I can sink my bare toes in while I nurse her in the middle of the night.

"Are you going to tell him?"

My body jerks over the words that crash into my lovely fantasies and fill me with blackness. "No."

"Why not?" Brody asks.

"Because he doesn't deserve to know," I tell him matter-of-factly. "Besides... I wouldn't even know how to contact him."

"Don't you have his phone number?"

"Nope. Deleted it several weeks ago and couldn't remember it to save my life. Don't want to remember it either."

"Seriously?"

"Seriously."

"I think you should tell him," Brody says.

Anger threads through me, and I hope the baby can't feel the terrible vibes coursing through me right now. Turning on Brody, I practically spit at him, "Why in the fuck would you think he even wants to know the sex of the baby? He made it pretty clear he doesn't want me... I mean her."

"Because he loves you, and I guarantee you that he loves her. He's just fucked up in the head. I mean... look at what he went through with his little boy."

I instantly regret ever telling Brody the full truth about Gavin's past. It was in my denial phase, because I was trying to come up with every justification for Gavin's abandonment. Now Brody dares to throw that in my face.

"He doesn't love me or the little peanut," I mutter. We started calling my baby "peanut" from the start, and now the nickname has stuck. That may potentially be her nickname for the rest of her life.

"I bet he loves both of you," Brody says firmly. "And you love him."

"No, I hate him. I hate him, I hate him, I hate him," I say, stomping my foot on the ground with each proclamation.

"I'm pretty sure you love him."

"No, I'm pretty sure I hate him."

Brody sighs and it sounds long-suffering. "Do you love the peanut?"

I give him a quick glance, just long enough to give him an exasperated glare. "Of course I love her. Stupid question."

"Then you love Gavin... at least a part of him. Because that baby is part Gavin."

Spinning on Brody, I poke him in the chest. "What the hell is your problem? You spent weeks cursing Gavin's name with me, threatening to put him six feet under if he showed his face around here again. Now, all of a sudden, you're his champion?"

Shrugging his shoulders nonchalantly, Brody says, "I guess I just feel for the guy a little... knowing his history and all. I'm sure he was terrified. Terrified of having another child and losing it. It's scary as shit having the responsibility of someone's tiny life in your hands. And he has more reason to be terrified than any of us do."

Turning away, I sneer. "What could you possibly know about it, Brody? Seriously... what could you possibly know?"

"I know a little something about it," he says smugly, and the hairs rise up on the back of my neck.

My head swivels slowly to him, my mouth hanging open. "Are you... is Alyssa...?"

"Pregnant? That she is," he says with a big grin. "But we haven't told anyone else yet so keep your trap shut."

"Oh my God," I shriek and launch myself into his arms. "Oh my God, oh my God, oh my God. That's wonderful. Oh my God. I'm so happy. We're going to have babies together. And you'll have a little boy, and they'll be sweet on each other... or maybe we should just betroth them. What do you think?"

"I think you're hilarious," he says as he gives me a last squeeze and sets me away from him. "But to get back to the point I was making... I think there's a good chance that Gavin was just terrified out of his mind and didn't know what to do. I think there's an equally good chance that he probably knows he fucked up, but has no clue how to fix it. I think you should contact him."

"So, I should be the bigger person is what you're saying?" I ask with some derision in my voice.

"I'm saying, Savannah, that you're the type of woman that will always be the bigger person. It's who you are, and I also know your heart... it's a forgiving heart. It's also a loving heart. You can tell me all you want that you hate him, but we both know it isn't true. Give him a pass on this one. Open the door and see if he'll walk back in."

Shaking my head, wanting to deny what he's saying, I still don't understand Brody's complete empathy with Gavin. "I don't get you, Brody. I figured you'd be the last person that would want to see him back in my life. You threatened to kill him so many times."

"Oh, when he comes back… and I'm betting he does, I'm going to beat the shit out of him for hurting you. Make no mistake about that. But then I'll forgive him, same as you."

I now mentally shake my head again so Brody doesn't see my outright denial, that I'm not willing to accept what he's saying. Not willing to accept what he's suggesting I do. Contacting Gavin is going to open me up to a potential world of hurt, because no matter what Brody thinks, I personally think Gavin is done with this baby and me. He has too much shit to overcome, and I'm not sure he has an ounce of hero-like qualities in him to admit his wrong and take the risk for something wonderful.

"Doesn't matter anyway," I say, surprised at how glum my voice sounds and how sad I feel inside. "I told you… I seriously don't know how to contact him."

"Well, then it's a good thing I know how," Brody says with a smirk.

"What do you mean?" I ask carefully, refusing to have even a moment's excitement over the prospect that maybe… just maybe, I could have a second crack at happiness with Gavin.

"He's doing a book signing in New York this weekend. You need to go see him."

"I couldn't possibly," I say, backing away with my hands held before me.

"You could."

"I can't."

"You can. You will."

Rubbing my knuckles over my breastbone to assuage the stab of pain I'm feeling there, the most I'll give Brody at this time is, "I'll think about it."

"What's your favorite memory of Charlie?" I asked Gavin as we lay in bed together one night before we fell asleep. It had become routine… Gavin would make love to me, or fuck me, depending on his mood and mine, and then we'd lay in the dark and talk.

Sometimes our talks were easy and lighthearted. Sometimes they were deep. I learned early on that Gavin never shied away from talking about Charlie with me, and I used every opportunity I could to learn more about his little boy that only had two short years on this earth. Because every detail I learned about Charlie let me understand the real Gavin Cooke all that much more.

Gavin chuckled as he stroked my shoulder. "That's an easy one. It was the first time he giggled. I was holding him on my lap… I think he was about three months old. His legs were

*so strong, and he liked to try to stand up as much as possible
with me holding him. He was facing me, with his little fist in
his mouth, and I was making some type of goofy noise and
funny face, or something like that. And this little giggle just
burst out of his mouth. I was so shocked... I hadn't heard
anything like that before. Can you believe it? I'd never heard a
baby laugh. It was miraculous. It was hilarious. It made me
laugh, and when I laughed... he giggled again. Then I laughed,
then he laughed, and we just sat there and laughed at each
other."*

*"Sounds like the best memory ever," I told him with a
smile on my face that he couldn't see in the dark.*

*"Want to know what my best memory is of you?" he
asked.*

"Lay it on me," I told him.

*"My best memory is of right now... of you asking me
about Charlie, and me remembering his laugh. Yes, my best
memory is of sharing that special moment with my boy, with
you."*

I sighed long and deep, and my heart cried with joy.

Setting my cup of tea aside, I get up from the
couch and wipe the tears that are streaming down my
face. I've been sitting here all evening, trying to decide
what to do.

Brody's words hammering at me...

He has more reason to be terrified than any of us do.

Then you love Gavin… at least a part of him.

Because he loves you, and I guarantee you that he loves her.

I have no clue if Brody's wisdom knows what the hell it's really talking about. But I know one thing that he is absolutely correct about. I do still love Gavin and because of that, I do need to reach out and give him a chance to explain himself.

Sitting down at the kitchen table, I open up my laptop and search out the cost of a flight to New York this weekend.

TWENTY-NINE

Gavin

Glancing down at my watch, I mutter a curse when I see how slowly time is moving by. Lindie nudges me in the ribs, leans over, and hisses at me, "Try to act like you're enjoying this. Try to act like you're happy to see your fans."

Looking up at the next woman in line, I plaster a smile on my face as she shoves my book at me. "Mr. Cooke... it's an honor to meet you. I loved *Killing the*

Tides so much. It's my favorite book of all time. I've read it seven times already, and oh my God... I can't believe I'm standing here talking to you."

I struggle to keep my smile in place, which has become a fucking chore I detest lately, and say, "That's very kind, love. Who should I sign this to?"

"Marie... sign it *To Marie, With Love*, if you don't mind," she gushes. "My friends will die when they see it. Oh, and can I get my picture with you?"

I hastily make out the inscription and stand up from my chair. I move around the side of the table and Marie plasters herself to me while Lindie takes our picture with the woman's phone.

"You weren't smiling," Lindie growls at me, so I put back on my plastic pose of flashing teeth and she snaps another photo.

"Perfect," Lindie says, and the woman squeezes the air from my lungs with a vicious hug.

"Thank you, Mr. Cooke. Thank you so much. You're amazing. Just the nicest man. Thank you so much."

Yeah, I'm a fucking really nice man. I'm so amazing that I left the woman I love, who is pregnant with my child. I left her behind and stuck my head in the sand for weeks, and now that my head is free, I don't know what the fuck to do.

Pain wracks my chest when I think of Savannah… all alone, pregnant, scared. I ache to talk to her… to touch her. I'm going crazy with wonder… how is she doing? How is the baby? And yet, I'm too fucking scared to even pick up the phone to call her.

There hasn't been one day that has passed since I walked out of my home… walked away from Savannah, that I didn't regret my actions. At first, my deepest regret was in hurting her. It was something I didn't think I had the power within me to do. Yet, I let my anger drive my actions. I let my anger drive my car all the way to the airport, where I boarded a plane for London. I cursed at Savannah in my head so many times for getting pregnant, even though I know it was an accident. I cursed her for making me fall in love with her, and then doing something so stupid as to ruin it all.

Then I turned the anger inward and castigated myself for my selfish actions and shortsighted vision. As the weeks rolled by, there wasn't a day that didn't dawn where I picked up my phone to call her several times. I chickened out, time and again, because I knew there was ultimately a point where Savannah would grow to hate me, and there would be no point in trying to work around that.

Then my deepest regret came when I realized that I had a baby coming. My own flesh and blood…

my DNA... my heart, was growing inside of Savannah's belly every day. I was missing out on every single thing, and my regret festered and then turned into bitterness.

I became a dark, selfish asshole once again. I drank too much and got high a few times, enjoying the numbness it brought me. The only aspect of my prior life I didn't sink to was the women... the countless, nameless women. I had no desire for them, because everywhere I looked, I saw Savannah's face.

Savannah's sad, fearful face. The face I left her wearing when I walked out.

I see her everywhere. Every woman standing in this line wears her face... because I want it to be so. I would kill to get just one real glimpse of her again.

Another book is shoved under my nose, and two young women stand before me. I can tell by the nervous looks on their faces that I won't have to overly engage with them. I vaguely note about another thirty people standing in line, which means I have another good hour to an hour and a half of this shit before I can be done with it. I told Lindie this morning... no more signings. I was done with this shit for good.

She just shook her head, gave me a smile, and said, "Whatever you want, Gavin."

I know damn well she probably went and booked me on another one right then.

"Who should I make this out to?" I ask the woman who handed me the book.

"Stephanie," she says breathlessly, and I force the plastic smile in place.

"Sure thing, love," I tell her, scrawling some meaningless words before handing the book back to her. "Thank you for reading it."

The girls giggle, nod, and look as if they are about to say something, but then they slide off to the side.

Turning to look at Lindie, I lean in to her and whisper, "I swear to fucking God, if you book one more of these, I'm firing you."

She doesn't say anything, just smirks at me.

I put the smile back on and raise my face up to meet my next fan.

And everything I ever wished for in life stands right before me.

My head spins, my world tilts, and the floor seems to shake underneath me.

Savannah.

She stands on the other side of the table... three feet from me, clutching a copy of my book to her chest. Her amber eyes are anxious, and she's chewing on her bottom lip. I can feel the smile slide off my face as I stare at her.

And she stares at me.

I want to leap across the table and grab ahold of her. She's so fucking stunning, and my parched eyes run down her body. She's wearing a brown, wool, wraparound dress that has a sash tied over her stomach with her black, wool winter coat unbuttoned over it. I know that she's over seventeen weeks now, because I've been marking it on my calendar, but I can't tell that she's pregnant. I don't see a swollen belly, but then again, it could be hidden by that damn sash across the middle of her stomach and her bulky coat.

Is she pregnant? Did she have an abortion? The thought makes me sick to my stomach, but no… Savannah would never do that.

Never.

My mind spins with something to say.

How are you, Savannah? No, too trite.

You're looking well, Savannah. No, too cold.

God, I fucking miss you, Savannah. No, too desperate.

Savannah opens her mouth to say something, and I wait with my breath held deep in my lungs. Her eyebrows furrow inward, and I'm dismayed by a slight sheen of tears that form in her eyes. She snaps her mouth shut, looks at me a moment more, and then spins away as she drops the book to the floor, practically running down the line of fans and toward the entrance of the bookstore.

"Savannah," I call out to her, but she doesn't stop.

Lurching out of my chair, I spring over the top of the table and practically knock over the next woman standing there.

"Sorry," I mutter as I reach out a hand to steady her and then take off after Savannah.

"Gavin," Lindie yells out at me. "Get back here… you have fans waiting."

I don't pay her any mind. I can vaguely hear her offering apologies and saying, "He'll be right back."

My shoulder hits another person standing in the line as I scramble after the mother of my child. Another muttered apology.

I veer to the right to avoid hitting the next person, cracking my knee on a table stacked with books.

Fuck that hurt.

I curse viciously, causing gasps all around, and push onward.

When I get to the entrance doors, I burst through them and out onto the New York City sidewalk, where dozens of people are walking by. I look left and right, desperately searching for Savannah.

There… there, she is. I can see her long, brown hair swaying back and forth as she walks at a brisk pace up West 18th Street.

My mad dash continues, squeezing past people, knocking shoulders, and calling out apologies. I finally start to catch up to her at the intersection of Park Avenue where she has to wait for the light to turn green.

"Savannah," I yell.

Her head snaps my way, and fear fills her eyes. She hastily turns right and starts running south down Park Avenue. But my legs are longer and she's in my sights now. In four long strides, I catch up to her and grab ahold of her elbow, spinning her toward me.

"Savannah—"

Throwing my hand off her with a vicious shrug, she starts walking away from me again.

I jump forward, grab her upper arm gently, and pull her back around. "Savannah… for God's sake, will you just wait a minute?"

Her eyes flash with anger, and she snarls, "Get your fucking hand off me."

"No," I tell her adamantly. "Not until you stop and just talk to me for a second."

"I don't want to talk to you," she seethes, trying to pull free again.

I refuse to give her up though and hold firm. "Yet you came here to see me."

"A mistake," she says sadly, pulling free of me once more.

I don't even give her a chance to take a step before I have her again in my grasp, turning her to face me. "Please... just wait a minute."

I'm not sure if it was the begging quality to my tone or if she's just worn out, but she doesn't try to pull away again. Instead, she just stares at me sadly with those big, brown eyes, and I want to hug her so bad.

Keeping a firm grip on her arm so she doesn't jet away again, I ask, "How are you? Is everything okay?"

She lets out a big gust of air from her lungs and tugs her arm from me. I let her go, giving her the space she wants, but prepared to lunge at her if she tries to run again.

"I'm fine," she says.

"The baby?" I ask, my heart in my throat. Because I need her to tell me about the baby.

"She's fine," she says reluctantly. "All is well."

She? A girl? And she's fine.

"A girl?"

"Yes, a girl."

"We're having a girl?" I ask again in wonder, as my gaze flits around at the city life around me.

A girl.

Unforeseen pleasure wells up inside of me. I can't help the smile... a true smile... the first one in months, that grabs ahold of my face.

"We're having a girl," I say in amazement.

"No," Savannah snarls at me. "I'm having a girl. You're having nothing."

She turns away... to run from me again.

And again, I grab her... spin her back to me one more time.

"Don't," I beg her. "Please don't go. Stay... talk to me."

"I can't," she says. "I can't do this. I thought I could... but seeing you... I just can't."

"You can," I tell her urgently. "Just give me a minute—"

"Gavin," I hear from behind me, turning my head to see Lindie jogging up toward me. "You need to get your ass back in the store. You have fans waiting."

Savannah uses the opportunity to once again jerk out of my hold. She looks at me with beseeching eyes, and now it's her turn to plead. "Please… I'm begging you, Gavin. Just let me go. Stay away from me. I can't do this with you."

Tears well up and spill from her eyes, making crystal tracks down her cheeks. My heart breaks wide open, because I can hear the finality in her voice.

"Gavin!" Lindie yells at me, and I turn to see her glaring at me. "Have you lost your mind? This is completely inappropriate. Get back to the fucking store, now."

I turn back to Savannah, prepared to make my case to her one more time, but she's gone. I catch sight of her hair… half a block down as she briskly walks away from me.

"Gavin," Lindie snarls at me.

"For fuck's sake, I'm coming," I yell at her, but I don't move until Savannah is completely gone from my sight.

Sighing, I turn and walk past Lindie… heading back to the bookstore. She fortunately stays silent and doesn't berate me for my behavior. I pull my phone out of my pocket and dial Savannah's number. She doesn't answer but I don't expect her to, so I leave a message.

"Savannah… please talk to me. I'll come to you after the signing. Or you can come to me. I'm staying at the Mandarin Oriental. Room 877. Please… I'm begging you. Let's talk. I have so many things I need to say to you."

I hang up… not knowing what else I can do at this point.

I walk back into the bookstore with Lindie, making my apologies as I walk past the line of fans. When I sit back down at the table, I put the smile back on my face. Except this time, it's not as plastic.

This time… it's coming naturally to me.

I saw Savannah… and she looked marvelous. And though she wouldn't give me the time of day, the fact of the matter is, *she* sought me out. So she must still care… at least a little bit, to have come all this way.

And… I'm having a girl. A little baby girl.

My smile gets brighter as I look up and greet the next person in line.

And so, here it all begins.

At least, I hope this is the beginning.

I booked the earliest flight I could out of New York the following day. Savannah never did return my calls. Yes, calls as in plural. I left her seven more voice mails, but she was proving to be stubborn.

I had to assume she flew back to North Carolina, and I was in hot pursuit. I pull the rental car up to The Haven, carefully following the dirt driveway around to the back. I'm immediately relieved to see Savannah's car sitting beside a large truck. No one is in sight.

I park and shut off the car. Gripping the steering wheel hard, I lay my forehead against it and take in a deep breath.

It's do or die.

As I get out of the car, the back door to the kennel opens up and Brody walks out. He makes immediate eye contact with me, and I'm relieved to see a slow smile come to his face. He walks toward me with purpose. Two feet away, he offers me his hand.

I reach out to shake it, returning a smile of my own. His shake is firm. He pumps my arm twice, and then pulls me in for what I think may be a man-hug, which is weird, but then I see his other hand balled into a fist and flying toward my face.

He catches me square on the jaw, rocking my head hard to the right, and releases his hold on my hand at the same time. I go flying backward, completely caught off guard by the sucker punch. I stumble back into my car and slump halfway down the driver's door before I catch myself.

Brody isn't done though. He's striding toward me, anger blazing out of his eyes.

Rubbing my jaw gingerly, I flex it and find it's not broken. I hold one hand out in front of me, a silent plea for him to hold up, because I didn't come here to fight with Savannah's bestie.

"Okay… I deserved that," I admit.

Brody at least stops his advance, but he looks like he wants to murder me. "You deserve a lot more than that, you piece of shit."

I drag myself up the car and get into a standing position, because I'm pretty sure I'm going to need to defend myself at the least.

"Probably," I tell him. "But do you really want to pound me into the ground before I can make things right with Savannah?"

"You can't make things right with her. It's done, and you need to leave."

"I love her," I tell him simply.

Brody snorts and throws his hands out to the side. "Oh, well gee… that just makes everything better, doesn't it?"

"Look, mate," I try to reason with him. "You can beat me to a pulp, but I'm still going to see Savannah, and she is going to listen to me. I'm not going to let up until she forgives me and lets me back in. So, if I have to take an ass-whooping from you to get to

Savannah, so be it." I hold my arms out and to the side. "Take your best shot."

"With pleasure," Brody snarls, and then lunges at me.

"Enough," Savannah says from behind me, and Brody immediately stops his forward progress. I turn and there she is.

My Sweet.

Looking like she wants to murder me as much as Brody wants to.

Sighing... because this looks to be a long day, I say, "Hey, Sweet. What does a gent have to do to get a few moments alone with you?"

THIRTY

Savannah

Oh, God.

He's here.

He actually came after me.

The realization of what that could possibly mean almost knocks me over. Did he come after the peanut or me? Both?

Gavin walks past Brody, eyeing him warily, and approaches me. Then he's there... in my space, inches away from me and staring down with unfathomably beautiful and tortured eyes.

"We need to talk," he says quietly.

I feel the pull of him… I'm in danger of being mesmerized, and my broken heart is afraid of getting crushed. "There's nothing to talk about anymore. That time is gone. It expired twelve weeks ago when you walked out."

"Don't say that," he rasps out. "Don't fucking say that."

"Well, what do you want me to say, Filthy? Welcome back. Glad you could spare me some time?"

His lips curve upward slightly, and he looks amused. "You called me Filthy?"

"So what?" I grumble.

"That's an endearment. You should be calling me any number of vile names, but you chose not to. You gave me an endearment. I think you're still sweet on me."

I want to slap that look off his face, and I want to kick myself in the ass for that slip of the tongue, because Gavin sees me a little too well. He always has.

Reaching down, he takes my hand softly in his. "Let's go to our house. Let's talk."

Not missing the way he says "our house," which causes all kinds of weird feelings to stir up inside of me, I start to pull away, but his hand tightens.

"Gavin... I don't want to."

Gone is the amusement and his look goes hard. He turns and starts walking back to his car, pulling me along behind him. "And I don't really give a fuck, Sweet. Give me the damn courtesy of an hour of your time."

We walk past Brody, who is leaning back against his truck, his arms crossed over his chest as he intently watches this play out. He pins Gavin with a deadly stare and then lifts one hand to point at him. "You and me, boy. We're going to finish this later."

Gavin gives him a curt nod, and I wholly surprise myself when I snap at Brody. "Oh, knock it off, Brody. You're the one that wanted him to come back, you dumbass."

Stopping dead in his tracks, Gavin turns to look at Brody in surprise. Brody just throws his head back and laughs, then looks back at Gavin. "I almost pity you, dude."

The entire drive to Gavin's house is in silence. I sit hunched in the passenger seat, my arms hugging my chest, and my gaze out the window. My mind swirls with the potential of all the things that Gavin may end up saying to me, and I try to harden my heart against them. I don't want to hear those things. I've made my peace, done my healing. I did the phases of grief... denial, anger, bargaining, depression... a little more anger thrown in for good measure, then acceptance.

It's done.

I'm done.

Except, I'm completely overwhelmed just sitting next to Gavin. My heart pounds, my hands sweat, and butterflies flutter in my stomach. Or is that indigestion? Could be both.

When Gavin turns into his driveway, he slows the car to a halt and looks at the broken realty sign still laying on the ground. Clearly, no one has noticed my vandalism and fixed it.

His head swivels, and he pins me with a direct stare. "Your handiwork?"

Shrugging my shoulders, I flippantly respond, "I have no clue what you mean."

Gavin snorts in response and continues up the driveway. "Right."

Because there's no escaping the inevitable, I dutifully follow Gavin up the stairs and into his house. His house. *Not ours*, I affirm to myself.

Throwing his keys on the kitchen counter, he walks into the living room and comes to a dead stop. His shoulders stiffen and his hands clench. "Where are the horses?"

I don't respond. Not going to make this easy on him.

He turns to me, and his eyes are sad. "What did you do with the photographs of the horses you gave me?"

I glance over at the southern wall of the living room where I had hung them over the fireplace. It's starkly blank, almost mocking Gavin that everything I ever gave him I took back. "Probably the county landfill, I expect," I say coldly.

"You threw them away?" he asks in astonishment.

"It was this whole anger thing I went through. That came right in between 'denial' and 'bargaining.' But I didn't just throw them away... I pulled them off the wall, put them on the back deck, and destroyed them with a hammer. Then I took the little itty bits of wood, glass, and paper, and threw them away. You know what it's like, right? To throw something away?"

"I know a little something about it," Gavin says softly, his eyes even sadder and shit... now I'm feeling sorry for him.

"Don't even give me that 'poor me' look, Gavin. You have no right."

Sighing, he grabs my hand and walks to the far side of the living room, pulling me along. When he reaches the big, overstuffed chair that sits in the corner, he releases my hand and lowers himself down. I stand there, two feet from him, and watch as he leans back and plants his feet on the floor, legs slightly apart. He props his elbow on the chair casually. Lowering his chin into the palm of his hand, he looks at me with determined eyes and says, "Okay... let's have it."

I blink at him. "Let's have what?"

"Well, you're obviously pissed at me. You need the chance to get it off your chest... lay into me. So let's have it."

Standing there with my arms wrapped around my stomach, I look down at him primly and say, "No thanks. I've made my peace with what happened between us."

"Bollocks, you have," Gavin says calmly. "In case you haven't forgotten, let me remind you. You told me you were pregnant. I was a complete arse and blamed you entirely. I think I even called you stupid for doing so. I never once gave you the benefit of the doubt, I left you under the pretense of needing time to think, and I drove away from you. Straight to the airport without a backward glance, boarded a plane, and flew to England."

"Stop it," I say softly, because I don't need the recap.

He ignores me. "I left you high and dry, alone while you were pregnant. I stayed away for twelve long weeks and never contacted you once to see if you were okay."

"Enough, Gavin," I say with a little more force, dropping my arms and curling my hands into balls.

"I left you, and you were scared... alone... unsure of what to do. You were heartbroken, angry, and sad."

Digging my nails into the palm of my hands, I glare at him.

"You cried and broke things," he says, his voice hard and menacing. "You cursed me and then cried some more. Come on, Sweet... let me have it, because I sure as hell made it clear to you, by my actions, that neither you nor our daughter were important to me."

"She is not your daughter!" I scream at him, my chest rising and falling with anger and bitterness. My eyes fill with wetness, puddle deep, and then spill over. I take a deep breath and let it out, and then do it again, until I feel more in control.

My voice is a bit more rational when I repeat, "She's not your daughter. You didn't want her, and now you have no right to her."

Gavin stares me... his eyes wide, skin pale. Pain takes hold of his face... crumbling it right before me into a million pieces, and my heart lurches. I open my mouth to take back those cruel words, because no matter what... I didn't mean that. I never meant that.

With lightning-fast speed, Gavin lurches forward in the chair and grabs me around my waist. My hands fly to his shoulders for balance as he pulls me in between his legs while he moves forward to sit on the edge of the cushion. His hands are fast... going to the hem of my sweatshirt, yanking it upward to the bottom of my breasts, exposing my stomach, which is swollen in the lower portion. He stares at my belly, his eyes filled with remorse.

Leaning forward, he kisses my stomach so softly that I barely feel it. Turning his head, he lays his cheek against my skin and wraps his arms around my waist to hold me tight to him. I squeeze my eyes shut against the hauntingly beautiful image of the man before me, humbled against my womb as he hugs his baby and me.

"She is my daughter," he murmurs. "I always wanted her. I may have been scared, but I always wanted her."

Hesitantly, I move my hands from his shoulders to his head, slipping my fingers in his cool, dark hair. I press against his head... pushing him into my stomach a little harder, and he gives a stuttering breath.

"I am so sorry, Savannah," he says with so much anguish that I don't think I can take it. I feel wetness on my stomach, and I know it's tears from his eyes.

"Oh, God," I croak, gripping his head tighter.

"So sorry," he murmurs, turning to kiss my belly again. "So sorry. So very fucking sorry."

My own tears start again, and I let them freely fall. I let them fall… let them pour out all of my past anger and hurt…I let them slide down my cheeks and beg them to take away the bitter betrayal I've been feeling.

Gavin lifts his head and tilts his head back to look at me. His eyes are wet… tortured. "I don't deserve your forgiveness. A man can never do worse than abandoning his love when she needs him most. I did that, and I don't deserve a drop of your kind heart. I don't deserve for you to put your hands on my cheeks and tell me it will be all right. I have no right to ask for assurances or for a place in your life. I don't have a single thing I'm entitled to right now, and yet… I'm begging you, Savannah. I am begging you with everything in my soul to please tell me it's okay. To please forgive me, and let me back in. I will do anything you ask and, I swear, I will never let you down again."

Gavin pushes off the chair and drops to his knees, his face pressing into my stomach again as he kisses my skin, wetting it with more tears.

He presses the words into me… straight through the skin and muscle that protects our little peanut. "Please forgive me, daughter. Please forgive your father for his weakness. I swear I'll never leave you again. Please ask your mommy to forgive a man for being scared and weak. For having too many demons in his closet. I'm begging you… please."

"Stop it," I cry out and grab him by the hair again, pulling his face away. He sits backward on his haunches, and I drop to my knees with a straight spine so we're face to face. "Please stop."

Gavin blinks at me, sending a fresh wave of tears down his tortured face. I bring my hands up and wipe them away, giving him a sad smile laced with the very forgiveness he is begging for. "It's okay, Filthy. It will be okay. It's going to be fine. I promise."

I lean forward and touch my mouth to his, continuing to whisper. "I forgive you. I understand. It's okay."

When I pull back, his face is disbelieving of my words. I can see he's still too disgusted with himself to believe the truth of them. I cup his face with my hands and give him a little shake. Leaning in closer, I look straight through his eyes... I look straight into his heart. "Hear me... I forgive you. We'll start again... all of us... together."

I wait for it... watching closely, and finally, I see his dark eyes lighten. I see him accept what I'm saying, and I watch... all within the depths of his beautiful gray eyes, as he finally understands that his sins have been forgiven.

Gavin's arms come around me... one around my lower back and the other with his hand gripping the back of my head. He pulls me in close and holds me tight as I bury my face in the crook of his neck and inhale him deep.

"Thank you," he whispers simply. "Thank you."

We stay like that... for minutes, for hours... I have no clue. All I know is that this very moment, I've wiped the slate clean and I'm not going to think another moment on the hurt he caused me. I'm only going to think about our future together and building it strong.

Gripping me by the back of the hair, Gavin pulls my head away from his shoulder and stares at me. "I love you, Sweet. So fucking much it hurts." His other hand comes to rest over my stomach. "And I love our daughter, too. With the last breath in my body, I love her and I can't wait to meet her. And I'm scared,

Sweet. You know that's why I ran, right? Because of Charlie... I'm just so scared."

"It's okay, baby," I croon to him as I lay my own hand over his while he strokes our baby through my skin. "It will all be fine. I promise."

"I believe you," he says, leaning forward to kiss me. It's a tentative kiss and utterly lacking Gavin's confidence. He's hesitant, not sure of where the boundaries lay.

I open my mouth to him... I slip my tongue inside his, and that tells him it's okay. That I want him the way I know that he wants me. The way that he craves me, as I crave him.

Pulling me in tighter and tighter still, his mouth angles and he delves for a better connection. His tongue is so warm, and sweet, and I've missed it so much. His mouth moves from mine, skims my cheek, my jaw... he whispers in my ear how much he loves me, and then he kisses me again.

His hands stroke my belly, up to my breasts, which are sensitive. My nipples pucker hard between his hand and the silk of my bra. Magically... smoothly... with only the way that Gavin can do, he removes all of my clothes and pushes me down onto the living room rug. Kneeling between my legs, he places his hands on my stomach and gently rubs the swell there. He watches his hands, mesmerized, as he cradles his daughter for the very first time.

Lifting his eyes to mine, he says, "You know she's going to be spoiled rotten."

I smile at him, a true smile for the first time in weeks, and it causes his breath to hitch.

"Oh, Sweet," he says reverently, returning a grateful smile to me. "I missed that smile."

"That smile missed you," I tell him. "*I* missed you, but you're back now."

His hands slide up my stomach and cup my breasts, but his eyes never leave mine. "Do you love me, Sweet?"

"I love you, Filthy," I assure him. "No matter what… I never stopped."

"I missed hearing you call me that," he admits, plucking at my nipples and finally letting his gaze drop to my breasts. "I missed a lot of things."

"Time to make up for it, don't you think?" I ask boldly.

He turns his hot gaze back to me. "What did you have in mind?"

"I want you to dirty me up a bit," I tell him honestly, and I'm rewarded by his hand going between my legs.

Oh, yes… I missed this a lot.

"Something like this?" he says as he pushes a finger inside of me, groaning at the ease with which he slides in.

"A lot like that," I breathe out harshly.

His eyes burn into me. "Or maybe you want my tongue here?" he asks as he pushes and pulls his finger against me.

"Filthy," I pant with burning need. "No more words. Just show me."

Gavin scoots backward and brings his face between my legs. He takes a hand and strokes it over my stomach while he lowers his mouth to me.

"I love you, Savannah," he says softly just before he covers me.

"I love you, Gavin," I gasp, and then I'm lost to the man I love.

EPILOGUE

Savannah

"Seriously, Gavin... is a blindfold really necessary?" I ask, trying to figure out where he's driving me by the turns that he's making. I'm completely lost.

"You don't seem to mind when I make you wear one in bed," he says smartly... with that crisp, British accent that is just one of the many things I adore about him.

I blush at the reminder, because yes… I do love when he blindfolds me so I can't see what he's doing to my body. It removes that precious sense of sight, and only lets me hear and feel. It heightens everything.

My legs squeeze together in yearning.

I feel his hand on my stomach, rubbing it lightly. He calls it my baby bump, but I call it my baby boulder. I feel like a whale. Look like one too, I imagine.

My life is still measured in weeks, but they are infinitely better than what they used to be.

At seventeen weeks, Gavin insisted I move in with him permanently and carted all of my stuff over himself. Casey was okay with it, because she made a shit pile full of money when she sold Gavin the house and didn't have to depend on splitting the rent with me anymore.

At nineteen weeks, my parents came to visit so they could meet Gavin. They loved him and while quietly making love to me so they wouldn't hear us in the next room over, he said, "I adore your parents. I have a new family now."

At twenty weeks, we had my next prenatal visit. We both cried when we saw the ultrasound and Gavin kissed my belly, despite the gel they had squirted all over it. "You're a beauty, little Clare," he had said with a thick voice. I cried again.

At twenty-two weeks, Gavin's parents came to visit. That first night, I sat astride Gavin and rode him slowly. This is his favorite position now, so he can see my swollen stomach and watch my eyes. "I adore your parents, too," I had told him.

He told me, "Less talk, Sweet. More fucking."

At twenty-six weeks, Gavin insisted I stop working at The Haven. This resulted in a fight of epic proportions and only after he called Brody and got his assurances that I wouldn't do anything too strenuous, did he finally relent on letting me stay.

As if he really had a say-so in what I do.

And here we are now… at twenty-nine weeks, and he has my fat ass in a car with a blindfold over my eyes, driving me to who knows where.

God, I love my Filthy.

Finally, the car comes to a stop. I wait patiently for him to open my door and lead me out. He holds one of my hands with his and keeps his other on my lower back to carefully guide me.

"Step up, Sweet," he says when we reach a curb, and I blindly follow with trust in his voice.

We take a few more steps, and he releases me. "Just a second."

I hear keys rattling in a lock, and then the squeak of a door swinging open. He takes ahold of my hand again, the other on my back, and leads me inside of a cool room. Walking me several paces inward, he turns me back around one-hundred-and-eighty degrees and finally removes the blindfold.

When he peels the black material away, I blink into the bright light, and realize I'm looking at a clear glass door that looks out onto the street where his Maserati is parked. I start to turn around, but his hands grip my shoulders and he says, "Just wait."

Then he turns me just ninety degrees to my right. I see a long, blank wall, painted in bright white. I can see gray, industrial carpet underneath my feet, but the room we are in appears to be empty. He turns me around again, another ninety degrees, and I see the back wall with a closed door that leads to God knows what.

Finally, he turns me the last ninety degrees to my right, and I inhale a deep breath of surprise. The entire wall is a painted mural... and not just any mural. It's a replica of the picture I had taken of the baby Corolla horse frolicking in the surf.

My heart immediately clenches in guilt for destroying the pictures I had taken and hung in Gavin's house. But I had rectified that situation. I made more prints and had Gabby replicate the frames. The replacements now hang over our fireplace once again.

I pull away from Gavin's hands and walk closer to the mural. The tiny horse takes up the entire wall, and whoever painted it wasted not one single detail to the fine hairs on his mane as they bounce with his movements, to the spray of the salt water that flies off his back hooves as he kicks out.

Turning back to Gavin, I murmur, "This is incredible. Who did this?"

"An artist that I flew in from Miami. Pretty awesome, right?"

"Awesome doesn't even do it justice," I say with disbelief as I look at the mural again.

"Come on," Gavin says, taking my hand. "I want to show you the rest."

"The rest of what?" I ask as I pull back against him. "What is this place?"

He beams at me brightly. "It's your new photography studio."

I blink at him, confused, and totally not understanding a word he says to me. "But I don't have a photography studio."

"You do now, Sweet," he says as he tugs on my hand and leads me to the door on the back wall. "You can use this space out here for a lobby area, or it's large enough we can partition it and create some additional space for you to do portrait work if you want."

Pulling me through the back door, he says, "Wait until you see this."

He leads me through another room, and I gasp. "How did you do all of this?"

"Had to hire someone to tell me everything I'd need," he says, and I spin around to look at the darkroom he created for me. "But you can develop all of your stuff here when you get back to doing your wildlife photography."

Custom-built shelving holds everything I'd ever need to process a print. I wouldn't have to go to the local community college to borrow their equipment ever again. It has everything... an enlarger, a safelight. Supplies galore... easel, tongs, processing trays. Bottles to hold the processing fluid, funnels, paper... even a little print squeegee.

"I don't know what to say," I whisper as my fingers glide across the enlarger.

Gavin walks up behind me and he puts his hands around my overly large waist, linking them over my huge girth. "This is where you say thank you."

Turning in his arms, I say, "Thank you, my sweet, filthy boy. I love you."

"I love you, too," he murmurs before he kisses me. "Do you like?"

"I love," I assure him. "But why now? What brought this on?"

He shrugs his shoulders. "I just figured if you had your own place, you could do more photography and because you love it so much… you really need to do more photography, love."

"But I have a job. I help you with all of your stuff."

"But that's not your passion, Sweet. You need to go after your passion."

"You're my passion," I tell him and kiss him again. He kisses me back and pushes me backward into the table.

"Speaking of passion," he says against my lips. His hand comes up and grazes against my breast. So freakin' sensitive nowadays that I can't help but arch into him. "I'm thinking we could make use of this table right now."

Yes, please.

"Baby… you know how to say all the right things," I tell him with a grin and start to work at his belt buckle.

"I know how to do all the right things too," he assures me as he bats my hands away so he can lift my shirt over my head. "Give me just a minute, and I'll prove it to you."

I can't help but sigh in anticipation.

Yes, please.

If you enjoyed *Sugar on the Edge* as much as I enjoyed writing it, it would mean a lot for you to give me a review.

NEWSLETTER SIGNUP!!!
Don't miss another new release by Sawyer Bennett!!!
Sign up for her newsletter on her website,
and keep up to date on new releases, giveaways,
book reviews and so much more.

Connect with Sawyer online:
Website: www.sawyerbennett.com
Twitter: www.twitter.com/bennettbooks
Facebook: www.facebook.com/bennettbooks

Books by Sawyer Bennett

The Off Series

Off Sides
Off Limits
Off The Record
Off Course
Off Chance

The Last Call Series

On The Rocks
Make It A Double
Sugar On The Edge (Coming Soon)
Shaken Not Stirred (Coming Soon)
With A Twist (Coming Soon)

The Legal Affairs Series

Objection
Stipulation
Violation
Mitigation
Reparation
Affirmation
Confessions of a Litigation God (Coming Soon)

The Forever Land Chronicles

Forever Young

Books of the Stone Veil

The Darkest of Blood Magicks
To Catch a Dark Thief

Stand Alone Titles

If I Return

About the Author

USA Today Bestselling Author, Sawyer Bennett is a snarky southern woman and reformed trial lawyer who decided to finally start putting on paper all of the stories that were floating in her head. Her husband works for a Fortune 100 company which lets him fly all over the world while she stays at home with their daughter and three big, furry dogs who hog the bed. Sawyer would like to report she doesn't have many weaknesses but can be bribed with a nominal amount of milk chocolate.

Made in the USA
Middletown, DE
20 June 2017